Pelican Books

Advisory Editor for Linguistics: David Crystal

Stylistics

G. W. Turner was born in New Zealand in 1921
and received an M.A. from the University of
New Zealand in 1948. He trained as a librarian,
then worked for six years in academic and
public libraries. From 1955 to 1964 he held a
post in the English Department of the University
of Canterbury, New Zealand, and since 1965 has
been Reader in the Department of English at the
University of Adelaide. G. W. Turner holds a
Diploma in English Linguistic Studies from
University College, London, and has contributed
a number of articles on Old Icelandic phonology,
Australian and New Zealand English, and
grammatical topics to learned journals.
His publications include *The English
Language in Australia and New Zealand* and
Good Australian English.

Stylistics

G. W. Turner

Penguin Books

Penguin Books Ltd, Harmondsworth,
Middlesex, England
Penguin Books Inc., 7110 Ambassador Road,
Baltimore, Maryland 21207, U.S.A.
Penguin Books Australia Ltd, Ringwood,
Victoria, Australia

First published 1973
Copyright © G. W. Turner, 1973

Made and printed in Great Britain by
Hazell Watson & Viney Ltd,
Aylesbury, Bucks
Set in Monotype Times

Contents

1. Language, Style and Situation

'Hello, darling', says a man to his wife. He says 'Hello, darling' to his neighbour's wife. He says 'Hello, dear' to his wife. An old lady says 'Hello, dear' to her pussy-cat. I write to the Commissioner of Taxes, beginning 'Dear Sir'. A young man says 'Hello, darling' to another young man. I call you 'Dear Reader'. I address the Commissioner of Taxes as 'Darling Sir'. A young man says 'Hello, dear' to another young man. A man says 'Hello, dear' to his neighbour's wife. I call you 'Darling Reader'. An old lady says 'Hello, darling' to her pussy-cat.

All very friendly. But we know that not all these events are equally likely to happen. This is because we have sifted from our experience of people saying things a pattern of language and another pattern of circumstances in which language is used, and we expect the language to fit the circumstances. We can see that in many cases words are interchangeable, that cats, unlike commissioners of taxes, may equally well be called 'dear' or 'darling', but we also know that these are different words, and that in other circumstances one word might be more appropriate than the other. Our knowledge of our language is immensely complex; we carry with us not only a knowledge of a vast, intricately patterned code, but also an experience of its varying surrounding circumstances. This guides us in making choices from approximately similar items in the code to fit particular occasions.

We know what language is, and we also know that it varies according to circumstances. Linguistics is the science of describing language and showing how it works; stylistics is that part of linguistics which concentrates on variation in the use of language, often, but not exclusively, with special attention to the most conscious and complex uses of language in literature. *Stylistics* is not a stylish word, but it is well connected. The French write of *la stylistique*; the Germans discuss *die Stylistik*. *Stylistics* means the study of style, with a suggestion, from the form of the word, of a scientific or at least a methodical study. The word allows the useful derivative *stylistician* for one who makes a methodical study of the principles of style. The stylistician is thus distinct from the stylist (sometimes markedly).

We know what language is in the sense that we can identify it or simply construct a sample of it. We would agree that I am using language now, though there is, when we think about it, something unusual about this language. As I sit at a desk in an outer suburb of Adelaide, looking from time to time out of my window on a day more overcast than we usually have, rather cold, in fact, for September, to see wind stirring our loquat tree and the gums beyond it, you are in London, or Canberra, or Leeds or Kuala Lumpur at another time and in circumstances quite unknown to me, so that the way you and I are using language in the present discussion is not the most normal one. As a matter of fact, it is more abnormal than I have suggested, since I have later revised and amended the words I wrote in Adelaide, looking out from time to time on a colder, more overcast day in Hampstead in March, taking account of comments made by two editors on a first draft of my text. Writing is a special, careful, elaborated, shuffled, pruned and tidied form of language, very different from the everyday, spontaneous, precarious adventures of speech which make up, and have made up, most of the world's linguistic activity and are in that sense 'normal language'. Yet the language of a philosopher or grammarian at his desk has often been chosen for description by grammarians and writers on the philosophy of language.

The grammarian who describes his own orderly, reflective language describes only one kind of English. He writes not *the* grammar of English but *a* grammar of English. He usually knows this, of course, though the schoolboy who accepts the grammar book as revealed truth may grow up with troublesome notions of correctness which condemn much of the language he really uses. It is certainly not to be thought that the grammarians and lexicographers who laboured to isolate or establish a 'correct English' from the flux of varied uses of language about them were unaware of other varieties of English. Dr Johnson, in the preface to his dictionary, notices the main types of variation that are noticed now. But the purpose of grammatical description is to bring orderliness and tidiness into a conception of language, and to do this it is necessary to begin by isolating one particular variety for systematic description. The most available, and the most manageable (because it is written, permanent and visible), is the formal written style of the scholar's own trade. This learned style is also the best described in the grammars of Latin which were the inevitable models for the first descriptions of modern languages. In our time, linguists have turned their attention to spoken language and its grammar, but they have frequently retained in their analysis the simplicity that goes with an approach to language through one single variety, this time by dismissing written language without further analysis as a mere partial reflection of speech. The grammars based on both speech and writing have tended in practice to concentrate especially on those patterns which are common to written language and formal speech.

Again the grammarian is not to be condemned. He is not interested in the surroundings of language; he does not want to know that I am now in Hampstead and you are in Smiths Falls, Ontario. In this he is like the mathematician who believes that if A or B alone can dig a garden in one hour, they will together finish the job in thirty minutes flat. No pauses for talk, no tangling of forks or argument about who begins at the sunny end enter his schematized world. The mathematician happily discusses a world which is patently absurd, a world in which people run baths by turning on two taps of different sizes and leaving the plug out.

For similar reasons, to concentrate attention on the essentials of a formal pattern, the grammarian is happiest in a world where the nuance and detail of real life and real language are subdued. From the ancient and medieval logicians he has inherited such favourite basic sentences as 'John runs', and with these he begins his work. Everyone knows that this is not real language, just as writers on elementary physics know that their friction-free models do not resemble the genuine problems of an engineer. No particular situation comes readily to mind in which the statement 'John runs' is likely to be usefully made. We think of no motive a speaker could have for saying it or interest it could have for a hearer. That is its merit. It eliminates certain variables, allowing the grammarian to get on with grammar.

How, indeed, could the grammarian, or, for that matter, the stylistician, begin to describe the intricate totality of a speech act? Consider, for example, two men standing together by the bar in the club-house of a golf-club. It is an overcast day in September. There are bottles on the shelves behind the bar. The lights are on, reflected in the bottles. Glasses have left wet rings on the counter. One of the men, Mr Alfred Appleby, an architect, notices that two of the wet rings touch, making a neat figure eight. He says to his companion, Mr Charles Plumtree, a draper, whose eyes, he notices, have been drawn by his own gaze to the wet rings, 'Makes a neat figure eight.' Mr Plumtree says 'It does.' As this conversation lapses, Mr Appleby says after a while, 'I hear your young John was doing very well in the hurdles at the school yesterday.' The reply is 'John? No, that was Roger, the younger boy. Roger's the hurdler. John runs.'

This, though I left much detail out, is already too much to deal with. To give ourselves a text of manageable length, let us play back and examine more closely only the last moment of this incipient conversation, 'John runs'. We could describe exactly where and how each man was standing as it was said, how many bottles were on the shelf, how old the men were, where the club-house was, where the men had gone to school and their careers in detail. Mr Plumtree's vocal movements could be analysed in all their complexity. We could note that the fading sound of the last word *runs* was made with the side rims of the tongue in close contact with the upper side teeth, and the tip and that part of the tongue which is just behind the tip pressed against the bony (alveolar) ridge behind the upper teeth in a way that allowed an audible sibilant escape of air, the nasal passage being meanwhile closed. The vocal cords had been vibrating while the *n* of *runs* was sounded, and this vibration continued into the portion of the word spelt -*s*, which was thus actually a *z*-sound, but with the voice cutting out before the sibilant sound ceased, so that, more finely, it was a *z*-sound terminating in a somewhat relaxed *s*-sound . . .

Now it is clear that this is likely to become a chaotic description of a scene, and to be both too full to comprehend and yet demonstrably incomplete. It is clear that some selection of essentials is necessary. Thus, unless the study is a special study of the exact sounds of speech, a phonetic study, it is unnecessary to analyse in detail the particular production of the last sound of *runs*. It is enough to note that it is a particular representation of the sound we hear at the end of *buzz*, in the middle and at the end of *roses* or at the beginning of *zero*. However they may vary in exact detail in particular productions, we recognize these sounds as *z*-sounds, or, to use the technical term, as the 'phoneme /z/'.

We do not consciously hear all the fine variations in particular pronunciations that a modern phonetician's machinery can measure. We sometimes ignore what we do hear, reinterpreting it in terms of an expected pattern. Such variant pronunciations as 'Empire Stape Building' or 'Hybe Park' are common in rapid speech, and are so much part of our language that they are taught to foreign learners to eliminate the over-precise flavour that a foreigner's speech often has, but few speakers of English are aware that they make these adjustments (technically called assimilations).

In other words, we interpret particular instances of language by referring them to a general scheme. We think of *stape* as a particular realization of *state*. In this, the grammarian or the scientific linguist proceeds as we all do. He, too, sifts from his experience of people saying things an abstract pattern of language, a 'form' and its 'formal elements'. The grammarian leaves to the phonetician the sound waves of physics, dealing himself with the elements of pattern for which the physical sounds are a basis. Grammar generalizes, finding similarities in pieces of language superficially different. It goes on to group 'John runs' with 'Dogs bark' in a wider concept 'subject plus verb', though the similarity between the two sentences is really very abstract. Grammar moves ever away from the particular to the general, ignoring the differences between male and female, childish and adult voices, or that recognizable twang that immediately tells his friends that Charlie Plumtree is talking. Perhaps when Mr Plumtree corrected Mr Appleby's mistake about the favoured sports of his boys, he spoke in the slightly chilled tone one uses when friends fail to distinguish one's very different and individual sons, but the grammarian puts such tones on one side as something additional to language proper (as 'paralinguistic features') to isolate an essential pattern of sounds and proceed to a methodical discussion of grammar. The grammar of 'John runs' will be built on an assumption of a sequence of seven minimal elements, or phonemes, together with the pauses, stresses (the varying 'weight' of the voice) and intonation patterns (or 'tune' of the voice) which unite such sequences into meaningful speech. Grammar will ignore such distinctions as 'male voice', 'chilly tone' and the voice quality which announces Charlie Plumtree's presence through a closed door.

Such distinctions are not, however, meaningless. We understand a chilly tone just as well as we understand the message 'John runs'. The tone of a message is sometimes the first part to be understood and was the only part of Othello's words that Desdemona had understood when she protested 'I understand a fury in your words, but not the words'. The speech of an actor or an evangelist depends for its effect on nuances outside the bare scheme of language. Even written texts have their particularity, appearing in a particular typeface and existing before they reach the printing press in a succession of handwritten and typed versions. When I wrote this paragraph in its first draft, the sentence I am now writing began with the second word in a line of my handwriting. As the paragraph is rewritten, typed and printed, this position changes. This does not matter (though such things perhaps explain the cold unfamiliar rhythms which seem to emerge when one first sees one's work in print), and we would agree that the position of words in their lines in one of the drafts of the present book is a 'paralinguistic feature' of no significance. Yet the latent significance of such a detail is brought out in poetry, where lines end and begin at points determined by the writer, and these line-ends take on significance in the special circumstances of poetic language. In children's picture books even the turn of a page may be carefully planned by the author.

Grammar leaves out part of real language and we feel that what it leaves out, the detailed particularity of particular occasions, brings us nearer to what we mean when we talk of 'variation' or 'style'. Can we simply say that the very setting up of a grammatical scheme isolates for us the companion study of stylistics? Is grammar what is said and style how it is said? Can style be defined as what grammar leaves out?

Only if these rough ideas are a good deal refined. The true nature of style is elusive and will need subtler nets than this to catch it. A very basic objection to this simple definition is that if by grammar we mean any attempt to find a scheme or pattern in language, such an approach would at the most allow us to contemplate style, not to describe it. The study of style, stylistics, must, like other branches of linguistics, generalize. Even to mention a 'chilly tone' is to classify Mr Plumtree's very individual pronunciation. In attempting to particularize, it adds a detail to the generalizations we can make about language: tones may be 'chilly'. We find an uncertainty principle at the very foundation of stylistics which ensures that however nearly its goal, if this is the particularity of language, is approached, it will never be reached. We might make narrower and narrower generalizations but we generalize to the last, until there is nothing left to do but quote. The lover of literature who fears that the academic critic will corrode poetry into a dust of arid comment worries unnecessarily. The full integrity of texts is guaranteed because it is impossible to capture particularity by multiplying generalizations.

Stylistics must therefore deal with a particularity it can never reach, ever indicating and lighting up what it cannot capture. Details are described in terms of other details; variations in the scheme of language are schematized. Merely to name 'variation' implies a scheme to vary from. The stylistician needs to begin with a theory of the linguistic scheme and relate it to particular speeches and writings, even if he is ultimately justified as the linguist not of our abstract competence in language but of our particular performances.

A distinction resembling the distinction between competence and performance underlies much of modern descriptive linguistic theory, and since F. W. Bateson once gave it as his opinion that it is the only useful contribution that linguistics has made to the study of literature, we had better look at it. F. de Saussure, in many ways a founder of modern linguistics, made a distinction between *langue* and *parole*: the language, thought of as an abstract pattern or scheme, and speech (to adopt the usual, somewhat unsatisfactory, translation of *parole*) or individual uses of language on particular occasions. The form 'John runs' belongs to the *langue*, Mr Plumtree's particular reproving pronunciation of it to the *parole*. The difference between *dear* and *darling* is a difference within the *langue*, but if a man whispers 'Darling!' in a particular way to a particular girl on a particular occasion we contemplate the *parole*.

Clearly the kind of distinction Saussure has made is useful for stylistics, but it does not immediately isolate stylistic choices. Evidence for stylistic choices is found in the *parole*, but an attempt to describe the nature of the choices that are made takes us back, as soon as we begin to use general terms, to the *langue*. Stylistic choices, like any other linguistic phenomena, are manifested in *parole* but described with reference to the *langue*. We cannot therefore merely take the relation of *langue* and *parole* as the model for an abstract scheme and stylistic variation.

One difficulty is that we cannot always agree whether what we observe belongs to the linguistic scheme or not. The relationship between scheme and variations is not given and absolute, but, like Mr Appleby's figure eight in the formal theory of wet rings on bar counters, a pattern discerned in language by linguists and, less methodically, by the users of language. There are, accordingly, several possible kinds of relationship between linguistic scheme and variation.

The most ambitious way to relate grammar and style is to try to incorporate all variations within the scheme by outlining general patterns of variation. Even the whispered performance of 'Darling!' is not inaccessible to generalization. Whispering can be described phonetically and its meaning discussed. Perhaps the man had reasons for not wishing to be overheard. Whispering is so often associated with secrecy that a man with acute laryngitis asking the doctor's wife 'Is the doctor in?' risks receiving the (also whispered) reply 'No – Come in.' On the other hand, the whisper perhaps showed strong emotion, and emotion is another reason for whispering. We might imagine that the hero in a melodrama, discovering the full extent of the villain's villainy, would whisper the words 'You devil!' (magnifying his whisper to a stage whisper to suit the needs of the theatre). Whispering, then, is not absolutely different from such recognized grammatical categories as questions or commands; at least a describable linguistic phenomenon correlates with describable general situations. To include everything in a 'grammar' is to risk an untidy and incoherent grammar, perhaps, but we shall see later that modern grammars are quite capable of establishing a hierarchy of grammatical categories and of deriving a multiplicity of surface phenomena from a coherent set of 'deep' structural forms by precisely defined operations. There may be little usefulness in including such phenomena as whispering on the surface fringe of such a grammar, but it is not theoretically impossible.

An all-inclusive approach, if totally successful, would abolish the distinction between scheme and sporadic variants by bringing all variation within the scheme. The user of language would find everything he could ever need in the multi-purpose kit supplied by the super-grammarian. His only remaining choice would be to take it or leave it.

But this is a real choice, introducing a second possible relationship between scheme and variations. It is possible to depart from an accepted scheme, whether all-inclusive or not, to produce a novelty by a creative jump. Dylan Thomas, writing in English but using the phrase 'farmyards away', extends the usual rules of

English in which phrases of 'distance away' normally begin with specific measures of length, as in 'miles away'. Creative leaps of this kind are not confined to poetry but are also found in slang and in technical language. When a wingless flying machine was dubbed a 'flying bedstead', words were brought together that had normally been kept apart to add a new idiom to the scheme of English, and the first humorist to say that his mate was 'as silly as a square wheel' went even further in joining unlikely yokefellows. A scheme of language is never complete and static, because language is always being put to new uses and adjusted to them, or resharpened for old uses, particularly for occasions where people like to be emphatic. Vocabulary, the least rigorously systematic part of language, is especially subject to innovation in this way.

Literary language establishes yet another special relationship with the scheme of language by using linguistic elements to build new schemes of its own, adding new rules of metre and line length, word order and the choice of vocabulary to the existing rules of ordinary language. These new schemes multiply the possibilities of scheme and variation in a complex way, allowing departures from ordinary language in accord with the literary scheme and departures from the literary scheme in accord with ordinary language.

The superimposition of literary schemes on the scheme of ordinary language creates a very interesting stylistic study because the two schemes are consciously played off one against the other, but the existence of multiple schemes is not in itself special to literary language. The English language is itself a complex interrelation of many different schemes. Scots English varies from American English and both from the English of the Caribbean. On a time scale, Old English (Anglo-Saxon) has a quite different grammar from Modern English and there is an infinite number of stages of development linking the two. Each individual user of English controls several different forms of his language. We speak and write, read legal language or a book on science, understand a ceremonial speech or the slang of our area and generation. Some of these differences are perhaps to be discounted in a study of style, since Old English is not available as a possible way of writing now and Burns's choice of Scots or Southern English for a poem is doubtfully a matter of style, but dialect mixture within a single text and the varieties of his language controlled by a particular speaker to suit particular occasions have a surer place within stylistics. In the relation of writing to speech there is even something of the conscious interplay of schemes found in poetry, a justification, perhaps, for a feeling that writing is particularly associated with literature.

Older grammarians were inclined to reject all but a few of the schemes of English, usually narrowing their attention to formal written language, and often regarding all departures from their chosen scheme as an unclassified array of 'errors', but the nature of grammatical study does not preclude the study of spoken language or the less socially influential dialects, and recently linguists have been readier to elaborate the schemes of these varieties of language. As a result another possible distinction between grammar and style is seen to be less absolute than it appears at first sight. Both grammarians and stylisticians are aware of variety in language, and since both work through generalizing, both seek tidy descriptions of the order within the variety by recognizing a series of schemes of language. Yet in their approach to variety the grammarian and the stylistician remain distinct. The grammarian is interested in each scheme separately and for its own sake; the stylistician is interested in comparing schemes, relating them to their contexts and observing the intricate patterns emerging from the interference of one with another.

Faced with a schematic difference, the two proceed in different ways. Suppose the difference noted is that between a standard pronunciation of *singing hymns* and a pronunciation we may represent as *singin' 'ymns*. The grammarian may describe either, but as they belong to different schemes, he describes them separately. He will want to know whether the pronunciation *'ymns* represents a total loss of /h/ in the speaker's dialect, and, if it does, this will be relevant to the 'phoneme inventory' or number of phonemes in the dialect. The replacement of the final *ng* of *singing* by *n* is not a total loss of *ng*, as *ng* remains in the middle of the word. A stylistician is not concerned with this argument but will be more concerned with the possibility that the two pronunciations of the phrase will be known to a single speaker and will want to know their difference in social effect. The stylistician deals primarily with what the users of language know when language is used, ignoring hidden grammatical generalities, just as he normally ignores etymology and the forgotten history of languages. If a 'dropped *h*' and a 'dropped *g*' have the same effect, it is not stylistically important that one is a difference in phoneme inventory and one not, though it is of grammatical importance. This is not to say that grammar will not reveal in clear detail many stylistic effects that are sensed vaguely and impressionistically without it; it is just that ultimately the relevance of such grammatical information to stylistics is justified by an awareness among users of language of *some* effect. This may be absent in etymological truths or truths about phoneme inventory, truths which have other kinds of usefulness than the stylistic.

Because a grammarian deals with one scheme at a time, and the internal coherence of the scheme itself is the subject matter of his study, he is happiest with pure dialects and straightforward styles. The implication of more than one scheme at a time or the merging of pure dialects into standard languages, with resulting irregularities (like the varying pronunciation of *one* and *stone*) on the one hand and the artificial imposition of regularity on the other, seem somewhat 'unnatural' to him. The stylistician has different tastes. He welcomes an implication of dual or multiple schemes in a single text, since this greatly complicates the possibilities of choice and subtlety of effect.

Nevertheless a stylistician can, and very often does, work, like the grammarian, within a single scheme. The grammarian's scheme allows choices within it. It sets up systems of choice: active and passive, statement, question and command, variant word orders or words of similar meaning, like *dear* and *darling*. Even detectable variations in the pronunciation of individual sounds may be consistent with the preservation of a single scheme of phonemes. (We say in these cases that a speaker has a different 'accent'.) All these are variations within a single scheme, say, 'standard English'.

If the grammar is subtle and adds statistically based indications of the rarity or frequency of the choices it enumerates, we may decide that the stylistic study of a pure variety of language can be merged into the grammar as a component of the grammar, but even then some might prefer to say that a strictly stylistic discussion concerns not what choices are available in the language but the particular applications that writers or speakers have made of these potentialities. In this view stylistics would deal with performance, not competence, and would be a study of texts, not the potential of language. In this view grammar still leaves something out, to form a subject matter for stylistics.

Grammar, taken in a wide sense to mean all formal analysis of language – that is, all attempts to arrive at the general pattern or scheme found in the sounds and words of language and their arrangement – has been a central concern of linguistics, especially in our time. What grammar leaves out has therefore intruded later as a region of special difficulty in linguistic studies and remains an underdeveloped area of such studies. Since the variables that grammar eliminates are the purpose and circumstances and detailed particularity of speech, linguists have experienced difficulty in developing adequate theories of meaning and style.

The study of meaning and style will have to bring back what grammar leaves out. These studies will not work in opposition to grammar, however, nor be independent of it, since it is grammar that will define their starting point. The grammarian isolates the forms and constructions to which meaning can be attached and establishes the norms against which variation can be clearly marked. It is by being based in a coherent theory of general linguistics, of grammar in the wide sense, that stylistics as a branch of linguistics can aim ultimately to be more soundly based than those discussions of style which trace a web of stylistic effects, that is, in our view, a series of departures, without a coherent theory of what is departed from.

In the meantime, because the linguist's difficulties with meaning and style are partly of his own making, arising from his starting point and preoccupation with the general form of language, he will be challenged – and helped – by workers in other disciplines. He has been helped by the philosopher studying problems of meaning with different preoccupations from his own, and looks with growing interest in the direction of the literary critic, who has long been interested in style.

The literary critic begins with a particular text, and even if he has his own doubts about the relevance of the circumstances in which the whole text was composed, he is always alert to the purpose and circumstances of each detail within it; he sees each part, each line and word, in context. This is why 'John runs' appears to be unliterary as well as unlifelike. It suggests no context, either in literature or life. Literary language is language in context, words in relation to other words. Each detail of a literary work takes its quality from the whole work. 'Put out the light' is an undistinguished sentence in isolation, but not in *Othello*. They are the right words in the context. 'Mistah Kurtz – he dead' is not a grand statement, but it has deep seriousness in the context of Conrad's *Heart of Darkness*.

Sometimes a context is merely implied by the words, as it usually is in the opening words of a modern novel. Virginia Woolf's *To the Lighthouse* begins '"Yes, of course, if it's fine tomorrow," said Mrs Ramsay', and already the setting is strongly enough indicated for us to judge the appropriateness of the words. Sometimes, it is true, an isolated observation is of literary value even when its context is not known or recalled. We might remember 'Queens have died young and fair' without needing to remember the rest of the poem to appreciate it, but, if this is allowed, it is because the words relate to the whole human context. Literature, especially poetry, tends towards such universally valid statements, so much so that it is a mark of the outstanding non-poet, William McGonagall, that he is always specific about dates, names and places, but to say that poetic statements are of very general context is not to say that they are without context. In any case, memorable fragments, if they are weightier than a proverb, probably carry some memory or implication of the context which reinforced them in the whole work in which they had their full richness of meaning.

The literary critic, then, is more concerned with the particularity and circumstances of language than the mainstream of theoretical linguists have been. The critic makes one abstraction when he separates the work of art from the circumstances of its production and does not want to know that a poet's tragic view of life arose from a persistent toothache, but, within the work, words retain for him the particularity of their setting. When defining his view of style, the critic will welcome definitions which do not neglect the setting of language.

A formula that has satisfied many is Swift's 'proper words in proper places'. Taken from its own proper place – and not everyone who uses the formula refers on each occasion to 'A Letter to a Young Gentleman Lately entered into Holy Orders' where it has its context – this formula is capable of enough different meanings to accommodate most approaches to the theory of style. It could even describe a grammarian's material, since 'they runs' would be judged deviant on the grounds that *runs* is not the proper word to use here, and 'run they' would be deviant because the words are not in their proper places. Swift, however, talked of style: 'Proper Words in proper Places, makes the true Definition of a Stile', and though he continues 'But this would require too ample a Disquisition to be now dwelt on', we feel certain that he did not have in mind merely the correct choice of a plural verb with a plural subject and the linking of the two into a sequence meaningful in English. This much is prior to style. It is given by the language, leaving no choice, and, though it does not appear in all definitions, an element of choice seems to be basic to all conceptions of style.

Since Swift goes on to condemn the use of obscure terms which were not accessible to some of a clergyman's audience, and to distinguish 'elaborate Discourses upon important Occasions, delivered to Princes or Parliaments, written with a View of being made publick' from a 'plain Sermon intended for the Middle or lower Size of People', it could appear that he had in mind the fitting of discourse to the social situation in which it operates, but when later in the same letter he writes 'When a Man's Thoughts are clear, the properest Words will generally offer themselves first; and his own Judgment will direct him in what Order to place them, so as they may be best understood', we must take him to refer to the use of the right words in the right order. This rightness will not merely be grammatical, since 'Judgment', not merely knowledge of the language, is to direct the writer. It is recognized that the grammatical system of a language will often allow more than one choice, that several 'correct' ways of saying 'the same thing' will be available.

We need not doubt this. A sentence in a sports commentary might be 'Now Smith hits the ball', but this might equally properly be 'Smith now hits the ball' or 'Smith hits the ball now'. We may feel that 'the same thing' is said by 'Now the ball is hit by Smith' (and its variants) or simply by 'Now the ball is hit'. All these choices were available to the announcer, given by the grammar of his language. Grammar sometimes allows apparently free choices in word order, or allows transformations of a basic form into forms which are accepted as equivalent. In all such cases, there are likely to be slight differences of emphasis or very fine shades of meaning, but it is not possible to insist on absolute identity of meaning in what we choose to call stylistic variants. To do so would demand a very refined theory of meaning, and abolish the subject matter of stylistics altogether.

Such minor decisions as the placing of *now*, which have very little influence on the meaning, emphasis and suggestive power of language, might seem to be random decisions. I believe that I make quite a random decision when I use *anybody* or *anyone*. If typing from a handwritten draft, I might easily type *anyone* where I wrote *anybody*, and vice versa. Other people might be different from me in this matter, having an unconscious preference for one or the other word. There may be many such unconscious preferences in all of us, ultimately caused by complex elements in our makeup that can hardly be analysed even with the aid of such modern devices as psychoanalysis and the psychological study of personality.

This brings us to another definition of style, to Buffon's

celebrated 'Style is the man himself', or, as William Puttenham wrote in an earlier age, with emphasis on the habitual nature of such apparently random choices, 'Style is a constant and continual phrase or tenour of speaking and writing'. It is true that we do very often recognize the 'voice' of someone we know when we read his writing, and even 'get to know' a writer we have not met by reading his work. We are least likely to have this feeling when we read writing that is very stereotyped, when we read a writer who cautiously relies on clichés, for example, or one who is obliged to use set formulas in a legal document. We are most aware of it in the writer who chooses appropriate words and forms carefully. Though it would appear at first that the careful writer would be less likely to be making 'unconscious decisions', we must assume that along with his conscious choices, for which he could perhaps give good reasons, the habit of choosing, rather than piecing together set expressions, carries over into the minor unconscious choices. These, instead of being entirely random, must be subtly determined by the psychological makeup of the particular writer or by the total linguistic context formed by the work in which they occur. Possibly it is only a few small or pervasive details that suggest the full human complexity of the writer, just as a few marks on a stone or in the pattern of wallpaper will sometimes allow us to 'see' a human face of rich character. Style in this sense is more easily recognized than analysed, more easily caught in an impressionistic phrase than revealed in detailed grammatically or statistically described complexity, and when rigorous descriptive methods are used their success will depend greatly on the ability of the investigator to choose the right details to count or describe.

A personal style, once it is formed, may be imitated by others, either in pastiche, where salient points, often exaggerated, are selected for imitation, or, more respectfully, in the formation of a later writer's style, where the more striking idiosyncrasies are likely to be avoided. The parodist seeks as his target the writers of most individual tone and recognizable style, and these same writers, because their style is a defined and shaped one, are no bad models for the apprentice who can retain their manner without their mannerisms. That Johnson is easily parodied few would deny, but his strong rhythms have taught many how to write.

An influential writer suffuses his influence through a school or leaves his stamp on an age or even a language. The concept of personal style is thus easily extended to a concept of a period style or the style of a given language. It is even possible to be uncertain whether an individual or a more general style is being discerned. Students of Middle English cannot be sure whether stylistic similarities in *Pearl* and *Sir Gawain and the Green Knight* indicate a common author or a regional style.

Swift and Buffon are two among a multitude of literary men who have offered definitions of style. Their definitions, freely interpreted, may stand as the expression of two rival approaches to the subject. They agree in stating or implying that style has to do with making choices, conscious or otherwise, which are not entirely determined, or not so far as we can ascertain determined. This much agreement could hardly be avoided. An omniscient Being might need no theory of style in this sense, only an inconceivably complex deterministic linguistics, but human beings can achieve tidiness in description only if they leave something to 'style' in order to arrive at firm outlines in grammar, lexicography and the theory of linguistic variety.

A stylistic choice cannot by definition be said to be determined in the way that agreement between a plural subject and a plural verb is determined by the rules of the English language. Nevertheless, such choices can to some extent be explained. It is possible to ask what controls choice, making one choice more likely than another. Swift's definition implies such a question in a way that Buffon's does not. Buffon forgoes any claim to say why a style is of a particular kind. He asserts the essential particularity of a particular writer's work. Swift's 'proper places', with its hint of context, draws attention to the relations of a text, or part of a text, to its setting. Swift's definition allows that a man might have different styles on different occasions; Buffon, interpreted rigorously, does not. Swift's slogan can be used to justify the sociological theorists of style, the linguists who study the socially selected varieties of language. Buffon's definition stands behind the statistician who identifies an author by means of word counts. One approach is explanatory, the other descriptive.

Both the explanatory and descriptive approaches have their place in a total view of style. We need first to know what styles and varieties there are, with a description of the forms occurring in each style and an indication of their frequency. Before these needs are supplied, an adequate grammatical description is necessary to identify the forms to be described and counted. Merely to count the frequency of nouns, for example, would not distinguish such grammatically and stylistically variant sequences as 'the transmission of the information in the discourse' and 'the branches of the trees in the forest'. When the items to be counted are well defined, however, counting can be of help. If we notice that Dr Johnson often begins sentences with a clause beginning with the conjunction *that*, it is of value to ask how often. If we know that scientific English frequently makes use of the passive construction, it is illuminating to find out how frequent this construction is in selected texts.

Since these counts describe particular performances only, we need further statistical information about the language itself before our counts can be illuminating. How often do other writers use passives or *that*-clauses? If there are choices in language, there are probabilities, and it is the task of the statistician to give exact descriptions of probabilities. Even such basic concepts as a 'rare word' or a 'common word' are statistical concepts. There are statistical methods for dealing with probabilities that change as a context is built up, so that statistics can be linked with performance as well as with the linguistic scheme. To take a simple illustration, if I am about to spell an English word, the probability that I will use a particular letter to begin it, say *n* or *g*, can be roughly measured with a ruler and a good dictionary; if I choose *n* to begin with, the probability that the next letter will be *g* becomes zero; if I reach the stage *notwithstandin-*, the probability that the next letter will be *g* becomes certainty. In a similar way a sequence of words, e.g. 'This box is hermetically . . .', may make the occurrence of a following word almost certain.

Poets may use such near certainties to slip in a surprising variant. Dylan Thomas's 'as happy as the grass was green' is an example, though since 'farmyards away' may be instanced as an intuitively similar example, we do well not to insist too much on the linear sequence of the probabilities. The important thing is that statistics allows us to give a precise meaning to the statement that a form, even if not grammatically deviant, is unusual or unexpected in its context.

Statistical methods lead to very precise descriptions but they are not, even when they correlate several variables and describe the probability of words in context, explanatory. It is precise to say that in a given year a man had a main meat dish in 85·71 per cent of his dinners and that in 14·29 per cent of his dinners the main dish was fish – it is more explanatory to point out that he ate fish on Fridays.

Explanation in stylistics depends on examining the circumstances of language, the situations in which it is used. Variations in style are measured against variations in setting, and where the two appear to be interdependent, style is to that extent explained. In this view style is not a matter of free, unfettered choice, but it is at least partly controlled by setting. Students of linguistics have included within stylistics a description of such varieties of language as technical language, colloquial language or written language, together with such sublanguages as the language of telegrams, newspaper headlines, advertisements or knitting patterns. All these styles can be related directly to the social setting or circumstances in which the language is used.

By limiting freedom of choice, context narrows the range of potential meaning of words, making them precise, or bringing them into focus. When a telephone operator says 'Hold the line, please', the total diversity of meaning of the word *line* in English is irrelevant; in this context its meaning is simple and determined. The group of words 'hold the line' becomes in this context a completely fixed formula of precise meaning. The more restricted the application of a formula, however, the more precisely the formula implies its context, so that even in isolation 'hold the line' suggests a setting in the world of telephones, and so its meaning, narrowed in one dimension, is enriched in another as it takes on connotations of the whole modern business world and the world of long-distance telephone calls. Thus the most stereotyped language of a highly organized urban community unexpectedly provides rich poetic effect in W. H. Auden's Christmas Oratorio *For the Time Being*, where the world of Christ's birth is made vivid as it is related to our own in a radio announcer's phrase 'You have been listening to the voice of Caesar', or the words of officialdom 'All male persons who shall have attained the age of twenty-one years must proceed immediately . . .'

Perhaps only recently have poets so escaped from the confines of a special poetic diction that they can draw on the total resources of language in this way. Perhaps it is not surprising therefore that established literary stylistics has not been much interested in the styles most directly subject to the pressure of circumstances, the 'varieties' of linguistic study. The context and meaning of language are inevitably assumed in literary discussion, but it seems that the only methodical examination of the setting of language that has entered into literary discussion of the details of style is an analysis of meaning.

One important approach to the study of style is based on an analysis of meaning into its 'denotative' and 'connotative' elements. In this view the words *obstinate* and *resolute* might denote the same objective situation but the 'connotation' is different. This is to analyse meaning into a stylistically neutral 'cognitive meaning' and an 'expressive' or 'affective' element which is the concern of stylistics. It could be objected that this analysis reflects an older concept of language and literature, still dominant when the theory was first developed in the first decade of this century, before T. S. Eliot lodged his famous complaint against the 'dissociation of sensibility', and that not all stylistically interesting literary effects are readily classified as 'expressive' or 'affective'. Is an elegant proof in algebra expressive? What of the laconic speeches in Norse sagas? When Grettir was advised not to stay at a haunted house because, if he were not destroyed himself, every bone in his horse would be broken, he said that he could always get another horse. Is this reply factual or expressive?

Inevitably the 'connotations' of language prove on closer analysis to be understood from the particular nature of the situations or contexts in which the language is used, or else such contexts are inferred from the language. I may guess variously at a man's political background according to whether he remembers President Johnson as 'resolute' or 'obstinate', and I would certainly want to interpret such terms as 'retreat' or 'planned withdrawal' with knowledge of the circumstances in which they were used. When at a conference on style in language at Indiana University in 1958 Roman Jakobson, discussing the expressive element in language, instanced the case of a former actor of Stanislavsky's Moscow Theatre, who was asked at his audition to make forty different messages by diversifying the expressive tint in the Russian words for 'this evening', we notice that the success of the enterprise was assessed by the success of his listeners in correctly decoding the messages, that is, in inferring the appropriate situation of each utterance from its sound.

In England the term 'expressive' has been less commonly used than another term, 'emotive', originated by A. Marty in Germany in 1908 but especially used in English-speaking countries after the appearance in 1923 of *The Meaning of Meaning* by C. K. Ogden and I. A. Richards. Some years ago the isolation of 'factual' and 'emotive' elements in meaning had considerable but often unfortunate influence on the teaching of English in schools. It became linked with a worthy admiration for clear scientific and technical prose, and a perhaps oversimplified suspicion of the guile of advertisers (who work in subtler ways than ordinary liars) until *emotive* itself became an emotive word and the chief observable result of introducing the term into English classes was a hardening of pupils' natural suspicion of poetry, which, they alleged, was emotive, and, like advertising, to be distrusted.

The proponents of a theory need not be held responsible for its misapplication, and perhaps the currency of the terms 'factual' and 'emotive' did something to dispel a simplified idea that meaning is merely the attachment of a particular word to a particular 'thing'. It at least introduced into the general knowledge of schoolboys an awareness that language carries information about speakers as well as the 'outside world', that as well as saying 'roses are red', I might say 'I am happy', and that if I go on to say 'roses are beautiful', it is a real question whether my third statement is to be grouped with the first or the second. This is not, by the way, to prove that any of the three statements is deficient in meaning. It is rather that some parts of the situations described by language are more directly observable than others.

We think and feel, and use language to induce parallel thoughts and feelings in others. Possibly neither thoughts nor feelings are ultimately objective. To see a figure eight in two wet rings is perhaps as subjective as to feel anger at an unwiped counter. A figure 8 itself might equally well be seen as a pair of circles joined, or as an S with the ends joined by a curved line. We communicate, in language, not reality but a pattern in reality, not raw emotions (except perhaps in such interjections as *ouch*) but a pattern in emotions. All language does both, though some language, the language of science being an obvious example, is especially concerned with the pattern in facts, while other language, lyric poetry being an equally obvious example, concerns itself especially with the pattern of feeling. Neither specialization is pure; the scientist obviously enjoys his white-coated detachment, communicating a delight in objectivity, and the poet must find some objectively describable situation to represent his feelings, a pattern of images or a story, the carrier which T. S. Eliot has called the 'objective correlative', selected to invoke and organize appropriate feelings.

In practice, the best writers who have analysed style in terms of 'expressiveness' have interpreted the term very widely. Stephen Ullmann includes within the province of expressiveness 'everything that transcends the referential' and goes on to particularize 'emotive overtones, emphasis, rhythm, symmetry, euphony, and also the so-called "evocative" elements which place our style in a particular register (literary, colloquial, slangy, etc.) or associate it with a particular milieu (historical, foreign, provincial, professional etc.)'.

Such a definition seems to be wide enough to permit unimpeded investigation of all that is relevant to the study of style, though if the word 'expressive' is interpreted so widely, we are perhaps merely replacing the word 'stylistic' with another word which is explanatory only in a misleading way. The 'evocative' group of effects is better related directly to those elements in the social situation which are broad enough and general enough to be described in general terms, while the earlier group of effects named by Ullmann, though ultimately traceable to subtler differences in the total situation, can provisionally be grouped as options left available to speakers and writers within the grammatical pattern of the language, or meaningful variations in language which are omitted from the grammatical scheme. Ullmann usefully points out that stylistics has the same divisions as linguistics and that there are phonological, lexical and syntactic levels in the study of style. He distinguishes these 'inherent' effects from the 'evocative' effects such as the funny speech of foreigners or the flower girl's Cockney pronunciation in *Pygmalion*.

This approach seems to be sufficiently inclusive, and, at least in implication, sufficiently methodical to provide a framework for the present survey of the problems and achievements of stylistics. It is a procedure of analysis, inevitably fragmenting the total experience of language or literature, as any linguistic or critical investigation must, but allowing us to see stylistic effects in sharper detail than we usually do. This, like any other critical study, is a preparation, not a substitute, for understanding.

We begin by dividing language from its setting, as the grammarian does, but more consciously, retaining a preference for language with interesting meaning and assuming an awareness of meaning whenever it helps our analysis. This will be the basis for my next three chapters, descriptive chapters focusing attention on the possibilities of variation in the sounds, syntax and vocabulary of language. Within each of these chapters I will analyse further – analysing sound, for instance, into pause, syllables, stress, intonation and phonemic distinctions. These elements do not precede language or exist apart from it and all are in real language interdependent and related to other patterns of grammar and vocabulary and to their total linguistic context and the situations in which language has its natural being. This is true of any language but especially true of poetry, where all the interdependent forces of language are especially brought into harmonious balance. Yet each analysed element in a particular text both contributes to a total effect and receives from it, and what it contributes is precise enough to bear independent description, provided we always remember that we deal with one thread at a time in a complex pattern.

In later chapters I will attempt a more explanatory stylistics, looking more closely at the situation of language and its possibilities of variation, and attempt to draw together some at least of the variations in linguistic pattern and variations in situation.

Of course we know too little about these matters, and any synoptic study of style, like any other very general study, is premature. But there is room for style in stylistics and no study of style will ever be complete. At least no one (or nobody) need fear that our abstract schemes will replace or explain away the particularity of a poem – or of a greeting.

2. The Sounds of Language

The sounds of language may be studied with special attention to the speaker, the surrounding air or the hearer. In the first case we study articulatory phonetics, the movement of lungs, vocal cords, tongue, lips and other organs which initiate and modify the noisy outward breathing which is the physiological reality of language. In the second case, acoustic phonetics, attention is directed to the sound waves in the air, the physical reality of speech; and in the third case, auditory phonetics, we study the process of perceiving these sounds and the psychology of hearing.

Acoustic phonetics (suggesting etymologically a study of the hearer but in practice relating to the science of acoustics, a study of the physical, mathematically described vibrations in the air) might appear to be the most detached from mankind and hence the most scientific study of speech; articulatory phonetics might seem to be logically prior because until someone speaks there is no speech to analyse, but auditory phonetics might put in a counter-claim that the meaningful use of language presupposes the hearing of language. No one approach is clearly more basic than another and in practice an articulatory approach is customary in books about speech simply because it is easier to manage. The others are useful checks; acoustics may show, for example, that different articulations may produce a like sound while auditory phonetics reminds us that not all distinctions discernible in the physical vibrations of speech are heard. The human ear is selective. The Australian explorer Leichhardt observed in 1846 that Aboriginals whose ears were attuned to the slightest rustling of a snake in dry grass might fail to hear the approach of horses, which were to them unfamiliar animals.

If we can free ourselves from the prejudice induced by the alphabet, which leads us to assume from an early age that language is a linear sequence of discrete elements, we can learn to think of speech as a constantly varying flow of sound and notice that a number of different kinds of variation are at work simultaneously. Obviously when we pronounce the word *runs* we do not assume a posture for *r*, quickly shuffle into a new stance for *u*, hold it a moment before flipping into *n* and then *s*, later adding a tone to the whole, however useful such an analysis may be in describing the totality of what we do.

The most elementary variation we can make in the flow of speech sound is to switch it on or off. The distinction between speech and silence enters linguistics as the phenomenon of pause, as much a part of speech as rests and pause are a part of music. At the same time there is a 'pulse' in language, an opening and restricting of the flow of air, allowing the analysis of language into syllables. There is, further, a reinforcement of certain syllables, a stress pulse, and at the same time a variation in pitch known as intonation. Again the vocal cords may or may not come into operation. Voicing is (to simplify a little) switched on or off, dividing sounds into voiced or unvoiced sounds. Finally, lip and tongue movements, adjustments in the shape of the mouth and opening or closing of the nasal passage vary the sound of speech (with varying degrees of clarity through mumbling and poorly enunciated speech to the highly trained speech of the actor or good speaker) to produce the distinct sounds which are very roughly matched by the letters of our alphabet. It is likely that speech is first learned through a series of refinements such as these, rather than by the mastering of one distinct sound after another, though fond parents are apt to observe the achievement of recognizable sounds more accurately than the differences in pitch or rhythm which are at least equally important in communication.

Each of these stages in the analysis of language is important in the study of linguistics and of style. All are capable of infinite variation. The linguist must establish norms for his tidy description; the student of style will also note finer modifications of these norms which are of stylistic significance. Applied to the language of poetry, this stylistic analysis will become a theory of metrics; and applied to spoken language, with more emphasis on individual performance, it will underlie the theory of elocution. Some idea of the potential intricacy of these subjects will become apparent as we begin our discussion by looking at pause, which we have quickly described as the temporary switching off of speech.

Attempts have sometimes been made to give a very tidy description of the phenomenon of pause. In the seventeenth century, Simon Daines, a teacher of music as well as of speech, urged his students to count to one, two, three or four when pausing in reading, though as John Walker observed a century later 'nothing so regular fits the facts of language'. American linguists nevertheless revived, a generation ago, a concept of four significant pauses in English speech, and, in order to build up a concept of language based on scientifically observable data, posited that these pauses or 'junctures' were always audible. In this theory the smallest pause was not, as with Daines, that marked by a comma, but was the boundary between words, and this was to be audible too. That is, even a difference between 'a name' and 'an aim' was to be audible. It seems not to be strikingly so in practice, since older forms such as 'a napron' have been reinterpreted during the history of English as 'an apron'. On the other hand, the philosopher J. L. Austin probably went too far when he claimed 'In saying "Iced ink", I was uttering the words "I stink" .' This is because pause or 'juncture' is not manifested in actual language purely as silence, but becomes inextricably mixed with very slight but discernible variations in the quality of adjoining consonants or in a slight prolongation of a preceding sound, or, in the case of longer pauses, with patterns of pitch. These variations, even those that are slight, are audible, and are interpreted as pause, or at least, as in the case of Professor Austin's difficulties, as a boundary between words. Of course there is always a *potential* pause which differs in different structures. Very careful speech will distinguish 'a – name' from 'an – aim', 'the sons – raise meat' from 'the sun's rays – meet' and even make the purely grammatical distinction between 'Good – Friday films' and 'Good Friday – films'.

There is stylistic variation in speech both in the number of potential pauses that are actually realized and in the length of those pauses that are made. A measured or menacing speech may exaggerate pauses; a chatty, amiable prattle may 'run on' without them. A certain type of substandard speech is marked by the concentration of groups of words into short rapid bursts separated by pauses. Additional pauses, unrelated to structure, may distinguish hesitant speech or the special jerky speech adopted by some radio and television speakers who even pause after articles, as though searching for the – exact word.

The television mannerism is particularly noticeable when the pauses are without intonational support. In these cases the speech is cut off on a level tone and there is a genuine silence while we sense a tension in the vocal cords, sometimes audible in the 'glottal attack' of the resumed speech. In a list of such television pauses which I once began to compile, I included along with 'in connection–with' and 'links with–the arts' and 'I shall be–talking with her' such apparently normal exhibits as 'the low – unbroken line of trees', but in this case the word 'low' had a high level pitch and abrupt cut-off to make the pause prominent and unexpected.

Pause becomes especially important within the special schemes of poetic language. In poetry an expectation of pause is controlled by line division. If the line has an odd number of 'beats' (three or five), the pause is more evident than if there is an even number of beats (usually four). Compare

> How pleasant to know Mr Lear!
> Who has written such volumes of stuff!

with

> John Gilpin was a citizen
> Of credit and renown,

but even in four-beat lines some pause is likely to be felt at the ends of lines, and writers of free verse determine emphasis by line ends, directing a reader to pause or give weight to the words or groups of words isolated in lines.

In more traditional verse there are very often pauses other than those at line ends, the 'caesura' or pause within a line, as in

> She fear'd no danger, for she knew no sin.

The caesura may be variously placed, or the pause may be 'distributed' in a line with more than one pause:

> Thy wish was father, Harry, to that thought.

Some have argued that the caesura is not part of the metrical scheme of a poem, since the scheme does not lay down rules for the placing or even the existence of a caesura. It is true that the caesura seems to be less a part of metrics than the line-end, but internal pauses are in general part of what the poet, rather than the reader, determines, and to that extent are part of the scheme of a poem if not of poetry. Poets differ in their habits of using the caesura, and this differentiates individual styles, but also suggests that within a particular poet's work the placing of a caesura may sometimes become almost a rule. Pope favours a caesura after a second beat and hardly ever allows one after a fourth beat. His line

> Destroy his fib or sophistry – in vain!

is therefore, within his own work, 'deviant' or unusually emphatic. In Shakespeare, however, such a line would not be deviant at all.

For this reason the same metrical scheme (if in defining the scheme we exclude the caesura) may be a different thing in the hands of different poets. Each of the following pairs of lines concludes a Spenserian stanza:

> Evening must usher night, night urge the morrow,
> Month follow month with woe, and year wake year to sorrow.
> > – Shelley, *Adonais*, 21

> . . . *Be not too bolde*; whereto though she did bend
> Her earnest minde, yet wist not what it might intend.
> > – Spenser, *Faerie Queene*, III, xi, 54

> And all went merry as a marriage bell;
> But hush! hark! a deep sound strikes like a rising knell.
> > – Byron, *Childe Harold's Pilgrimage*, III, 21

Shelley usually, as here, breaks the alexandrine (six-beat line) in the middle, into two balancing parts, often with a hint of epigram or at least of alert intellect. In the quoted lines, a pause after the third beat in the preceding line prepares for the rhythm of the alexandrine, muting the impression of extra length into a mere slight swelling of the rhythm, appropriate to the mournful message of the words. The beats in the two lines fall into a pattern of three-two-three-three.

There is more complexity in Spenser's rhythm. Again the alexandrine is prepared for, by a pause after the second beat in the preceding line, but the remaining part of the alexandrine is longer than any group of words preceding it. Not all Spenser's alexandrines are of this shape, but those that are contribute to the leisurely, almost dreamy, impression which, despite the action in his story, is the particular impression we retain after reading *The Faerie Queene*. The quoted lines divide into groups of two, three, two and four beats, already a more varied pattern than Shelley's, but further complexity is suggested by the absence of pause between the lines, so that 'whereto though she did bend her earnest minde' seems to form a normal five-beat line in itself, straddling the basic metre, to make a complex ambiguous pattern of groups of two, three, four or five beats.

Byron's lines have no such ambiguity, though the contrast between a line without any compelling internal pause and the distributed pause in the alexandrine, combined with a pull of the normal pronunciation of the words away from the metrical accent, show a sufficiently individual pattern. To a modern ear Byron's lines perhaps seem the most contrived and Spenser's the most interesting, but whatever our judgement of the three effects, we are likely to feel that they are different, and that a metrics that merely describes lines and beats omits much that is distinctive in the metrical effect of specific poetic lines.

The discussion of pause in English poetry centres especially on the traditional five-beat (pentameter) line used by the major dramatists and poets for several centuries. In this verse the reader is induced to expect a pause at the end of lines or at least at the end of a couplet (a rhyming pair of lines) and to feel surprised if this expectation is disappointed by 'enjambement' or run-on lines (as in the example from Spenser, above). Since pauses may be of different length, there are degrees of enjambement. The expectation of pause is fully met if the line or couplet ends a sentence; it is reasonably fulfilled if a line ends a clause, less so if the line ends a phrase and not at all if the line merely ends a word. A line which breaks a word into its constituent parts, as Hopkins's

> I caught this morning morning's minion, king-
> dom of daylight's dauphin ...

is rare, and only in a dream could we meet

> Who would not give all else for two p
> ennyworth only of beautiful Soup?

A poet has in his control a double system of (potential) pauses, one controlled by grammar and the other by the ends of his lines. If the two coincide in 'end-stopped verse', there is a reinforcement of pauses; if they do not, there is a kind of counterpoint of the two systems. Such counterpoint is usual in poetry, and is perhaps what distinguishes 'poetry' from 'verse', but conventions of enjambement vary from poet to poet and from age to age. Pope characteristically finishes a sentence within a rhyming couplet, with an effect of neatness and wit, whereas Milton prefers a majestic sweep down a sequence of run-on lines. Modern poets even cross the once inviolate boundaries between stanzas.

It is well known that in the development of English drama the trend was away from end-stopped lines towards verse in which enjambement is frequent. Statistics of end-stopped and run-on lines are used to support the dating of Shakespeare's plays. The trend led to increased subtlety, but the end-stopped lines in Marlowe were not without grandeur, a relentless onward movement like waves breaking on a shore, since the lines ended clauses or major units within a sentence more often than sentences:

> Zenocrate, lovelier than the love of Jove,
> Brighter than is the silver Rhodope,
> Fairer than whitest snow on Scythian Hills,

> Thy person is worth more to Tamburlaine
> Than the possession of the Persian Crown
> Which gracious stars have promis'd at my birth . . .

By contrast, the developed Shakespearian line suggests the purling intertwining of currents in a swiftly flowing stream:

> Besides, this Duncan
> Hath borne his faculties so meek; hath been
> So clear in his great office, that his virtues
> Will plead like angels, trumpet-tongu'd against
> The deep damnation of his taking-off . . .

Nobody but a television commentator would pause at the ends of these lines; yet, perhaps, there is a hint of potential pause, with the associated tension that is felt in a commentator's pauses, providing an undercurrent of excitement that is missing from prose.

In Shakespeare's late plays enjambement becomes so frequent that it is doubtful whether a listener without a text can discern the ends of lines at all. If an internal pause comes regularly in the same place in several successive lines, there is even a false metre suggested, in which the caesurae may be taken as line-ends, as in these lines from Act I of *The Winter's Tale*:

> Is whispering nothing?
> Is leaning cheek to cheek? Is meeting noses?
> Kissing with inside lip? stopping the career
> Of laughter with a sigh (a note infallible
> Of breaking honesty)? horsing foot on foot?
> Skulking in corners? wishing clocks more swift?
> Hours, minutes? noon, midnight? and all eyes
> Blind with the pin and web, but theirs, theirs only.

The internal pause is, in these lines, more insistent than the pauses at the ends of lines, though, in this particular case, both are clearly present. It divides the five beats in the line into groups of three and two or, after the break at 'honesty', two and three. The regularity is a contrived one, to suggest a catalogue, a sameness which the observer sees in the activities listed. The change in the place of the caesura as the lines proceed prevents, in this case, the too insistent establishment of a false metre, and, by setting up a pattern of lines which lead from shorter to longer groups of words, allows the catalogue to swell into a more emphatic rhythm.

The decline of the traditional pentameter in favour of freer verse forms in contemporary poetry has diminished our expectation of traditional regularities, and has to that extent removed one source of effects from the poet's equipment. Nevertheless skilful uses of pauses within and at the ends of lines can still be found. Henry Reed in 'Naming of Parts' allows line-ends to fall in the middle of sentences, but in so doing he uses our tendency to pause at the end of a line to suggest the self-important pauses of an army instructor's speech, and also catches the quiet transition into daydreaming, followed by an appropriate catch of breath, in the listening soldier:

> This is the lower sling swivel. And this
> Is the upper sling swivel, whose use you will see,
> When you are given your slings. And this is the piling swivel,
> Which in your case you have not got. The branches
> Hold in the gardens their silent, eloquent gestures,
>   Which in our case we have not got.

These lines are modern in their relation between metre and syntax, since the traditional pentameter usually favours a greater syntactic division at the line-end than within the line. If pauses within lines are more prominent than those at the line-end, the line will break apart. This is, indeed, part of the effect in Yeats's line

> Things fall apart. The centre cannot hold.

All language has pauses; in verse they need to be more patterned than the pauses of prose, or we will simply hear prose.

Consider the following lines from a play:

LADY ALLWORTH [*aside*]: I am glad to hear this. Why then, My Lord, pretend you marriage to her? Dissumulation but ties false knots on that straight line by which you, hitherto, have measured all your actions.

LOVELL: I will make answer, and aptly, with a question. Wherefore

have you, that, since your husband's death, have lived a straight and
chaste nun's life, on the sudden given yourself to visits and entertain-
ments? Think you, madam, 'tis not grown public conference? Or the
favours which you too prodigally have thrown on Wellborn, being
too reserved before, incur not censure?

LADY ALLWORTH: I am innocent here, and on my life I swear my
ends are good.

LOVELL: On my soul, so are mine to Margaret.

Well, any questions? I mean, are you suspicious about anything? Because I have deceived you in this quotation by printing
as prose what is normally printed as verse. The lines are from
Massinger's *A New Way to Pay Old Debts*, Act IV Scene i, a
play ostensibly in blank verse. John Middleton Murry observed
that Massinger is 'almost as remote from true blank verse as was
the prose of Congreve'. It is, in fact, good prose. Unlike Congreve,
however, it can be fitted into rhythmical five-stress lines. You
perhaps suspected this when reading such sequences as 'And on
my life I swear my ends are good'. This was, however, not a
single line in the printed play, where the text reads:

> I am innocent here, and on my life I swear
> My ends are good.

Though stress occurs regularly, no natural pause marks the line-
end. Here is Lady Allworth's speech in its proper form:

LADY ALLWORTH: I am glad to hear this.
Why then, My Lord, pretend you marriage to her?
Dissimulation but ties false knots
On that straight line by which you, hitherto,
Have measured all your actions.

In written poetry, as in other writing, pause is partly indicated
by punctuation, more regularly in earlier, especially dramatic,
writing than in present practice, where, for example, the very
frequent occurrence of a pause between a subject and its predicate
(if the subject is at all long) is left unmarked. In some Anglo-
Saxon manuscripts a raised dot was used by scribes to mark a
break between units, and this practice continued in Middle
English manuscripts. It probably indicated a pause and associated

intonation, and in the sixteenth century was interpreted, in Sir
Philip Sidney's words, as 'That *Caesura* or breathing place in
the middest of the verse'. Sidney's contemporary, Puttenham,
observed that 'The very nature of speech (because it goeth by
clauses of severall construction and sense) requireth some space
betwixt them with intermission of sound', and noted the varying
duration of such intermissions in three values, comma, colon and
period. These terms in early use (and the term *period* even now)
were used both for the punctuation mark which indicated a pause
and the syntactic unit which the pause marked off. It is a reminder that pause cannot be dissociated from other elements in
a description of language. It has close relations with syntax and
intonation, and within metrics (the systematic study of the sound
of poetry) with stress and the syllable. It will be convenient to
delay further discussion of pause until something has been said
about these.

The syllable pulse in language is marked by an alternating
restriction and release in the outward flow of air which produces
speech. The primary impulse seems to be produced by muscles in
the chest; it is made audible by vibration of the voice for at least
part of every syllable, and further restrictions, heard as consonants, usually mark its boundaries. The relatively unobstructed
central part of the syllable is heard as a vowel or, exceptionally,
the equivalent *l*, *m*, *n* or *r* without vowel heard in one kind of
pronunciation of *bottle*, *bottom*, *button* or an American pronunciation of *butter*.

The structure of syllables varies from one language to another.
In Maori, the syllable consists of a single vowel, or a single
consonant followed by a single vowel. There is no other possibility. New words, borrowed from English, are adapted to this
pattern, *register* becoming *rehita* or *Auckland Akarana*. In
English, syllables can be more complex, with up to three initial
consonants, as in *strive*, and up to four or five final consonants,
according to whether the word *sixths* is pronounced with a pure
'th' as in *wraith*, or with an intrusive 't' as in *eighth*. It is, incidentally, a measure of the stylistician's indifference to defining
the exact boundaries of linguistic schemes that the difference

between the two pronunciations of *sixths*, though it divides English speakers into two groups with a different basic syllable structure, is scarcely to be accounted a stylistic difference. This is because it normally passes unnoticed. Even when differences of this kind are noticed, they are not always understood as differences in syllable structure. In a certain type of American 'black English', final consonant clusters are simplified, so that 'he picked me up' is pronounced as 'he pick me up', but speakers of standard American English are likely to interpret this as uncertainty of grammar rather than a difference in syllable structure (and base many prejudices on the misinterpretation).

The stylistician deals with what the users of a language know and notice, and the users of language have a general, rather than an exact, awareness of syllable structure, feeling that some languages (Italian, especially) are more 'musical' than others, or recognizing that *five sixths* is 'harder to say' than *a half*, noticing, probably, the 'restrictiveness' of stop consonants (*p,t,k,b,d,g*) more than the continuants (*l,m,n,r,s,f* and other sounds which can be prolonged). Awareness of all these things is likely to be sharpened and made more precise in poetry.

Syllables vary in 'length' or duration. The syllable *band* is longer than *bat*, both because there are more sounds in it and because we tend to lengthen the pronunciation of the *a* before the voiced sounds *n* and *d*. In the same way, *seed* has a longer vowel than *seat*, though few of us notice this because length of vowel alone does not distinguish words in standard English.

Though we do not consciously notice the difference in the duration of the vowels in the words *seat* and *seed*, we are not, perhaps, entirely unaware of it. Most people, in my experience, quickly notice the difference when it is pointed out to them. In some forms of English there may be pairs of vowels which are distinguished mainly by differences in their length. For some speakers, *cut* and *cart* have so nearly the same quality that a drawled *cut* would hardly be distinguished from a normal pronunciation of *cart*. Experiments in Australia showed that students listening to a series of tape-recorded pronunciations of the word *banner* with a short or lengthened pronunciation of the *a*, tended to interpret the version with short *a* as the word meaning 'flag' and the version where *a* had more duration as a word meaning 'someone who bans something' (a prominent figure in Australia, of course).

A linguistic scientist writing a systematic description of English may find it economical to ignore these indistinct patterns in vowel and syllable length and discuss the difference between *seed* and *seat* entirely in terms of a voiced and an unvoiced consonant, but it seems that those who use English have some (usually unanalysed) awareness of the differences in duration as well, so that these differences may enter legitimately into stylistic discussions.

They perhaps help with the difficult poetic problem of scanning Milton's line

Rocks, caves, lakes, fens, bogs, dens and shades of death

in which *caves*, *fens* and *dens* ought, according to the metre, be more prominent than *Rocks*, *lakes* and *bogs*. Clearly it is not, in this line, a difference of stress, until the words 'and shades of death' are reached. Yet we feel that, though the catalogue is given weight by suspending some of the conventions of metre, the words are in the right order metrically. Perhaps this is because the words *caves* and *fens*, with voiced consonants to end them, are longer than *Rocks* and *lakes* with unvoiced consonants, and this establishes the metre. Even *bogs*, though voiced, is perhaps shorter than *dens*, as a stop is shorter than a continuant, so that the rhyme linking *dens* and *fens* is not the only clue to scansion but an extra brace in an already rhythmical sequence.

Again, Pope's unfair parody of the alexandrine (six-stress) poetic line

That, like a wounded snake, drags its slow length along

illustrates some of the ways in which lengthened syllables can cause delays along the line. He uses diphthongs (gliding vowel sounds, which, other things being equal, are longer than monophthongs, or 'pure' sounds) in *like* (longer than *lick*) and *snake* (longer than *snack*); he uses syllables ending in continuant sounds (*long* is longer than *log*), sometimes combined with another voiced sound (*drags*, *wound-*). *Drags* is particularly effective in slowing the line because it is placed in a position where we would expect a short unstressed syllable. This throws *its* into unstressed position, next to the metrically unstressed *slow*, so that a sequence of four consonants, *-ts sl-*, three of them continuants, must be pronounced between the dislocated 'beats' *drags* and *length*. The 'distributed pause' at the commas offers two more occasions for delay.

The length (or 'quantity') of syllables was more important in early English than it is now. In modern English, apart from some Elizabethan experimenters, length of syllables does not enter into the theoretical metrical pattern of poetry, but the number of syllables does. A regular line in English verse traditionally has a fixed number of syllables, most commonly eight or ten. The number of syllables in a word is therefore of importance for poetry. This may seem straightforward; obviously *bake* has one syllable, *baker* two and *bakery* three. But how many syllables are there in *practically*? Or *familiar*? In older poetry, we may need to ask, further, what was the pronunciation, when the poet wrote, of words that may have changed in pronunciation since his time. When Chaucer wrote

> Un-to his faire fresshe lady May

he wrote a metrical ten-syllabled line, because *-e* in *faire* and *fresshe* made a syllable, comparable in sound to the modern *fairer* and *fresher*.

It is argued whether the syllabic sounding of final *-e* was general in the English of Chaucer's time; it need not have been, since poetry has often retained for its own purposes pronunciations no longer current. Milton's lines

> In notes, with many a winding bout
> Of linked sweetness long drawn out

would be ruined if we failed to give *linked* its second syllable.

Perhaps partly through a misreading of Chaucer, critics until the eighteenth century worried about the English language as an instrument for poetry because of the number of monosyllables in it. Perhaps we can recover the anxiety by reading a line of Chaucer such as 'He coude songes make and wel endyte' as a modern 'He could songs make and well indict'. We would hardly think Chaucer a musical poet then, and if there was not yet much other verse in English to match the still well-remembered classical poets, we might easily lack confidence in English as a language capable of enough regularity for serious poetry, just as some people smile today when Sophocles is translated into New Guinea Pidgin English.

Pope's well-known

> And ten low words oft creep in one dull line

may be thought to attack monosyllables, but, if so, he is unfair again, since the dragging nature of the line does not arise from its monosyllables alone, but from the delaying clusters of consonants (as -*ft cr*- in 'oft creep') and in the choice of syntax (numeral plus adjective plus noun) which obliges us to give almost equal stress in actual performance to syllables which the metre requires us to count as unstressed and those which the metre requires us to think of as stressed. This would not be true if he had written an equally monosyllabic

> And lo! The words are ten and make a line.

or, if this seems insufficiently poetic, it is not true in his own description of the Denizens of Air in *The Rape of the Lock* who

> Waft on the breeze, or sink in clouds of gold.

It seems that the criticism of monosyllables, at least in the eighteenth century, may really have been directed mainly at the choice of monosyllabic forms where these were alternatives to disyllabic forms, the choice of *linkt* rather than *linkèd*, for example. Here the shortened form resulted in a collision of consonants which might have seemed awkward to pronounce, though it has since become standard. Latin-derived words also allowed the consonant cluster of *linkt*, in a word like *distinct*, but in Latin itself vocalic endings to this stem prevented the further accumulation of consecutive consonants as another word followed.

Eighteenth-century writers seem to have preferred a preponderance of vocalic sounds. Swift would have entrusted the future of the language to women, because in an experiment (which really ought to be repeated) in which men and women were asked to produce nonsense words, he found that men produced clusters of consonants while women produced words reminiscent of Italian. Objections seem less often to have been directed at contractions, equally monosyllabic, which brought vowels together or simplified a sequence of vowels, and poets continued to admit the useful *th'* and *e'er* and *o'er*. Among Pope's lines of ten monosyllables, some are the result of such contractions, for example

> Thinks what ne'er was, nor is, nor e'er shall be

from *An Essay on Criticism.*

It remains difficult to recapture a concern about monosyllables which is found in writers on language from Spenser's time to Pope's. If we compare the eighty lines of Keats's *Ode to a Nightingale* with the first eighty lines of Pope's *The Rape of the Lock*, we find, certainly, that Keats has four entirely monosyllabic lines to Pope's one, but Pope's sixteen lines where one two-syllabled word varies this pattern are not notably different from Keats's eighteen; Pope has twenty-three lines where two disyllables vary the pattern to Keats's eighteen, not a marked difference considering the balanced nature of Pope's verse. In fifteen of Pope's lines and nine of Keats's there are three disyllables. Keats more often (nine times to Pope's three) has a single three-syllabled word, but a three-syllabled word occurs along with a disyllable almost equally in the two poets (fifteen lines in Pope, thirteen in Keats). More striking differences can be found among poems, of course. In Ben Jonson's simple 'Drink to me only with thine eyes' seven of the sixteen lines are monosyllabic and each of the other nine is varied with a single disyllable. We may contrast T. S. Eliot's 'Mr Eliot's Sunday Morning Service', where of thirty-two eight-syllabled lines none is monosyllabic, only four have a single disyllable and one line consists of a single word. Whereas in the eighty (longer) lines of Pope or Keats, only ten different types of line were found by relating syllables to words, Eliot's thirty-two lines show fourteen such types. No word, including compounds as words, in Pope or Keats had more than four syllables, but three of Eliot's lines contain words of five or more syllables.

It would seem then that the syllabic structure of words does in extreme cases have a discernible stylistic effect, but since it does not clearly separate poets as different as Pope and Keats, it is of less importance than the earnest early debates about monosyllables might lead us to expect.

In prose style the choice or avoidance of polysyllabic and sesquipedalian words is still often discussed. We now like simple words, but monosyllables in prose were once less admired than they are now. James Harris in the eighteenth century thought that to close a sentence with 'to set it up' or 'to get by and by at it' was to introduce 'Rabble at the close of some pompous Cavalcade'. One suspects that the little words were rabble because they had no classical or noble French origin, and that where early writers condemned English for being monosyllabic, Harris dislikes monosyllables for being English. Rhythmically 'to get by and by at it' (if the weight comes on the second *by*) is indistinguishable from 'commend its propriety'. Of course, it would be possible to pronounce 'to get by and by at it' with a different emphasis, with the weight on *at*, so that the rhythm would now be nearer to 'agreeably constructed'. There is, then, one difference between a sequence of monosyllables and a rhythmically similar polysyllable. In the polysyllable, the weight (or 'stress', to use the more technical word) is fixed, but in a sequence of monosyllables there is potential variation. Polysyllabic prose is therefore likely to be more rhythmically exact than 'simple prose', unless the writer using shorter words can so control his rhythms that it is clear to the reader where the stress should fall. In poetry it is one of the functions of metre to control emphasis in this way. In Pope's

In ev'ry work regard the writer's End
Since none can compass more than they intend

a witless reading with emphasis on *writer's* (not reader's) and
they (not we) is prevented by the emphasis normally given to
rhyming words. The prose writer, without this aid, has to control
the incidence of main stresses by means of syntax, and, indeed,
in a long rhyming poem, a regularly recurring emphatic stress
would begin to lose its force, so that a poet too will use syntax to
shift, sometimes, the expected main stress from the line-end, as
Pope does in

Some to church repair
Not for the doctrine, but the music there.

Inevitably a discussion of syllables tries to drift into a discussion of other variables in the complex interrelated sound effects
which a poet has to manage. We have begun to discuss stress and
in the term 'emphatic stress' surreptitiously introduce another
element, since analysis would show that intonation enters into
this concept. We do well to remember the interrelationship of
the threads we are trying to sort out, but must now attempt to
isolate the concept 'stress' in language.

It is easier to point to the existence of stress than to discover
its phonetic nature. It is easy to hear that *baker* has stress on the
first syllable, *cadet* on the second. *Contract* has stress on the first
syllable if a noun, on the second if a verb. The phrase 'on the
whole' has stress on the last syllable. 'After all' traditionally has
stress on the last syllable, but a recent tendency is to place stress
on the first. The 'weight' of a stressed syllable usually appears as
an increase in loudness, but not always. 'Thank you' is normally
pronounced with stress on the first syllable, and this is still true
in a possible pronunciation in which that syllable becomes
inaudible ('kyou). There is still a chest pulse, or residual pulse,
which is felt as stress by the speaker and even sympathetically felt
as such by the hearer, despite the absence of any audible sound.
In the same way it is possible to 'hear' silent beats in music, and,
according to one theory of metrics, in poetry.

An Elizabethan poet and musician, Thomas Campion, noticed

s.–3

that English lines of five feet 'hold pace with the Latines of sixe', thinking this greater length perhaps due to the 'heaviness' of monosyllables in English, but associating it with rests in music. In our time, the phonetician David Abercrombie has more clearly suggested that an English pentameter (five-stress line) is in reality a six-stress line, and that the pause at the end of each line is in essence a 'silent stress'. Enjambement, or a run-on line, is then seen to be an audible displacement of a silent stress. The theory of silent stress perhaps proves useful in describing nursery rhymes, which do not fit very well into classical patterns. Try it out:

> Hickory dickory dock (tee tum),
> The mouse ran up the clock (tee tum);
> The clock struck one and down the mouse ran.
> Hickory dickory dock (tee tum).

My bracketed 'tee tum' need not be pronounced but simply 'felt' as a silent stress.

Traditional metrical theory assumes a simple opposition between stressed and unstressed syllables. For this theory a syllable is stressed if it has stronger stress than the syllable following it. In poetry the word *penitential* is a simple sequence of stressed, unstressed, stressed, unstressed syllables. It is evident that in English this is a simplification of the actual facts of language, since the main stress on the third syllable is stronger than any other, though the first syllable has more stress than the second or fourth.

If we accept traditional metrics we must assume that poetry has added a scheme of its own, a metrical scheme, to the scheme of ordinary language, but, in so doing, it disregards some of the describable scheme of ordinary language. Part of what metrical theory leaves to stylistic variation is therefore part of what a scientific linguist includes in his description of English stress. In Lewis Carroll's couplet

> I sent to them again to say
> 'It will be better to obey'

both lines have the same metre, iambic tetrameter, that is a line of four 'feet' each consisting of a (relatively) unstressed and (relatively) stressed syllable. But the lines sound different, and it is obvious that this is because in the first line stronger stresses occur on the first, third and fourth beats than on the second, whereas in the second line there is more weight on the second and fourth beat. In this case the linguist can provide for the critic an exact description (if he wants it) of the varying degrees of stress that give lines their particular 'style'.

Some linguists have wanted to do more and have urged critics to abandon traditional metrics in favour of a description based on more than two stresses. Usually linguists have urged four significant degrees of stress, shown in the phrases 'lighthouse keeper', where each stress is less strong than the one before it, or 'light housekeeper' in which the strongest stress follows the second-degree stress, -keep- has less stress than either, and the final syllable less still. They point out that in English (but not in, for example, Spanish) there is a tendency to give equal duration to each group of syllables containing a main stress. If the number of stresses is the same, it may take no longer to say 'My són-in-law's a líghthouse-keeper in América' than to say 'My són's a clérk in Léeds', though one sentence has more than twice as many syllables as the other. If, then, a 'beat' in poetry falls on a syllable with weakened stress, the duration of the line and the relative length of its parts may be altered, and the theory of metrics does not tell us this. Hopkins, with his theory of 'sprung rhythm', appears to have been making a similar point, though he was concerned especially to point out that if a line has a fixed number of stresses, any number of unstressed syllables may be allowed. In 'The Wreck of the Deutschland' each stanza ends in a line of six stresses, but a varying number of syllables controls varying effect in

> The sour scythe cringe, and the blear share come

or

> With the burl of the fountains of air, buck and the flood of the wave.

It is possible to base poetry directly on the 'isochronic principle' that the time elapsing between stressed syllables in English tends to be uniform. It may become fully uniform if ambiguous stress, a metrical stress on a phonetically weakly stressed word, is avoided, along with subtleties of caesura. This seems to be the principle underlying the curiously attractive rhythm of Louis MacNeice's 'Bagpipe Music':

> Annie MacDougall went to milk, caught her foot in the heather,
> Woke to hear a dance record playing of old Vienna.
> It's no go your maidenheads, it's no go your culture,
> All we want is a Dunlop tyre and the devil mend the puncture.

Each line sets up eight insistent beats, the last a 'silent stress', the others falling on words with main or secondary (not third- or fourth-degree) stress. The stresses are variously placed in terms of syllables, but are regular in their timing, so that the words 'no go', falling together, become lengthened to provide a drone, while sequences like 'Annie MacDougall' demand a more rapid skirl of syllables. But possibly the usefulness of the isochronic principle in explaining a poem so distinctive in its rhythm is not an argument for its wider use.

Counter-arguments in favour of traditional metrics are available. It is worth setting up a scheme which gives a single ground-plan for all the lines in *Paradise Lost*, even if a great deal of easily described variation is left to stylistics. The theory is enough to distinguish *lighthouse-keeper* (two trochees) from *light house-keeper* (an iamb and a trochee) at least. It is not necessary for a metrical scheme to include all the details of a linguistic scheme, since stylistics, as we have seen, is able to deal with an interplay of schemes or a superimposition of one pattern on another, provided the stylistician understands both. The linguist is right to offer his help, but not necessarily right to ask that traditional schemes be abandoned.

It does mean, however, that the traditional iambic pentameter very seldom comes near in sound to the theoretical basis 'de DUM de DUM de DUM de DUM de DUM'. In all of Wordsworth's sonnet on Westminster Bridge, this scheme is felt in the background but never once fully realized until the poem comes to rest in the last line

> And all that mighty heart is lying still.

Nevertheless it is possible that if a crowd in Trafalgar Square could be induced each to chant a different iambic pentameter line, the result would be a surging justification of the traditional metrical theory. (Experimenters might find it easier to super-impose readings on a tape.)

Traditional metrical theory admits the possibility of 'inversion' of a foot. In

> Law in his voice and fortune in his hand

we cannot give the first *in* more weight than *Law* and so we say that the first foot is inverted and that instead of the expected beginning 'de DUM de DUM' we have 'DUM de de DUM'. This variation of the scheme allows a poet control of emphasis, but traditional metrical theory does not include in its theoretical scheme a more important means of controlling emphasis. Among the five beats in a pentameter line, one is very often weaker than the others. In Johnson's line (above) for example, the second *in*, though stronger than the syllable following it, is phonetically no stronger than the first *in*. The phonetic weakness of this beat, like the initial inversion, directs our attention to the more semanti-cally important words, *law*, *voice*, *fortune* and *hand*, but tradi-tional metrics explains only one part and not the other of this marshalling of emphasis. Here then is a new justification of attempts to introduce a full phonetic theory with its four degrees of stress (or at least three of them) into poetic discussion. If such a theory is not adopted, the discussion of the stylistic variation in individual lines will need to deal with 'weakened stress' which a poet may place variously or not at all, as he places a caesura or inverted foot, within the limits of a basic metrical pattern.

If a student in my classes cannot understand Pope, I ask him to read some aloud. If he begins

> 'Tis hard to say if greater want of skill
> Appear in writing or in judging ill

in a stolid chant of five equal stresses per line, we discuss how to read Pope aloud. Once the second line is read with more stress on *writ-* and *judg-* than on *-pear* and *ill* (though these have more stress than *or*), problems of understanding will be found to have disappeared. The varying stresses in this line are not the optional ornaments of a particular performance; they must be understood if the poem is to be read meaningfully. They are open to precise theoretical description, and if the abstract metrical theory of the literary critic leaves them out, this must be one place where the linguist can be of use, by providing a language for discussing in an exact way the 'stylistic variation' within a metrical scheme.

In Anglo-Saxon poetry, a line consisted of four stresses and a varying number of unstressed syllables. The line was divided into two half lines, each with two stresses, by a caesura. The heroic words uttered at the Battle of Maldon will illustrate:

> Hige sceal þe heardra, heorte þe cenre
> Mod sceal þe mare, þe ure mægen lytlað.

The lines mean 'Our resolve shall be the firmer, heart the bolder; courage shall be the greater as our strength dwindles'. If scholars will look the other way, I will give a very rough indication of the pronunciation, since the sound of the lines is important for the present discussion. Chant them with enjoyment; no Anglo-Saxon will hear you. (Stress the syllables marked with an accent, passing more quickly over the others – do not pronounce the *r*'s I have used to indicate vowel quality.)

> He´eyer shairl the haírdrer, haírter the kénrer
> Móde shairl the máhrer, they oorer máyen liílath.

It is usually assumed that this four-stress line is very different from later English poetry. It is of course different. Until Hopkins revived something of this old style, the number of syllables in a line was regulated in a way foreign to Old English verse, and the caesura was less regularly placed. Yet, underneath the continental syllabic line in English, there has been, like a counterpoint, a hint of the old four-stress rhythm, because one beat in the penta-meter is so often weakened. There is perhaps more continuity in English verse than is commonly supposed.

A study of stress alone (or of syllables alone or of pause alone) in poetry alone could furnish material for a lengthy and often controversial book, but this book must not be lengthy and should not often be controversial, and so, regretfully, we leave these problems to glance at the next variable in language, intonation.

For a long time the importance of pitch or tune – technically called intonation – in English was not recognized, and it has not yet entered into the discussion of poetry. It was debated in the eighteenth century whether English words had tone like Greek words or whether, as Lord Monboddo thought, English had stress only, and was musical only in the way that a drum is. Thomas Sheridan, the elocutionist father of the better known playwright, was aware of the importance of tone, but did not clearly separate it from pause. He noted that a suspension or lift of the voice was combined with a short pause at points marked in writing by a comma. It is interesting to note that Sheridan's description, promulgated in America early in the nineteenth century by a now little remembered writer on speech called James Rush and later by a writer of a compendious *Grammar of Grammars* called Goold Brown, survives in the recent American theories of 'juncture' which similarly combined grammatically determined tone and pause. After Sheridan, John Walker introduced a more analytical study of intonation, separating it from pause and noting the essential difference between rising and falling tones. He is a rich source of detail about eighteenth-century ways of reading poetry and made the important point that intonation in English is not a property of words but of sentences or clauses. It is idle to argue whether the second syllable of *belief* is higher or lower in pitch than the first, though a generation had argued such points. The second syllable of *belief* usually has a higher tone than the first in the question 'Is that your belief?' and a lower tone in the answer 'That is my belief.'

The range of English tones can be isolated in more or less pure form by considering the sounds we can give to 'mm' used as a form of agreement and the like. This use of 'mm', with all its tones, seems by the way to be found in some other European languages, so that the following discussion can sometimes be used in classes for foreign students to link English tones with something known and make at the same time a friendly discovery that there are elements of a common European language other than the technical.

If the sound of 'mm' begins at mid-pitch and glides down the scale, it means 'yes', a simple agreement. If it begins at high pitch before gliding down it suggests a more emphatic, enthusiastic agreement. (Foreign students catch the excitement of discovery at this point, and produce fine enthusiastic 'mm's.) If 'mm' begins low and rises to mid-pitch, it suggests a question or an agreement with a built-in implication of 'Is that all right?' If it begins at mid-pitch and rises to high pitch, a tone of surprise is added to the question. If the 'mm' falls and rises again, a note of hesitation is suggested. A rise followed by a fall might represent a particularly enthusiastic agreement.

These tones enter into connected language as the 'moving' tones on emphatic words in a clause. In 'If John runs, I will jump' the words 'If' and 'John' have level tone, though 'John' has lower pitch than 'If', but on 'runs' the voice glides down and up. In the second clause, 'I' and 'will' are level in tone, though 'will' is lower in pitch than 'I', but 'jump' returns to the pitch of 'I' and glides downwards. (Other pronunciations are possible, of course; I regard this as a normal pronunciation in British English at a fairly deliberate speed.)

The fall-and-rise intonation is often used at the end of a clause which does not end a sentence and at other points where a comma would be used in writing. The suggestion of hesitation heard in 'mm' with this pattern is more specifically an indication that something could or will be added. The 'low fall' is appropriate at the end of a sentence, including questions beginning with *who*, *which*, *how*, *why* and similar interrogative words. The low rise is often used at the end of a question which can be answered with 'yes' or 'no', especially when inverted word order does not already signal a question. If the tone of a question beginning with *who*, *which* etc. rises, it asks for a repetition of information already given (Three cheers for Pooh! For who?) If a yes-no question has falling intonation, it seeks confirmation, e.g. 'I liked your book.' – 'Oh, have you read it?' We would expect both speeches in this conversation to have falling intonation. Since a rising tone may denote a question, a sentence pronounced with rising intonation may be a question even without the usual inversion of word order: 'You've remembered the tickets?' It might even remain a question with falling intonation ('You *have* remembered the tickets?'), though generally such questions are very easily misunderstood as statements unless the context makes the interrogative intention clear.

The high-pitched tones and the rise-fall are of stylistic rather than grammatical interest. They are expressive variations of surprise or pleasure or dismay. They are not easily transmitted in writing, though the use of italics or exclamation marks gives some indication of the appropriate reading. Italics may also be used to show that a moving tone falls on a syllable other than the normal or 'unmarked' last stress in a clause, if this is not evident from the context.

Some important distinctions in intonation are entirely unrecorded in writing. An early nineteenth-century rhetorician complained of a curate who read Mark iv, 21 (Is a candle brought to be put under a bushel or under a bed?) 'pronounced as to imply that there is no other alternative'. Logicians give the word *or* two distinct meanings, and these meanings are clearly kept apart in speech by intonation. 'Tea or coffee?' with rising tone on *tea* and falling tone on *coffee*, or with a falling tone throughout the sequence, implies that the choice is between these two items alone, whereas 'Cigarettes or liquor?' pronounced by a customs official with rising tone on both nouns, or on the word *liquor* alone, leaves open the possibility that further items might attract his interest, and does not imply that one of the two items is necessarily thought to be present, as a rising and a falling tone would.

A writer, even a poet very concerned about the sound of his writing, cannot lay down an intonation for his reader except where this is prescribed by the grammatical structure of what he writes and its context. A poet could in theory provide a score to his text but it seems that, despite the availability of adequate phonetic notations, no poet has yet thought of doing this. Perhaps the absence of a poetic theory of intonation has allowed the neglect of this part of the technique of poetry by poets and by critics. No doubt the child who chants 'Three cheers for Pooh! For who? For Pooh!' is aware of an interesting intonation pattern but he forgets this before he can discover Browning's more intricate patterns:

> 'Were you happy?' – 'Yes' – 'And are you still as happy?'
>   'Yes. And you?'
> 'Then, more kisses!' – 'Did *I* stop them when a million
>   seemed so few?'

The coming of free verse brought new opportunities for control over pause, and, by implication, intonation, but a new poetry also brings a new doggerel, not this time lines 'one for sense and one for rhyme' or a jigging rocking-horse metre, but a fragmentation of speech into a succession of short low-falling tone groups. It would be interesting to investigate how much mediocre contemporary verse is a reiteration of this despondent melody of hollow men.

The old verse forms could imprison a minor talent but a better poet used the pattern as a ground base for other patterns of the kind now liberated by free verse, among which patterns of syntax, implying patterns of intonation, were dominant. A comparatively uncomplicated and regular example is Dr Johnson's poetry with its favourite device of balancing a divided against an undivided line, two short groups against a longer one:

> Must helpless man, in ignorance sedate,
> Roll darkling down the torrent of his fate?
> Must no dislike alarm, no wishes rise
> No cries attempt the mercies of the skies?

This is, among other things, a balance of two short tone groups against a longer tone group in each couplet. The mood is gloomy but not self-pitying, because the pattern is strong enough to control the feeling (and, of course, both in meaning and in their rising intonation the questions modify the potential despair of the words). We are not surprised when the next line begins 'Inquirer, cease'.

Goldsmith, gentle, melancholy, occasionally mischievous, uses the same metre that expressed Johnson's strong feelings and stronger restraint. Thackeray talks of Goldsmith's 'tremulous sympathy'; how does this reside in black marks on paper and their interpretation by a reader's inner voice? I think it lies, perhaps, in an ambiguity of intonation, suggesting but not demanding certain intonations, so that along with the seriousness and sensitivity of a great man we catch the informal modulations of an intimately conversational voice:

> Thus to relieve the wretched was his pride,
> And e'en his failings lean'd to Virtue's side . . .

Pride probably requires falling tone, though a rise is also possible, but *e'en*, requiring a fall, perhaps a high fall, on *failings*, suggests a rise on the following *side*. It is like a change to 'intimate tone' in a formal speech. Again:

> Yet he was kind, or if severe in aught,
> The love he bore to learning was in fault . . .

could just possibly be spoken with a series of falling tones, but again we sense the possibility of the quieter low rising tone on *kind* and a forgiving rise on *severe* and again, perhaps, on *fault*. Thackeray's 'tremulous sympathy' captures this effect rather well, though Thackeray, who thought our love for Goldsmith 'half pity', missed the underlying strength that resides in his effective mastery of the heroic couplet which forms a background for these effects. Goldsmith can write strongly, can address the Muse of Poetry:

> Thou source of all my bliss, and all my woe,
> That found'st me poor at first . . .

(perhaps with a 'tremulous' rise on *first*, admittedly, but any way mischief now intrudes)

> . . . and keep'st me so.

We can compare Johnson and Goldsmith very well because

Johnson contributed the last four lines of *The Deserted Village*. Here are the last six – note how the ambiguous intonation of 'Though very poor' contrasts with the firm tone of the four lines that follow:

> Teach him, that states of native strength possess'd,
> Though very poor, may still be very bless'd;
> That trade's proud empire hastes to swift decay,
> As ocean sweeps the labour'd mole away;
> While self-dependent power can time defy,
> As rocks resist the billows and the sky.

Modern poets have discovered many new subtleties in verse form and the iambic pentameter line has lost its dominating appeal. But not all its tunes have yet been played:

> What pleasures have great princes? These: to know
> Themselves reputed mad with pride or power ...

This is perhaps as near to a unique rhythm as we will find in a modern poet – with its apparently rhetorical question immediately answered, its subtle tension between a possible metrically regular pronunciation with emphasis on *have* and a more likely accumulation of (ironically) majestic weight on the sequence 'great princes', its double pause isolating 'These', perhaps inviting a firm low level tone for this word, the ambiguous tone of 'know' which seems to rise, expecting a pause, but catch itself as 'Themselves' appears, and to link itself with the following line, so that until you count syllables you are sure this line is too long. It was a modern poet, A. D. Hope, who wrote these modern pentameters.

Prose, as well as verse, has a rhythm, analysable into patterns of pause, stress and intonation. But it does not have metre. Huxley's railway passenger in *Eyeless in Gaza* who, lulled by the wheels of the train, began to read 'To stop the train pull down the chain penálty for impróper use five pounds, FIVE POUNDS, FIVE POUNDS', deformed prose which already erred with its hint of verse in its opening words. Classical writers, recognizing the importance of rhythm in prose, described some of the most common prose rhythms in terms of poetic feet, unwittingly launching an artificiality in writing among their followers, who took their generalizations as prescriptions. Prose writers must steer between the extremes of being insensitive to sound, and so losing control of emphasis and subtle meaning, and of being so concerned with sound that emphasis and subtlety echo vacuously among meaningless words. An early nineteenth-century elocutionist who wrote of his subject 'When we say that there is no person or station which it cannot adorn, we assert, that we neither exaggerate on the one hand nor diminish on the other' catches the shape of communication without its substance.

An important function of intonation in speech is to show the connection between parts of a sentence or between separate sentences. The proverbial 'Never venture, never win' is pronounced with a rise or fall-rise at the word 'venture'. In written style, the intonation is likely to be replaced, and the connections between units made explicit, by conjunctions: 'If you never venture, you will never win'. Links between sentences can to some extent be made explicit in a similar way, by using connectives such as *therefore, thus, on the other hand,* or words referring back to a previous sentence (as the word 'similar' does at the beginning of this sentence). There are, however, stress and intonation links as well which are 'felt' even by the silent reader, if he understands the text. A repeated word is likely to have reduced stress and is unlikely to be the word with 'moving tone' unless the repetition is emphatic. Thus in the sequence 'Books are essential to education. The price of books is therefore a matter of social importance', the word *books* in its second occurrence will be lightly stressed, whereas in the sequence 'Books are essential to education. The price of tobacco is without social importance', the word *tobacco*, introducing a new idea, has stress and falling tone. The rule holds good even when an idea is repeated in a synonym and no word is repeated. The pronunciation of 'Snakes and lizards are inactive in winter. Both these reptiles are cold-blooded', with reduced stress on *reptiles*, indicates in a purely formal way that *reptiles* is similar in meaning to the phrase *snakes and lizards*. This, by the way, could help in a task which linguists have found difficult, to approach similarities in meaning through purely formal and scientifically observable indications. As a check, the 'Tea or coffee?' intonation indicates in a purely formal way a diversity of meaning.

The discussion of pause, syllables, stress and intonation has been rich in the suggestion of stylistic problems, but the next variable, the presence or absence of the voice, hardly enters stylistic discussion at all, since this difference is used in the pattern of English to distinguish one sound from another and so cannot usually be arbitrarily varied. The chief exception is in the combination of voice with pause to produce the *um* and *er* especially associated with hesitant speech, but also likely in thoughtful speech, and perhaps seldom entirely absent except in writing and a rather 'glib' style of speech. Pervasive voicing might possibly be heard in the speech of a grizzling youngster ('E zboiled my bezd zdamb'), since a grizzle is a continuous voicing with or without words added, but possibly an imperfect control of the tension of the speech organs in such speech merely gives an impression of voiced sounds. The 'funny foreign' speech of 'Hans Breitmann gife a barty' does not represent a real reversal of voiced and unvoiced sounds but such things as the use of intermediate consonants, ambiguous to English ears, without voice but also without 'aspiration', that minute puff of breathiness that helps English speakers to recognize the unvoiced stops, /p/, /t/ and /k/.

Though the presence or absence of voice is hardly a stylistic variable, variations in the quality of the voice, when it is used, are of basic importance in classifying the 'paralinguistic features' of speech, for example the whispering, breathy, husky, creaky, falsetto or resonant voice of particular utterances, and the laughs, giggles or sobs which further qualify their particular meaning.

Some pervasive effects in speech are produced by organs other than the voice. The nasal passage may be used generally or in the neighbourhood of nasal consonants to produce pervasive or local nasality. The term 'nasal' seems to have acquired a pejorative flavour in common use, perhaps because it is associated with sanctimonious speech, so that it is usually thought to be a distinctive mark of someone else's speech, American or Australian perhaps – though Australians often hear it in English speech. It does seem to be commoner in some varieties of English than others, but often varies from person to person, and is perhaps stylistic rather than schematic in most areas.

Generally spread or rounded lips may similarly be stylistic or the mark of a regional English. Speech with spread (smiling) lips is apt to seem affable. I have heard the theory advanced that New Zealand speech has spread vowels because in a new country everyone is expected to approach his neighbour with a democratic grin. (The stylistic, it seems, has become schematic.) The theory could equally well work in reverse. If Australians tend to use spread-lipped vowels (and they do), they perhaps seem matey fellows, and as this begets a friendly response when they are abroad, they live up to it, becoming indeed matey – at least until their normally flattened intonation patterns appear unnecessarily casual to their hosts.

Differences distinguishing the individual sounds of speech are outside the domain of choice and style, except where variations in their production are of stylistic interest. Not all the differences in sound habitually made by speakers of a particular language are heard consciously by its speakers. Like the Aboriginals of Australia, we might hear snakes and fail to hear horses. Nabokov dwelt on the different quality of the two /l/ sounds in 'Lolita', but few English speakers are aware of a difference between an *l* followed by *o* and one followed by *i*. Phoneticians hear different sounds at the beginning and end of *little*, but most English speakers are hardly aware of this distinction. Russians and Poles, who use the distinction to distinguish words, are sensitive to it. Even recognizable sound differences are not always heard in the flow of speech. Englishmen distinguish 'singing' from 'sinning', but a pronunciation 'The sung comes into this room' is not noticed as deviant. 'Shorpbread' and 'shorkcake' are both assumed to contain the element *short*. The child who wrote in an essay that she had done her 'upmost' probably spelt the word as she had heard it. This phenomenon, assimilation, does not seem to have suggested literary uses, even in such experimental works as *Finnegans Wake*, though it enters into the fun of 'Afferbeck Lauder's *Let Stalk Strine*.

Literary theorists are more interested in asking whether sounds have any inherent meaning. In general, linguists quickly answer that sounds as such do not carry meaning, that there is no meaning in the referential sense to the phoneme /l/, for instance, but some linguists have considered seriously the possibility that particular sequences have developed particular significance in particular languages. In English, initial *gl-* seems to be associated with sources of light in *gleam*, *glow*, *glitter*, *glint* – though not in *glossematics*.

On safer ground, certain words are clearly echoic in origin, *bang*, *crash* or *fizz* being obvious examples. Animal sounds, too, such as *bow-wow* are echoic, though still somewhat arbitrary, as French dogs say *tou-tou* and Dutch dogs say *waf-waf*. The *New Yorker* (27 January 1962) published an amusing article, 'Old McBerlitz Had a Farm', on the varying ways in which animal cries are represented in different languages.

Poets have made use of appropriate sounds to reinforce the meaning of verse. Goldsmith echoes sense with sound in

> The varnish'd clock that click'd behind the door

as Auden does, in the rhythm as well as the sounds of

> The clock on the wall gives an electric tick.

Tennyson's 'murmuring of innumerable bees' is famous, and John Crowe Ransom's reference to the Chicago meatworks and its 'murdering of innumerable beeves' does not show that the onomatopoeic effect in Tennyson is an illusion, but merely that sound in association with its appropriate meaning is effective. In fact Ransom does not even prove that much, since the intrusion of a stop sound into a line relying on a succession of nasals for its success could be taken to 'break the spell'. 'The murmuring of innumerable knees' would avoid this objection and show that sound and sense must combine for the sound to be effective.

Poets, like linguists, are more concerned with pattern than with raw sound, so that the echoing of sense in sound is less important in poetry than the patterns that can be made from chance similarities of sound in different words. The poet uses rhyme to emphasize the shape of his verse, marking line-ends and controlling the sense of expectation in his readers or hearers.

Some poets have scorned rhyme as a needless ornament, but it is an instrument of power in the hands of a good poet. Paradoxically, it both emphasizes and neutralizes the linear movement of language. All language exists in one dimension, in a succession of vibrations if spoken, along a line if written. A sentence does not exist physically all at once, but its parts are heard or read, as they are uttered or written, serially. Rhyme, by creating expectation in a hearer or reader, emphasizes this onward movement of language, but once a pair of rhymes is completed, we seem to look back at a static block of language. A sonnet does not seem to be a long succession of sounds (as it really is of course) but a square block of language to be contemplated as a whole.

Rhyme is paradoxical again in that it sets up expectations that are met and at the same time provides surprise. Once a rhyme scheme is established in a poem or in a poetic tradition, the hearer expects a recurrence of sounds, but he does not know which exact word will provide the chime. A poor poet slips into expected rhymes, until, as Pope put it:

> Where-e'er you find 'the cooling western breeze'
> In the next line it 'whispers thro' the trees'.
> If crystal streams 'with pleasing murmurs creep'
> The reader's threaten'd (not in vain) with 'sleep'.

A better poet finds words less frequently yoked in rhyme, perhaps different parts of speech or words of different grammatical composition. Adrian Mitchell links a contracted noun and verb with a plural noun and a personal name in:

> My girl Kate's teaching in the States,
> Lecturing from town to town.
> Pays her bills by, gets her thrills by
> Studying the influence of Yeats on Yeats.

Rhyme in poetry is a stylistic effect because a poet chooses whether to use rhyme or not, which kind of rhyme to use (whether grammatically different words or not) and which particular rhyming words to select. Rhyme is also found in advertising jingles (What is home without Plumtree's potted meat? Incomplete.), perhaps a kind of applied poetry, and, though not as a stylistic device in particular performances, in ordinary language. We use words once coined or adopted by a popular poetic impulse when we say *roly-poly*, *chock-a-block*, *namby-pamby*, *he thinks he's the bee's knees*, *lock*, *stock and barrel*, *claptrap*, *hobnob*, *helter-skelter*, or *fuddy duddy*. We find somewhat similar patterns in *see-saw*, *tip-top*, *wishy-washy*, *shilly-shally*, *mish-mash*, *sing-song*, *riff-raff* or *group grope*. One of Adrian Mitchell's poems is called 'Icarus Shmicarus', a poem on the unlikelihood that certain cautious people will ever attempt to fly. In this case the method rather than the ready-made term is given by the language, since any word can be contemptuously dismissed in this rhyming way, a legacy of Yiddish which interestingly introduces a new initial consonant cluster, *shm-*, into English.

It is easy to see that some of these popular items are rhyme and others are something else. It is, however, less easy to define a rhyme than to recognize one. I suggest that two words or groups of words rhyme if all sounds after the first sound in the last stressed syllable are the same. Not everyone would agree with this because it logically includes pairs of words of identical sounds like *bear* and *bare*. In French poetry, such rhymes are welcomed, and John Gower used them in English in the fourteenth century:

> He is a noble man of armes
> And yit no strengthe is in his armes

but they are usually avoided in later English poetry.

The definition accommodates pairs such as *believe/receive* or *penitential/deferential* where elements before the stressed syllable are different. The stressed syllable may be the last, as in *sad/mad*, or second to last, as in *sadder* and *madder* or third to last, as in *saddening* and *maddening*. Rarely it may be fourth to last, though if you are rhyming conventionally you would not do this intentionally. Byron in *Beppo* rhymes *Orientalism* with *sentimentalism*.

The elements of *tip-top* make a different pattern, less often used in poetry until Wilfred Owen showed its effectiveness:

> It seemed that out of battle I escaped
> Down some profound dull tunnel, long since scooped.

This effect is called 'consonance' and relies on similar consonants both at the beginning and end of the stressed syllable, with a difference in vowel sound. It is found in Hopkins's 'I caught this morning morning's minion' in *morn-* and *min-*. The same line illustrates an opposite device of like vowels and different consonants, called 'assonance', in the syllables *caught* and *morn-*. It was assonance, rather than rhyme, which linked *heather/Vienna* and *culture/puncture* in Louis MacNiece's 'Bagpipe Music'.

Hopkins's richly wrought style can be used to demonstrate two further sound effects. In the words 'so fagged, so fashed, so cogged, so cumbered', the words *fagged* and *fashed* have the same initial consonant and the same vowel, to make what G. N. Leech has called a 'reverse rhyme'. Common language examples are 'cash and carry', 'part and parcel' or 'home and hosed'. *Cogged* and *cumbered*, however, share only an initial consonant. Such repetition of an initial consonant, or the choice of a set of words beginning with (any) vowel sounds, as 'age and age's evils', is called 'alliteration'. In post-medieval verse it is a sporadic special effect, but in Old English verse it, rather than rhyme, was the organizing principle of verse, since three of the four stressed words in a line were expected to alliterate:

> Mod sceal þe mare, þe ure mægen litlað.

Within Old English, therefore, the use of alliteration represented a free stylistic choice only in ordinary language, or in prose, where it was sometimes used to drive home points in sermons, but in poetry it was part of the extended scheme in which the poet worked.

Early English alliterative texts have usually been copied by hand many times, and may have become corrupt in the process.

If an expected alliteration is missing, a modern editor is tempted to assume corruption of the text. It is theoretically possible, however, that an occasional breaking of the rules was felt as stylistic effect by the original hearers of the poem, and, though a modern reader can learn to appreciate the alliterative pattern, he cannot recapture it well enough to become sensitive to such variation.

We are much better able to understand the reasons for deviation in our own verse. The patterns of sound available to a poet working within the English tradition are infinitely rich, and yet there comes a time when rhyme and regularity themselves become stale and new freedoms are sought and conventions broken. We see it already in Keats. Rhyme traditionally links stressed syllables, but part of the effectiveness of the opening verse in 'La Belle Dame Sans Merci', with its other-worldly frozen movement, comes from its linking of a phonetically (though not metrically) unstressed syllable with a stressed one:

> O what can ail thee, knight-at-arms,
> Alone and palely loitering?
> The sedge has wither'd from the lake
> And no birds sing.

Variations are effective partly because they oppose established patterns. When the old patterns are quite forgotten by the young, time will sift out those new metrical patterns that have lasting value; a new tradition will be established and opposed, perhaps by finding new value in traditions discarded long before.

3. Syntax

Theodulphus of Orleans portrayed Grammar with whip and shears – to spur the lazy and to prune faults. Modern grammarians are more concerned to describe language as it is than to lay down rules. We have discarded the shears, so that the reader of this chapter need fear only the whip.

Anyone is a grammarian, even if his technical vocabulary is undeveloped, who can point out that 'John runs' is a bit of language consisting of two other bits (or, with prompting, three: 'John', 'run' and '-s'). Grammar is very much concerned with bits consisting of other bits and the relation between the bits.

More technically we will talk of 'units' rather than 'bits', and since the word 'grammar' is often used widely for all systematic study of ordinary non-literary language, we will use the term 'syntax' for the placing and relationship of the units of language.

The relationship of the units within 'John runs' is clear enough. The elements 'run' and '-s' have a closer relationship than any other two elements. Some grammarians prefer to study varying forms of a word (*run, runs, ran, running*) in a separate study of 'morphology', especially for the classical languages, where the basic word is frequently modified by 'inflections' in this way. For English, many find it convenient to include *runs* in syntax, as *run* plus *-s*, and even *ran* as *run* plus *past*, where the element *past* in this case changes the phonetic shape of the basic word to *ran*.

Sometimes the relationship of units within a larger unit is less immediately evident. A pretty young student is not necessarily a student that is pretty young, and if the Queen wears an old gold dress, it is not because she cannot afford a new one, but do 'radical workers and students' include all students or only those who are radical? One purpose of the study of syntax is to detect and analyse ambiguity.

For the student of style, a study of syntax will reveal further areas of choice in language, but will also show that the occurrence of pause, stress and intonation is more often predetermined than a study of sounds in isolation would suggest. For the statistical study of style, a knowledge of syntax is indispensable if units bigger than phonemes are to be counted.

There is a widespread belief that in our time a new grammar has replaced traditional grammar. This is not entirely untrue, but it is often unhelpfully exaggerated. Attempts to make a systematic description of the English language have never achieved finality, and there is as much originality in, say, Jespersen's *Analytic Syntax*, a grammar written within the older tradition, as in the studies made today. Some modern studies have added to the traditional analysis of sentences into clauses and words a more rigorous theory of an intermediate unit, the group, corresponding to the rather vaguely defined 'phrase' of older grammar, and have emphasized the importance of a correct procedure in analysing language. This is simply a matter of dealing with each detail at the most convenient level. If, for example, we talk of transitive and intransitive verbs (and some verbs that might be either), we seem to suggest some invisible quality in certain words, but if we talk of transitive and intransitive clauses, this difficulty disappears, because we can see whether a clause contains an object complement or not. It may occur to us that if 'John runs a car' it is really the car that runs, but at least this isolates a more interesting problem.

It is common to base a study of syntax on the sentence, but though the term 'sentence' is quite familiar, it is really a less easily defined unit than clause. Though there is a stylistic difference between the sentence 'John runs, but he can't walk' and the pair of sentences 'John runs. Yet he can't walk', it seems a very small difference on which to base a theory of syntactic units. It seems that the coordinate sentence (one linked by *and, but, or, nor*) is intermediate in status between the pair of linked but independent sentences on the one hand, and the more integrated hypotactic sentence (one containing subordinating conjunctions such as *if*, *because*, *although*, *when*, *which*, etc.) on the other. There is even less cohesion within the sentence 'John runs; he's quite an athlete', where only a semi-colon in writing or a slightly truncated falling tone in careful speech indicates the unity of the sentence. Since in speech even two independent sentences may be run together in a single intonation group (e.g. 'I did. I told you,' with *moving* (see p. 56) tone only on 'told'), the difference between one and two spoken sentences may become very slight.

For this reason statistical and most other studies of style might more conveniently examine clauses than sentences. An acknowledgement of sentence structure can be built into such a study if it includes connectives with the clauses. Thus a writer using many clauses containing *if*, *that*, *although* or *while* will be detected as a writer who uses complex sentences. Another writer who often uses *accordingly*, *nevertheless* or *at the same time* probably uses shorter sentences. A study based on clauses may group these two writers as writers concerned with connections or separate them according to their sentence style, and is thus perhaps more likely to be revealing than a simple count of sentence length or analysis of sentences according to the number and kind of clauses in them.

This is not to discount the importance of the length and complexity of sentences in assessing a writer's style, but merely to approach these qualities in a different way. It would be difficult to exaggerate the importance of sentence structure in the European literary tradition. If we had to decide which of the legacies of Ancient Greece has meant most to Europe and mankind, we might well nominate the complex sentence. Along with Greek philosophy, there grew up a language able to express its fine distinctions and carefully ordered thought. Early and popular writing in any country is close to spoken style, with loose paratactic sentences (in which the clauses are simply laid alongside each other, as in 'Never venture, never win'). The loss of intonation in writing leaves paratactic sentences rather bare. G. Vinokur writes of the early popular Russian sentence that it is 'decentralized' and lacks 'syntactic perspective'. The word 'perspective' describes well the effect of subordination of clauses in the complex hypotactic sentence which the Greeks first taught Europe to write. Each clause in the hypotactic sentence was given its exact weight in a controlled way, and the ordering and connecting of clauses in Greek was able to be copied in other languages, though the words were different, so that, as we put it in non-linguistic terms, Greek civilization spread through Europe. The Romans imitated the Greek sentence and have spread it wherever Latin is an accepted subject in schools. If we feel now that, just as art appears to be losing all perspective, we witness a decline and fall of the classical sentence as the world relapses into journalism and barbarism, I have already indicated one way of taking a less gloomy view. Sentences, as well as clauses, are interconnected, and the journalist or popular writer undertakes a more difficult task of ordering shorter units than the complex sentence into paragraphs which have their own perspective. The conjunctions which link clauses into sentences will, in modern writing, be one important measure of the fluency and coherence of prose, but not the only one.

The theoretical importance of the connecting words of language has not passed unnoticed among practising writers. De Quincey believed that 'all fluent and effective composition depends on the connectives' and on 'an interdependency of sentences'. With the addition of 'effective', this claims too much, since, as De Quincey's own writing warns us, prose that is fluent and connected may yet lack a firm controlling plan, but he has revealed the secret of one virtue of prose – its fluency. He took the word 'connective' from Coleridge's praise of Johnson in *Table Talk*, 15 May 1833: 'A close reasoner or a good writer in general may be known by his pertinent use of connectives. Read that page of Johnson; you cannot alter one conjunction without spoiling the sense.'

The word 'connective' was used by James Harris in 1751 to include both conjunctions and prepositions; it might provide a useful term to include 'sentence connectives' as well, those words (called 'conjunctive adverbs' by William Ward in 1765) which link sentences, words like *moreover*, *therefore*, *further*, *besides, too, likewise, even,* as well as phrases like *on the other hand, because of this,* and perhaps even clauses like *Be that as it may* . . .

While connectives are most essential in writing, where intonation cannot be explicit, they are not confined to it. Antoine Meillet even noticed in France a tendency to elaborate connectives in speech, to use, instead of *et* 'and', the compound connectives *et puis, et alors, et de plus,* and instead of *ou* 'or', *ou bien.* Perhaps in spoken English there is some tendency to do this, to say *and another thing* or *and I might add* rather than *and,* for instance, but a closer parallel is found in the semi-literate elaborations *due to the fact that* 'because', *in the event that* 'if', *in spite of the fact that* 'although'. In some writing it might be necessary to emphasize connectives in this way, but more often the elaborate forms reveal a mistrust of the small words that are so significant to those more used to writing.

The disappearance of the long sentence from the general repertoire of writers on non-technical subjects makes such long sentences as still occur stylistically prominent. This one is from Joseph Heller's novel, *Catch-22*:

It was a night of surprises for Appleby, who was as large as Yossarian and as strong and who swung at Yossarian as hard as he could with a punch that flooded Chief White Halfoat with such joyous excitement that he turned and busted Colonel Moodus in the nose with a punch that filled General Dreedle with such mellow gratification that he had Colonel Cathcart throw the chaplain out of the officers' club and ordered Chief White Halfoat moved into Doc Daneeka's tent, where he could be kept under a doctor's care twenty-four hours a day and be kept in good enough physical condition to bust Colonel Moodus in the nose again whenever General Dreedle wanted him to.

In describing a brisk sequence of events and their results, a series of short sentences would be normal. The effect of this long sentence is of everything happening at once, a piece of interconnected Heath-Robinsonian machinery in complicated operation. There is some extra fun in using quite normal sentence extensions an abnormal number of times, as 'The House that Jack Built' does, in combining a traditional dignified length of sentence with words like *bust* and in ending it all with a triumphantly unemphatic 'to'.

Heller's sentence is not the traditional long sentence, the periodic sentence, which moved towards a delayed main clause. Heller begins with a main clause. In the study of style, the difference between the loose and the periodic sentence has long been thought important, so that it seems to be a defect in a stylistics of the sentence based only on clauses and connectives that the order of clauses in a sentence escapes comment. But it is not inappropriate to segregate the order of clauses into a separate discussion, because the stylistic principles underlying the placing of subordinate clauses in a sentence resemble those guiding the arrangement of sentences in a paragraph, and the arrangement of larger structural elements in a literary work. In all these cases, writers control emphasis and choose to keep a reader in suspense or not. In older manuals, suspense was thought entirely a good thing, but modern writers more often prefer to begin with main statements, adding qualifications afterwards. No theory counters the old praise of suspense, except for a suggestion by the grammarian Yngve that 'right-branching' qualifications, those that follow a main element, are more easily taken in by readers or hearers. This seems true of Heller's sentence and fairly widely in English, but there are difficulties in applying the theory universally. In any case, everyone knew that loose sentences were more easy to take in than periodic sentences.

A more general justification of loose sentences on stylistic grounds could be made. We might point out that a writer can, in the detail as well as the general structure of his writing, choose to keep his reader in suspense and create a sense of mystery, or he can give his main information early in his sentence or his story, losing a sense of mystery but increasing opportunities for irony as each successive detail is contemplated with a maximum awareness of relevant facts. The 'mystery' structure is more emphatic and tends to greater dignity (What God hath joined, let no man put asunder), but in ordinary use is somewhat humourless and tends to be pontifical. It is common in proverbs (If the beard were all, the goat might preach). But there are some proverbs, less sententious, more ruefully ironical, in which a main statement precedes (We never miss the water till the well runs dry). The present liking is for the rueful addition. Wilde's 'I can resist everything except temptation' or Shaw's 'We don't bother much about dress and manners in England, because as a nation we don't dress well and we've no manners' already set the modern tone, both in the loose order of elements and in an attempt to have things both ways, both mystery and irony. We are given the main facts to begin with all right, but are puzzled to know why, until the point comes in the qualification. The separation of irony and mystery is not absolute in sentences or in books. A mystery story of literary quality can be enjoyed for the ironies which become evident in a second reading.

A sentence of several clauses may often be seen as a stylistic alternative to a succession of its separate clauses. The elements of a clause are more interdependent than this, and if they occur in isolation are more likely to be considered truncated clauses rather than independent messages. 'Nice day' is an isolated predicate, but it implies a suppressed 'It is a . . .', and the 'It is a' is suppressed only when the situation or context makes it unnecessary. We would hardly begin a letter with 'Nice day' in isolation.

Even where the situation allows omission of the subject of a clause in this way, there may be danger of ambiguity. When Cornelia Otis Skinner opened in Shaw's *Candida*, he is said to have cabled her: 'Excellent – greatest'. She cabled back: 'Undeserving such praise'. Shaw replied: 'I meant the play', to which Miss Skinner returned 'So did I'. It will be noticed that even with the complete set of telegrams, we remain uncertain how Shaw really meant and Miss Skinner understood the first telegram.

The subject is regularly omitted only in 'non-finite' clauses, those consisting of an infinitive or participle. These are always dependent, and so always have a context. The commonest kind of finite clause with an omitted subject is the imperative clause, 'Run, John,' where the omission is normal. Even here, however, older grammarians supposed a '*you* understood' and the presence of the pronoun is available as a stylistic alternative 'You run off now, John.' From a stylistic point of view, we say 'Run.' is the 'unmarked form' or usual form, and 'You run.' the 'marked form', that is, the form which departs from the more expected pattern and the one in which we are more conscious of a stylistic effect; but, in setting up a grammar, we may choose to take this marked form as base, in order to arrive at a single tidy description of the finite clause. Most recent grammarians adopt this procedure.

The full finite clause, then, requires a subject and predicate. It is an appropriate statement-making unit and its commonest form resembles that of the logical proposition. In 'John runs', 'John' is subject, 'runs' predicate. The structure is not altered if for 'John' we substitute 'Roger' or 'The boy' or 'The young man' or 'A slithy tove' or 'One of the ten fine old stony warriors', but we cannot simply substitute any collection of words; not, for instance, 'will go' or 'if' or 'Hello, darling'. Any words (not themselves making a clause) that can be substituted for 'John' as subject of the clause are referred to in the following discussion as a 'nominal group'. (To keep the definition simple I include pronouns among nominal groups.)

In a similar way, for 'runs' we could substitute 'walks', 'is walking', 'ought to have walked' and other verbal groups, but not 'chases' or 'ought to have chased' unless we add to the essential verbal element (sometimes called the 'predicator' by British linguists) another element to complete the clause, say 'John chased Charlie'. We may use the same items in place of 'Charlie' that we used in place of 'John' earlier, that is nominal groups. These elements which complete certain verbal groups are called 'complements', specificially, in this case, 'object complements'. Clauses with an object complement are called transitive clauses.

There is another set of words and phrases, separate from those that can replace either 'John' or 'runs', that can be optionally added to either transitive or intransitive clauses. Such optional additions are 'quickly', 'now', 'in the morning' or 'with gusto'. I shall use the term 'adjunct' for this set. It is easy to remember a formula for the present view of clause structure, since the letters

S.P.C.A. give us the normal order in English of subject, predicator, complement and adjunct.

Stylistic variation in the clause comes from a varying of the order of the elements. Very commonly an adjunct begins a clause (like the one I have just written). In poetry, an object complement may precede its verb, as in 'Towers and battlements it sees' and in 'all the air a solemn stillness holds', where it is not entirely clear which nominal group is subject and which object, since both readings are meaningful and perhaps work together. Part of the object precedes the verb in Donne's

> The poor, the foul, the false, love can
> Admit, but not the busied man.

and Spenser places an object before a participle and another before a finite verb in a single line in

> On which when gazing him the Palmer saw,
> He much rebuk'd those Wandering eyes of his.

Such inversions are not uncommon in Spenser's language, but the complexity of this one, contrasting with the more normal word order of the succeeding line, perhaps emphasizes Guyon's long gaze at the two naked damsels sporting in the little lake outside the Bower of Bliss. Inversion of subject and object modifies the intonation of a line of verse, adding interest and emphasis but also delaying its onward movement. The possibility of ambiguity adds a further sense of difficulty, though inversions are least ambiguous when a pronoun is present. 'Him the Palmer saw' or 'Ten thousand saw I at a glance' are not ambiguous, but if we were to write 'Ten thousand saw Wordsworth at a glance', we might imagine the poet appearing before a very large meeting.

An initial adjunct in poetry may be followed by inversion of subject and verb, as in Keats's 'Much have I travell'd in the realms of gold' or 'Yet did I never breathe its pure serene' or 'Then felt I like some watcher of the skies', all from the sonnet 'On First Looking into Chapman's Homer'. Inversion of subject and verb after the word for 'then' was normal in Old English and survives in the prayer book 'Then shall the bishop say . . .'

Inversion after an adverb of time therefore has the dignity of archaism and perhaps retains a latent religious potential, to become evident in Dylan Thomas's 'A Refusal to Mourn the Death, by Fire, of a Child in London', with its initial 'Never' anticipating 'Shall I' in the tenth line:

> Never until the mankind making
> Bird beast and flower
> Fathering and all humbling darkness
> Tells with silence the last light breaking
> And the still hour
> Is come of the sea tumbling in harness
>
> And I must enter again the round
> Zion of the water bead
> And the synagogue of the ear of corn
> Shall I let pray the shadow of a sound
> Or sow my salt seed
> In the least valley of sackcloth to mourn
>
> The majesty and burning of the child's death.

The word *never* and its following inversion provide an important clue for understanding the syntax of this long unpunctuated sentence which forms the first thirteen lines of the poem. Having detected the main clause 'Never . . . shall I . . .', we separate 'until . . . darkness tells . . .' and perceive further that it is a darkness which made mankind, fathered life and humbles all things, and so on until all the rich imagery of the words is marshalled into a syntactic shape.

It will be noticed that in the line 'Much have I travell'd in the realms of gold' the verbal group is discontinuous. The verbal group is 'have travell'd'; the inversion places the subject between the auxiliary and the main verbal element. The discontinuous verbal group has long been English idiom, and had in early English some stylistic uses that have not survived. A medieval prose guide for anchoresses, the *Ancrene Riwle*, tells of a certain prattling type of anchoress who chatters to her confessor in the hope of being known and acknowledged among the wise. The author adds (in a word-for-word translation to preserve the syntax): 'Known she is well – he understands that she is foolish'. We are less likely now to use this effective method of emphasis idiomatically, but would probably write 'She is indeed known' or, colloquially, 'She's known all right'.

It would not do to look for reasons every time we find a departure in poetry from the most common order of elements in a clause. It seems evident that once poets are permitted inversions for effect, they will sometimes extend the licence and invert for rhyme. Fitzgerald's 'Ah, with the grape my fading Life provide' would not be a worse line if 'provide' preceded 'my fading Life', but 'died' and 'side' required a rhyming word. I have never thought Wordsworth's 'What wealth the show to me had brought' a good line, and always have to look it up to make sure it reads 'the show to me' and not 'to me the show'. But 'thought' needed a rhyme. Of course we must remember that we are particularly opposed today to 'poetic' language for its own sake. A century ago such language as 'Say not the struggle nought availeth' or 'If doughty deeds my lady please' (written earlier but admired enough to be included in Palgrave's *The Golden Treasury*) was a proper way to set the tone of poetry. But then, as now, inversions influenced the pronunciation of verse with their suggestion of pause at the beginning and end of a dislocated element, and 'What wealth the show to me had brought' is less smoothly pronounced than 'What wealth the show had brought to me'. Perhaps Wordsworth's line could be justified in this way, as an onomatopoeic expression of breathless admiration; but this seems to force an effect from an observed linguistic irregularity rather than feel the effect first and then seek its linguistic cause. We do not have to force effects from Pope's

When Ajax strives some rock's vast weight to throw

nor from Milton's description of Adam's meeting with Eve after her encounter with the serpent:

From his slack hand the Garland wreath'd for Eve
Down drop'd, and all the faded Roses shed

nor from Wordsworth's own

> Bliss was it in that dawn to be alive.

A skilful poet may allow the pause at the end of a dislocated element to coincide with the end of a line, and in so doing provide an expected pause:

> Let me not to the marriage of true minds
> Admit impediment

but at the same time set up against this normal line-end pause a sort of 'syntactic enjambement' which does not 'admit the impediment' we hear. The extension, with or without such pauses, of clauses beyond line ends is felt as an onward-driving movement in the sense of what is said. Such overflowing of clauses, especially if combined with inversions which postpone essential elements of a clause or sentence, can be used, as in *Paradise Lost*, to supply the element of expectation which in Pope is given by a rhyme scheme, or it can, as in many of Shakespeare's sonnets, combine with rhyme to transmit strenuous and onward-driving, yet supremely ordered, thought.

In our time, as the elaborate sentence declines in popularity and the rearrangement of elements within the clause becomes less fashionable even in poetry (though some dying twitches are to be found in journalism), stylistic interest centres increasingly on the smaller units which are composed of words and make up clauses, that is, on the 'group' (also called 'phrase'). The group is of three kinds, the nominal group, forming the subject or complement of a clause, the verbal group, and the adverbial group forming the adjunct of a clause. Since an adjunct of more than one word very often consists of a preposition followed by a nominal group (e.g. 'in that dawn'), interest centres especially on the nominal and verbal groups.

Just as, in a study of the sentence, it is convenient to think of a sentence consisting of a single clause as one kind of sentence, rather than to separate these sentences into a special study, so in discussing the group it is convenient to include the special case of a group consisting of one word, if we are discussing the function of that word in a clause. A noun or pronoun may form a one-word nominal group, a verb a one-word verbal group or an adverb a one-word adjunct.

When a group consists of more than one word, there will be one of the words more essential than the others, called the 'head word' or 'head'. It is the last word that would be given up in a very brief summary – a newspaper headline, for instance. The one-clause sentence 'The proud mother of the three boys has been revealing their detailed plans for the future' might form a headline 'Mother Reveals Plans', retaining the head word from each of the three groups forming the clause. (Headlines like 'Gunman Slays Three' are stylistically deviant, and felt to be so.) Notice that the head word of the subject determines whether the verb is singular or plural; it also determines the pronoun which could replace the whole group. 'The proud mother of the three boys' could be represented by the pronoun 'she'.

Words preceding the head word in a group are conveniently called 'modifiers' (sometimes 'premodifiers') and those following it are called 'qualifiers' or 'postqualifiers'. The structure of a group is therefore (M)H(Q), an essential head word and optional modifiers and qualifiers.

In the clause 'John and Charlie are running', we cannot isolate a single head word in the subject but must assume a compound group with two head words, replaceable by a pronoun 'they' and selecting a plural verb. (Alternatively we could regard it as a fusion of two clauses, 'John is running' and 'Charlie is running'.) The same analysis looks after 'Bread and butter are going up in price', but what about 'Bread and butter is good for you'? Here there is a singular verb and the pronoun 'it' would seem to be an acceptable substitute for the whole subject. A compound group is acting here as if it were a single-word group. Such shifts of function in grammar from one 'rank' to another (e.g. from group to word) are sometimes referred to as 'rank shift'. The phenomenon is sometimes of stylistic interest; in Adelaide, where bus tickets are furnished with noble thoughts to instruct the poor on their way to work, the writer or anthologist of the sentiments seems to like to play with rank shift for stylistic effect. Examples: 'If you expect to get something good, for nothing, you are likely to get something good for nothing' and 'I would rather be a has-been than a never-was, because a has-been has been and a never-was never was'. In the first sentence, the complement 'something' in the first clause has two qualifiers, 'good' and 'for nothing' (or, alternatively, 'for nothing' is an adjunct), while in the second clause 'good for nothing' is rank-shifted to behave as one word and become a single qualifier. The other sentence can be analysed for homework.

Since the elements of a group are defined by their position, there cannot be stylistic variation in the order of elements in a group as there is in a clause. Occasionally an element normally a modifier becomes a qualifier, as in 'the body beautiful', and there is some freedom in the nominal group, especially in the ordering of qualifiers, but generally the order of the elements in a group is determined. The rules which determine it are often very subtle and were seldom noticed by the traditional grammarian. B. L. Whorf called such rules the 'covert grammar' of a language, instancing as an example 'a big black hunting dog'. It is not easy to explain to speakers of an entirely different language why English does not allow 'a black big hunting dog'. What is the rule?

We can devise some general rules about the order of modifiers. Adjectives of colour are nearer to the head than adjectives of size ('little brown jug', 'big blue eyes', 'little red schoolbook'). So are adjectives of age ('little old man', 'tall young lady') and adjectives of nationality are nearer still ('recent American literature', 'a young Norwegian sailor', 'a tall Swedish girl'). In all these instances there is a process of classification. The head word indicates a class which is subdivided by each adjective in turn, so that a 'young Norwegian sailor' is first classified as a sailor, then assigned to a set of Norwegian sailors, and then, within that set, to the subset of young Norwegian sailors. We reject the possibility of making a set of young sailors first and then isolating the Norwegians as 'Norwegian young sailors'.

There is little conscious stylistic manipulation of adjective sequences of this kind, but the order of adjectives perhaps exerts a no less powerful influence on our thinking for being unexamined. In science, where points of style merge with scientific method, assumptions lurk in every pair of adjectives. The words 'a white powdery substance' imply that physical state is a more basic category than colour. If a phonetician calls the sound of /m/ 'a bilabial nasal consonant', he (perhaps unconsciously) considers its nasality more essential than, or prior to, its articulation with the two lips.

There is some logic in the word order of the general language. A little grey elephant is a grey animal but not a little animal. Size, being relative, is properly a less essential classification than colour. But perhaps a less useful mode of thought governs our placing of adjectives of nationality. Would 'recent Australian poetry' be better considered as 'Australian recent poetry'? Might we, outside South African English, encourage talk of 'black intelligent young men' rather than 'intelligent young black men', who are fenced off as a race apart before we make the classifications that really matter? These, however, are stylistic choices not currently available, and would represent a very basic dislocation of grammar so universally accepted that it is not even formulated as a set of rules.

Not all sequences of adjectives are structured in the way we have been discussing. Those that are so structured can be recognized phonetically by a greater emphasis on the following noun than on the adjectives and orthographically (with less certainty) by an absence of commas. The structure forms a single tone group with moving tone on the noun.

Adjectives following a noun seem to be more loosely structured (e.g. 'All things counter, original, spare, strange'), and so do preceding adjectives (sometimes separated by commas in writing) when the stress and (potential) moving tone fall evenly on adjectives and the accompanying noun, or when the adjectives are joined by *and*, as in Arnold's 'The unplumbed, salt, estranging sea', Shakespeare's 'bare ruin'd choirs' or Hopkins's 'bright and battering sandal'. If a different word order in these well-known lines is unthinkable, it is mainly for metrical reasons, though possibly even here because some hint of a process of classification is at work. Chaucer's 'verray parfit gentil knight', for instance, was 'gentil' (of noble birth) first, and so stands out above the poor parson, who was also in his way 'verray' (true) and 'parfit' (perfect).

The groups 'bright and battering sandal' and 'young Norwegian sailor' have in common that all relationships centre on the noun, either because each adjective separately modifies the noun or because each adjective in sequence modifies the group of adjectives and noun that follows it. But when I talk of 'my Old English students', I do not expect to be interpreted in either of these ways. Here the items 'Old' and 'English' first form a structure between themselves and this whole structure modifies the noun. With such structures even the most elocutionary delivery could not give equal weight to each element in the sequence. In writing, sometimes, but not always, hyphens indicate linked words ('eighteenth-century poetry'). We usually have no difficulty in understanding these complex structures when we meet them, and may not even notice the complexity of 'Russian-American relations', 'fifty-two three-quarter-inch galvanized steel pipes' or 'a red flowering South Australian bluegum'.

When the words *little* or *old* stand next to a noun, they may be lightly stressed to become little more than enclitics colouring the meaning of the noun with a tinge of the affection we feel for small or familiar things ('she's a dear little girl', 'the good old days', 'you're a funny old thing', 'a poor little bird', 'my old dutch'). This does something to supply a deficiency in our vocabulary, which lacks 'diminutives', the affective variants found in Scottish English (*mousie, beastie, breastie*) or Russian or German. The few examples standard English provides, names like *Johnnie* or *Charlie*, words like *hottie* (for 'hot-water bottle') and perhaps *usherette*, are less important to the language than unstressed *little*.

An American linguist, A. A. Hill, once devised the model sequence 'All the ten fine old stone houses' to illustrate the kind of modifiers that can occur in a nominal group. The word order is fixed, but the sequence will remind us of the other opportunities for stylistic choice in the modifier of a nominal group. The word *all*, for example, has its overtones; it is a favourite word of Milton's.

A full study of *all* and words like *some* which fill the same place in the structure of a nominal group would take us through much of the study of logic. Numerals, too, have associations, numbers like *ten*, *seven* or *three*. But stylistically the most interesting, perhaps, are *the* and *stone*.

A whole book, and a very readable and interesting one, *The Tell-Tale Article* by G. Rostrevor Hamilton, has been written on the word *the* in modern poetry. A more technical discussion of the word *the* in Yeats's 'Leda and the Swan' by M. A. K. Halliday can be found in *Patterns of Language* by Angus McIntosh and M. A. K. Halliday. The word *the* is chosen, instead of *a* or a plural without an article, to refer to something known, either universally ('the sun', 'the Bible') or defined within the nominal group ('the point I want to make', 'the King of France', 'the Dover Road', and perhaps long-established London names like 'the Edgware Road') or the general context. When Auden records the mood of left-wing England during the Spanish Civil War, he mentions 'the boring meeting' and 'the flat political pamphlet', where plurals 'boring meetings' and 'flat political pamphlets' would have been the normal choice of earlier poets. Auden's use invites us to think 'Ah, yes, how well we know it all'. Indeed, the frequency of *the* in subsequent poetry, added to its falling intonations, tended towards a universal boredom. We all, like Tiresias, have seen it all. We are not childlike Romantics any more. The crowd of golden daffodils, the rainbow in the sky, the clerk of Oxenford also – none of them are new that way.

Modern novelists have their own use of the word *the*. If I had been writing a novel about Mr Appleby and Mr Plumtree, I might have begun 'The two men were standing by the bar in the club-house'. What two men? You would not know yet, of course, but you would, like the good reader you are, be patient, expecting to be told a little later (and you would be told). The use of *the*, as though talking of people already known to the reader, in the first sentence of a novel immediately establishes intimacy, without the formal introductions of, say, *Mansfield Park*, as though we are just looking in on a scene that has been there before we looked in. The assumption of knowledge the reader does not really have, inevitably raising a half-conscious question 'What men?', 'What clubhouse?' establishes expectancy. The reader is not merely receptive but actively interested. 'The old man looked again, and more sharply, at the disused barn ...' Don't you wish I'd go on? There is also another more specialized use of *the*; 'the old man' if he is never named more specifically will remain an archetypal figure as in Hemingway's *The Old Man and the Sea*. Patrick White in *The Tree of Man*, though naming the characters, frequently uses 'the man' and 'the woman' in this way.

The place occupied by *the* in a nominal group can also be occupied by the demonstratives *this* and *that*, one pointing to an object close to a speaker, the other indicating something more distant. In writing, *this* and *that* are often equally possible, with stylistic difference. This is because facts or ideas without any locality in the literal sense are referred to, as at the beginning of the sentence I am writing. I could have begun 'That is because ...', setting the idea at a greater distance. There is a modern tendency to favour the more intimate *this*, even, in colloquial speech, in place of indefinite articles. I knew a boy who began the synopsis of any film he had seen with 'Well, there was this chap and this girl ...'

The word *stone* in 'All the ten fine old stone houses' differs from the adjectives *fine* and *old* in that it does not have comparison (seen in *fine/finer/finest*) and in that it is a stylistic alternative to a qualifier, 'of stone' ('fine old houses of stone'), where *stone* would be a noun. In 'stone houses' we have the 'noun used as adjective' of traditional grammar.

Stylistically we could regard the slot in the structure of a nominal group represented by *stone* as a qualifier that has been transformed into a modifier, just as in 'the body beautiful' we could see a modifier made into a qualifier. The tendency in English seems to be towards a preference for modifiers. The sequence 'the body beautiful' survives only because its stylistic oddity gives it usefulness for advertisers. Those qualifiers that remain tend to consist of a further nominal group attached to the head word of the enclosing nominal group by a preposition (a body with beautiful proportions) or a participle (a body designed by top-ranking automotive engineers).

Recent writers, especially in scientific and journalistic style, have shown considerable ingenuity in getting the qualifier containing a nominal group into modifier position. Instead of 'activity directed towards a goal' we have 'goal-directed activity', instead of 'participation by students', 'student participation', instead of 'retrieval of information', 'information retrieval'. In each case there is a gain in brevity but a loss in precision, because the precise relation of elements, indicated in a qualifier by the choice of an appropriate preposition, is obscured. 'Student expulsions' could (these days) be expulsions *of* or *by* students. There is most clarity in the shortened group when a possessive is a precise alternative to *of*. 'Tales of a grandfather' is in fact less precise than 'a grandfather's tales', since it could refer to tales told by or about a grandfather. With a little less precision, an available adjective may indicate a relationship. A Russian scientist is a scientist in or from Russia. There is most ambiguity when the head word of the transposed group is a word normally used as an adjective; a speech about the poor is very cloudily referred to as 'a poor speech'. In spoken language, emphasis can control interpretation; 'a Spanish student' pronounced with greater stress on 'Spanish' is a student who studies the Spanish language, but if stress is on 'student', he is a student from Spain. The example is a textbook one, but I have met it in real life. When a tactful Australian university administrator, wishing to place an unpopular opinion safely far away, quoted 'an English departmental head', he was asked to clarify his meaning by the head of his own English department. In such cases speech and a normal reading allow only one interpretation, and not necessarily the author's. You cannot preserve (and so may not detect) the ambiguity in reading. The children's page riddle 'Why did the boy tiptoe into the bathroom' – 'Not to wake the sleeping pills' cannot be read aloud.

The potential ambiguity in some nominal modifiers has not gone unnoticed among scientists. John R. Baker, writing in *Nature* (5 November 1955) objected to 'iron containing globules' (meaning 'globules containing iron'), 'non-formalin containing fixatives', 'the nucleus associated chromatin' and 'adenosine triphosphate activated actomyosin contraction (i.e. the contraction of actomyosin, activated by adenosine triphosphate). Baker thought this kind of syntax comparatively new to science (within the preceding twenty-five years), and thought it came from German influence via the United States.

Our most skilled transposers of qualifiers into modifiers are the writers of newspaper headlines. Here brevity is especially desired and occasional ambiguity tolerated, since a following text elucidates the headline. In practice a string of nouns may be quite intelligible; we understand 'Post Office Pay Dispute Inquiry Chairman Named' (*The Times*, 25 March 1971) more readily than 'the man in the chair at the inquiry into the dispute concerning pay in the offices for posting has been named'.

A possible reason for this is that a sequence of nouns (unlike a sequence of true adjectives) is complete at each point in the chain. There is a double structuring: a chairman is classified as an inquiry chairman, more specifically a dispute inquiry chairman, and so on, as with any other sequence of modifiers, but in this case the topic is also announced as the post, more specifically the Post Office, in particular Post Office pay and so on. This alternative structure is lost in the succession of qualifiers 'the man in the chair at the inquiry . . .' and so on, so that a long list of qualifiers, though not ungrammatical, is unlikely to occur. The mind would only take them in if there was a progression or pattern in the items, as in 'The feather on the wing of the bird on the eggs in the nest on the twig of the branch of the tree in the park in Hampstead in London . . .' and so towards the galactic addresses loved by schoolboys.

A qualifier may take the form of a relative clause: 'The feather which is on the wing that belongs to the bird . . .' etc. A special stylistic problem arises if a verb in a relative clause is normally followed by a preposition, since the rules of formal style decree that the preposition should precede the relative: 'Spade! with which Wilkinson hath tilled his lands'. This now sounds over-formal, and few would condemn Thomas Hardy for writing, in the preface to *Far from the Madding Crowd*, of a 'region which people can go to, take a house in and write to the papers from'. David Lodge, who is certainly not unaware of the style of novels, since he has written a book on the subject, begins his own novel *The British Museum is Falling Down* with the sentence 'It was Adam Appleby's misfortune that at the moment of awakening from sleep his consciousness was immediately flooded with everything he least wanted to think about.' The omitted relative and the terminal preposition announce a modern, unpretentious and colloquial style suited to ironical unheroic comedy.

The simplest form of both the nominal and the verbal group was represented by Mr Plumtree's words 'It does', made up of the most general pronoun and the most general verb. Both words are usually used without modifier or qualifier. The verb *do* normally disappears if a modifier is present ('it can', 'it will' etc.) leaving 'It can do (that)' or 'it will do (that)' as emphatic alternatives. A participle relates to *it* in Donne's 'Running it never runs from us away', and other pronouns sometimes have modifiers ('Lucky you') or qualifiers ('You of all people', 'I for one'), particularly in religious rites ('Thou who takest away the sins of the world') or religious poetry ('Thou mastering me God'). Shakespeare economically expands a pronoun in *The Tempest*:

> ... i'th'dead of darkness
> The ministers for th'purpose hurried thence
> Me and thy crying self.

The addition of 'two' to a pronoun does something to re-create the lost dual number ('we two', 'you two') which must have had a particularly intimate flavour in the Old English 'The Husband's Message' with its repeated 'which you two in bygone days often talked about'. Byron's 'When we two parted' is perhaps a modern equivalent. The modern expression is not a true dual, of course, because it is an optional stylistic device, not part of an obligatory system of pronouns. Traces of the habit of mind which made a thorough distinction of dual from singular and plural are rather to be found in the series *unilateral, bilateral*

s.–5

and *multilateral* and in the insistence that *either* can be followed by only one *or*, that *former* (not *first*) must be used of two things, and, more generally, comparatives (*better*, *elder*) rather than superlatives (*best*, *eldest*) are to be used when only two things are compared, or in the careful distinction of *between* from *among*. In all these cases the 'dual' frequently survives in careful formal style, though Jane Austen, talking of the two Miss Steeles, mentions 'the vulgar freedom of the eldest . . . the beauty or the shrewd look of the youngest', and Jacques Barzun, no apostle of permissiveness, writes in *The House of Intellect* (p. 237) 'May the best man win', where only two men compete. I think I read once that Karl Marx thought the Holy Roman Empire 'neither holy, Roman nor an empire'. If so, the translation would perhaps not be improved by a more meticulous grammar.

The English verbal group offers little opportunity for stylistic variation in its structure. The finite verbal group consists of a head word perhaps preceded by one or more auxiliaries with a fixed word order. Even questions retain this order with a minimum of disturbance (Compare 'John will have been running' with 'Will John have been running?'). Stylistic variation in verbal groups is found not in word order but in the choice of tense, the choice of aspect (for example, the difference between 'John runs' and 'John is running'), the choice of active or passive voice, the use of full or contracted forms (such as *won't* for *will not*) and the use of expressive alternative forms for future and perfect tense, forms which usually begin life as colloquialisms.

The sequence of tenses in modern European languages has probably been influenced by Latin practice, so that we tend towards a logical identification of past tense forms with past time, present tense with present time and future tense with future time. But many anomalies remain. Hearing a whistle, we say 'That will be the postman', meaning logically that it probably *was* the postman. We say 'Boys will be – whatever the current fashion is', meaning that they usually *are* (unless we preserve an older emphasis on *will*, making it a present verb meaning 'desire to'). We say 'When you're ready, we'll go', though 'will be ready' would be more logical. We say 'If this street was quieter,

I would work better' without reflecting that it *was* quieter before internal combustion engines and electronic devices were marshalled to counter the forces of scholarship.

Special problems of tense arise in writing, because written language is transmitted and received at different times. We now expect indications of time to refer to a writer's time. We may begin a letter 'It is raining and I have nothing to do, so I suppose I might as well write'. When this is received, the recipient knows that it *was* raining and the reluctant correspondent *had* nothing to do. King Alfred, in a letter accompanying copies of the *Pastoral Care* sent to his bishops, used the older Latin style, using tense from a reader's point of view: 'It often *came* into my mind what wise men there used to be in England.' When in the first chapter I wanted to point out that one of my sentences began at different places in a line in various drafts of this book, including the final printed version, I had great difficulty in deciding on tenses. The printing was still to take place (still is, as I write this) but would be completed when the passage is (will be) read . . . I'm still having difficulty.

In novels, the past tense becomes the fictitious tense:

Astronomers reported that the spring of 2173 A.D. was a sunny one. The population of Nullocus had just reached three full people to the square yard, which was all right if you had nice neighbours, but Wordsworth J. Einsamkeit was an autistic lad, who loved to wander, lonely as an updrawn wisp of smog, among the deep and gloomy gutters, little lines of sportive sewage run wild, below the walls of the megacities . . .

If you condemn my little attempt at science fiction, it is not because it is in the past tense. Olaf Stapledon in *Last and First Men* imagined a future retrospective narrator in telepathic communion with a present-day writer to explain his past tenses, but this device is unnecessary. We expect a past tense in stories. The use of a pluperfect ('population had just reached') is a device novelists, SF or otherwise, use to fill in background as they locate a scene at a particular time. I suspect that Aldous Huxley uses this device at the beginning of a novel more than most writers. If you had let me go on with my story, I would have written 'One day . . .' and used the straight past tense to describe an event.

An interesting and unusual use of tense, possibly influenced by SF, is seen in Robert M. Hutchins's recent book, *The Learning Society*. He uses a past tense as he describes current educational practice: '. . . in the closing decades of the twentieth century, the aim of educational systems throughout the world was to process the young for the scientific, technical, industrial nation-state'. As he wrote, and as I write, these *are* the aims of educational systems; his use of the past tense invites us to see current pre-occupations historically and recognize that the possibility of change is so much present that these aims are survivals from the past which are already doomed.

Older English, and perhaps the prehistoric Germanic language from which it grew, if Icelandic sagas preserve an older idiom, used verb forms now called past and present tense with a less detectable reference to time than they have now. Modern readers of *Sir Gawain and the Green Knight* are apt to find its tenses haphazard. We read (in a translation preserving original tenses): 'Thereupon the man in the woods turns his bridle, hit the horse with his heels as hard as he might, races over the clearing and leaves the knight there alone.' The only way we could render this in idiomatic modern English while preserving original tenses is to use participles, since we do not take present participles to refer to a writer's present time, but to the time of other events in the context: 'Thereupon the man in the woods, turning his bridle, hit the horse with his heels as hard as he could, racing over the clearing and leaving the knight there alone.' This translation even preserves a sense that the verb forms are not governed by any impelling logic, since there would be little difference if we were to translate 'hitting the horse . . . he raced' or 'hitting . . . and racing . . . he left'.

Other idioms than tense in the verbal group indicate some gap between strict logic and our usual conceptions of time. We often think of the future as 'the days ahead' as though we faced it; yet we may talk of our forefathers as 'those who have gone before (in whose footsteps we follow)', as though, like the speakers of the Bolivian Quechua language, we assuméd that the past, which we know more about, is in front of us. Auden has it the other way when he refers to 'Dead in hundreds at the back' who 'Follow wooden in our Track'.

Talking of logic, why did Mr Appleby say 'I *hear* your young John was doing very well . . .'? He was not hearing this as he spoke. We meet the same idiom with *see* ('I see in the papers . . .'). These are not true present tenses, as the contrast is with another present tense (*am hearing, am seeing*) rather than with the past; it is a difference not of tense but of 'aspect'. Similarly *heard* and *was hearing, shall hear* and *shall be hearing* differ in aspect. Mr Appleby's 'I hear' is a 'perfective aspect' and could be more precisely indicated in formal style by 'I have heard'. 'I am hearing' would be 'imperfective' or 'continuous' and could never mean 'I have heard'. An imperfective aspect emphasizes the process designated by the verb; a perfective looks forward to a result. 'We'll be hearing from you' is friendlier than 'We'll hear from you'; it savours more of the pleasure of receiving a message, with less insistence on its usefulness.

Passive constructions are normally ambiguous in aspect. In 'The old songs are all sung now', the word *are* could be replaced by *have been*, but not in 'The old songs are sung with a modern accompaniment'. If we encounter 'The floor is polished' in isolation, we do not know whether the reference is to a process ('The floor is polished every morning') or a condition of the floor ('Walk carefully; the floor is polished'). An interesting use of this inbuilt ambiguity in the passive is made by Gwyn Jones in his translation of *Hrafnkels Saga*. The text tells us that people were settling eastern Iceland at the time of the story, but historians have pointed out that it is unlikely that the settlement continued so late. Jones translates: 'Most of the land in the district was settled in Hrafnkel's day' – a tactful solution.

In recent but not in older English, an unambiguously imperfective or continuous passive is available ('The songs are being sung'). But this form is odd in not contrasting with an unambiguously perfective form. It is a newcomer to the language, not yet part of a symmetrical system of aspect. There is, moreover, no continuous form available for past (i.e. passive) participles used attributively (i.e. in a modifier). We cannot say 'a being sung song'. Usually participles in modifiers are interpreted with perfective meaning ('a bound book', 'a painted Jezebel') but there appears to be an imperfective meaning in 'the harrowed toad' and perhaps in 'Blown hair is sweet' and its analogue 'Heard melodies are sweet'.

Elements of the verbal group may join with pronouns or negatives to produce contracted forms (*I'm, he's, won't, can't don't, isn't*, etc.). Contracted forms may be said to exist only in speech and in the dialogue of plays and novels that set out to report speech, though when I have said this in lectures in recent years, my opinion has been productive of a certain amount of student unrest. My argument is that in formal writing one writes *do not* and *cannot* even if one hopes that an intelligent reader will read *don't* and *can't*. This is, of course, merely a spelling convention, and one perhaps which is destined to lose favour. At present *do not* would appear to remain the unmarked form in writing and *don't* to be marked as informal and chatty, but there are signs that *do not* will eventually be written only when a pronunciation with two separate words is to be suggested.

A. Meillet has pointed out that speakers of a language constantly develop new and expressive ways of indicating future and perfect tenses. The future includes an element of promise (shown in the use of *will* in English) but as, in many varieties of English, *will* becomes a simple mark of futurity, something more expressive seems to be required. We say 'I am going to . . .', until this itself is now becoming a simple and colloquially normal future. So with the perfect; we do not feel dispassionate about the completion of a task. 'I have written my essay' would be weak in conversation, where 'I've finished writing my essay' would be normal. Among the first phrases a child learns is 'all gone', and he goes on to 'this book's all torn' or 'I've got all dirty', where *all* is perhaps more than anything else an intensifier of the participle or adjective and emphasizes the completeness of the state described. Perhaps there is an echo of this to reinforce the normal grammatical meaning of Lamb's 'All, all are gone, the old familiar faces' or Vaughan's 'They are all gone into the world of light'.

Adjuncts and complements offer few opportunities for stylistic variation apart from those available within the nominal groups they may contain. An adverb may be with or without a suffix -*ly*, 'he came quick' or 'he came quickly', the former suggesting an older or more colloquial style, but the chief stylistic interest in adjuncts is whether and where they are used in the clause. A complement may have various extensions not found in a subject, such as an indirect object ('I give thee all') or the one illustrated by the anecdote of a pompous man who mistook a fellow guest for an attendant and demanded 'Call me a cab,' to be obligingly answered 'You are a cab, sir.'

The syntactic group takes on a special interest in poetry because the boundary of a group may or may not coincide with the boundary of a poetic foot, with subtly different stylistic effects. When Pope, writing playfully to Miss Blount, describes a vision of the city she had just left

Of Lords and Earls and Dukes and garter'd Knights

three of the four boundaries of poetic feet coincide with boundaries of syntactic groups, and the last syntactic group exactly occupies two poetic feet. When the vision fades

Thus vanish sceptres, coronets and balls

the boundaries between the one-word groups and those separating the poetic feet are out of phase except in the last foot. The rising iambic rhythm, instead of being reinforced, is countered by a falling rhythm in the words. Tones of disappointment disperse the tones of excitement.

It would be agreed that there is remarkable control of rhythm in Shakespeare's Sonnet 65, beginning:

Since brass, nor stone, nor earth, nor boundless sea,
But sad mortality o'ersways their power,
How with this rage shall beauty hold a plea
Whose action is no stronger than a flower?

Yet metrically the lines are not unusual. Only an inversion at the beginning of the third line varies a regular iambic pentameter rhythm. The individuality in the rhythm is in the arrangement of syntactic groups, and even words, in a particularly happy relation with the boundaries of metrical feet. Strength is asserted in the rising isolated groups in the first line, entirely in phase with the metre except for a semantically appropriate prolongation of the word *boundless* across a metrical boundary, which does not divide the foot with a boundary between syntactic groups. But *beauty*, *action* and the negated *stronger* each spill over the boundary of a metrical foot in a softer uncertain rhythm enhanced by a syntactic boundary in the foot they enter, and this rhythm is picked up in the fifth line of the sonnet 'O how shall summer's honey breath hold out' since, although 'summer's honey breath' is a single syntactic group, each word blurs a metrical boundary, and in this group of three nouns the words perhaps have more phonetic independence than in the group 'boundless sea'.

It is not of course suggested that poets choosing and rejecting lines as they write are consciously aware of the sort of analysis attempted here, which has never been part of metrical theory, though it describes real differences in rhythmical effect. The interplay of syntax and metre is noticed in Mrs Winifred Nowottny's *The Language Poets Use* in an analysis of the Elegy on the Countess of Pembroke, usually attributed to William Browne of Tavistock, and in more detail by G. N. Leech in *A Linguistic Guide to English Poetry*. Dr Leech suggests that unstressed syllables are especially short if linked syntactically to a following stressed syllable, and uses the terms 'leading syllable' as in 'Boys and girls come out to play' and 'trailing syllable' as in 'Peter, Peter, pumpkin eater' for the two kinds of unstressed syllable syntactically defined.

An analysis of the superimposition of a metrical scheme on the (potential) phonetic patterns associated with syntactic groups may seem to take us some distance from what users of a language know and notice. But the analysis is devised to explain effects that are experienced by readers of the poems. The effects precede the explanation and that is all that is demanded to maintain the principle more roughly stated earlier in the form that 'stylistics deals with what the users of language know and notice'.

An attempt at a more exact definition of what is known by users of language would bring us into a no-man's-land of current linguistic debate. What *is* known? I have dealt mainly with sequences of words as they are on the page and the patterns we can find in their arrangement, and this seems a safe way to keep to what is known. But occasionally I have talked another way, saying that 'the body beautiful' could be regarded as a sequence containing a modifier which has become a qualifier, for example. What does this mean? It means that beneath the pattern we see, the surface pattern, lies another pattern, a 'deep' pattern, which is felt to be a truer representation of the 'real' grammar of the sequence. 'The body beautiful' is seen as a stylistic transposition of 'the beautiful body'.

This way of discussing grammar, an assumption of a surface and a deep grammar, is at least a tidy way of dealing with less usual constructions, and perhaps it is more, perhaps part of 'what speakers know'. We continually make and understand sentences that we have not met before, so that 'what we know', our linguistic competence, must include an understanding of the principles of generating sentences. We do not learn each new sentence as a boy without Latin learns his school motto. Language is less mechanical than a meccano set, but resembles a meccano set more than it resembles a box of manufactured toys.

Readers will perhaps assume that this preamble is to introduce Transformational Grammar, but a concept of deep and surface grammar is wider than the particular formulation of rules to generate sentences that we associate with Noam Chomsky. It is compatible with the British terminology I have drawn on in this brief outline and forms part of a systematic presentation of a British approach to linguistics in John Lyons's *Introduction to Theoretical Linguistics*. The terms 'surface grammar' and 'deep grammar' were used by C. F. Hockett in *A Course of Modern Linguistics* in 1958.

The distinction is obviously useful for the theory of stylistics. It formulates a 'what' is said and a 'how' it is said in exact terms.

By way of example, Richard Ohmann has pointed out that the sentence from James Joyce's story 'Araby', 'Gazing up into the darkness, I saw myself as a creature driven and derided by vanity' could be written, with obvious loss of 'style' but no change in content as 'I gazed up into the darkness. I saw myself as a creature. The creature was driven by vanity. The creature was derided by vanity'. This is the content of Joyce's sentence; the 'working up' into the actual form we have is the contribution of Joyce's style.

Writers will notice that Ohmann's hypothetical synthesis somewhat resembles the process of 'writing up' jotted notes or amending rough drafts where interlinear additions and cancelled passages are likely to resemble the blocks Ohmann sets up to explain a finished sentence. Perhaps also the hypothetical synthesis reflects the historical evolution of written style, if examples of Indian legends reported by Wilson D. Wallis and Ruth Sawtell Wallis in *The Micmac Indians of Eastern Canada* correctly represent the style of the original telling: 'Gluskap made the first canoe. He took as his model the breastbone of a bird. He procured a bird by killing it with a stone. From its flesh he had a good dinner.' These four sentences could be rendered in modern literary English as 'Gluskap made the first canoe, taking as his model the breastbone of a bird which he had killed with a stone to provide himself with a good dinner.' Retellings of Australian Aboriginal tales can be found with a structure of short sentences comparable with the Micmac example above, but caution is needed before assuming that their unelaborated style represents the idiom of the original teller, since such stories are sometimes collected as versions in Pidgin English, and there are examples of Greek legends rendered into Pidgin English for use in New Guinea schools which would not claim to reflect accurately all the resources of Greek prose.

The general analysis of sentences into constituent clauses, which is not new and was part of my own primary-school education for which I have ever been grateful, not only teaches the young how to write but also provides a useful language for elucidating difficult passages and describing ambiguities. Readers find difficulty with Auden's lines from 'The Wanderer':

> There head falls forward, fatigued at evening,
> And dreams of home,
> Waving from window, spread of welcome,
> Kissing of wife under single sheet;
> But waking sees
> Bird-flocks nameless to him, through doorway voices
> Of new men making another love.

It is helpful to see that we have here three clauses with main verbs *falls*, *dreams* and *sees*, and that *head* is the subject in each case: head falls . . . and (head) dreams . . . but (head) sees. . . . It dreams of home, of waving, of spread and of kissing. The poem is not finally ambiguous because only one meaning is satisfying, but the difficulties arise when we follow wrong clues given by words which in isolation are ambiguously noun or verb (*dreams*), participle or verbal noun (*waving, kissing*). The justification of syntactically difficult poems like this one or Dylan Thomas's 'Refusal to Mourn the Death, by Fire, of a Child in London' is that we begin to respond before we fully understand; we do not only contemplate a finished thought and mood but experience the ordering of thought and mood ourselves as the initially isolated, but already powerfully affective, elements fit into place and we understand the syntax.

The temporary checking of the reader becomes something of an intellectual game with the visual patterning in the poems of William Carlos Williams and E. E. Cummings, who recall the curiously attractive notice in *Our Mutual Friend*:

> Errands gone
> On with fi
> Delity By
> Ladies and Gentlemen
> I remain
> Your humble servt.
> Silas Wegg.

True ambiguity rests on a permanent failure to find a single satisfactory syntax. A single surface structure reflects more than one deep structure. 'He decided on the boat' might mean 'he chose the boat' or 'he came to a decision while on the boat';

'some more convincing evidence' might mean some additional evidence of a convincing kind or some evidence that is more convincing; 'the proper study of mankind' might mean (out of context) the proper way to study mankind or the proper thing for mankind to study.

There is a form of facetiousness which finds unintended meanings in something that is said:

> I dislike giggling schoolgirls, don't you?
> I don't know. I've never giggled one.

and wit may reside in formulating a sentence with a surface interpretation which does not too thoroughly hide another intended meaning: 'I shall lose no time in reading your book.' An advertiser may play with ambiguity, devising the slogan 'Rest assured' to advertise a mattress. These uses have their place, but what place has ambiguity in more extended writing?

For the writer of scientific prose, ambiguity is a cardinal error to be avoided. The scientist, detecting ambiguity in 'some more convincing evidence' amends his text to 'further convincing evidence' or 'some evidence that is more convincing'. In this the scientist and the literary man have only recently been thought distinct. It has always been part of literary study to notice ambiguities and historical literary study tried to solve them by deciding on the more likely interpretation. Even now students of Old and Middle English are never, it seems, allowed to solve a 'crux' (a difficulty in interpretation) by deciding that all suggested interpretations are to be accepted at once. In the unpunctuated texts of early English this would sometimes allow a notable richness of response.

A new approach to literary texts became prominent when the acceptance of ambiguity as a normal form of poetic statement by Robert Graves and Laura Riding had been publicized by William Empson's *The Seven Types of Ambiguity*. It was not merely a new answer to old questions but a new way of asking questions. Instead of asking 'Does the text mean this or that?' with a 'Tea or coffee?' intonation, implying that only one answer can be chosen, critics began to ask 'Can the text mean this or that?'

with a 'Cigarettes or liquor?' intonation, seeing a text as a bag of mysteries not advertised on the surface. (There is some debate whether the author knows what he has packed.) To take an example, in Marvell's lines:

> Meanwhile the mind, from pleasure less,
> Withdraws into its happiness

should we understand that the mind is less because of pleasure or that because of less pleasure the mind withdraws? The answer now was to be 'Both – and what else can you find?'

Those whose task it is to seek ambiguity are unlikely to give unambiguous definition to a favourite word, and as a fashionable method is pursued the term is stretched to include things it ought not to include and sometimes comes to mean little more than 'complexity'. It ought not to mean language that does not exactly specify its context, or all language, even the most precise legal document, will prove to be normally ambiguous, and poetry, because it aims to be universal, will be most ambiguous of all. It ought not to mean the merely puzzling or riddles will be called ambiguous, but riddles are precise in their interpretation. It ought not to be based on a modern misunderstanding of older forms of language, since it is our task to master the language of an author before we set up as his critic, though, if we are discussing fine shades of meaning in delicate balance, it is a formidable task in historical linguistics to discover how older linguistic forms were likely to be apprehended by their contemporary readers. Finally, and most difficult to separate from true ambiguity, it ought not to mean the rich interrelations between the parts in a syntactic structure, the delicate balance which is lost in a translation. Since any modern punctuation will sometimes limit the interpretation of an Old English text to one of several possible syntactic configurations, we should perhaps accept the text unpunctuated to appreciate its less precise but richer syntax than our own, but this looser construction is not true ambiguity. Post-finally, in case it needs to be said, ambiguity should not be confused with irony.

Strangely the promotion of ambiguity has not led to a rehabilitation of the pun, and neither does it refer to various possibilities that may be realized in performance (as in what I called the 'intonational ambiguity' of *The Deserted Village*, p. 59), so that in practice ambiguity in literature ought to mean what it means in linguistics, ambiguity in syntax, a surface structure which can be derived from more than one deep structure.

Undoubtedly the method has invited abuse, both in the low-powered accounts of literature by those who find ambiguity an attractively permissive concept and in the displays by more strenuous talents which vaporize an apparently clear stream of discourse into a prismatic cloud of unsuspected meanings, but the introduction of the concept of ambiguity has equally undoubtedly widened the range of critical techniques, and if it so far lacks precision as a literary term (since the medieval magic number seven is not the last word in linguistic classification) linguists and critics may fruitfully work together to give it definition.

A lead is given by Mrs Nowottny, who makes a convincing case for seeing ambiguities in Marvell's poem *Mourning*, but this poem questions the sincerity of a woman's tears for her dead lover, and this could hardly be done with brutal directness. It is a special kind of poem, and Mrs Nowottny carefully emphasizes Marvell's 'ironical insistence on keeping silent about his own judgement'. She is also well aware that true ambiguity in literature is rarer than the word 'ambiguity' in current criticism, but her analysis of *Mourning* and the further examples she goes on to give are the more valuable for her precise statement of the distinctive qualities of ambiguous texts.

The concept of 'deep structure' does more than revive a traditional analysis of sentences into clauses and elucidate the double meaning of syntactically ambiguous sentences. Richard Ohmann does not end his analysis of Joyce's sentence with such clauses as 'the creature was driven by vanity' or its deeper active form 'vanity drove the creature'. The word *vanity* is a derived noun with an underlying structure '(someone is) vain', just as *darkness* presupposes '(something is) dark'. The analysis of 'nominalizations' of this kind as transformations of underlying sentence-like structures is very important for stylistic study. For one thing it explains the paradox that as technology and therefore the content of writing has become immensely more complex, sentence structure has appeared to become simpler. It is appearance only. Sentences are now less complicated than in the Ciceronian period, but not less complex, just as an electric motor is less complicated but not less complex than James Watt's steam engine. 'Abstract nouns' formed from adjectives and verbs abound and may be used to achieve a miniaturization of complex structures. 'A pay-dispute inquiry' condenses the information that (someone) inquires (why people) dispute (about how someone) pays (them). It becomes clear why a mere count of nouns or sentence length would not be an exhaustive study of a writer's style.

There is some tendency for a subject in an underlying clause to become a modifier in a group containing a nominalization and for objects to become qualifiers. Thus 'John drew Susan' could be nominalized as 'John's drawing' or 'a drawing of Susan'. Perhaps this is why 'student participation' seems a more accept-able and natural modern idiom than 'character portrayal', since the latter reverses in its surface structure the order of elements in its deep structure.

Our current understanding of the relation between deep and surface grammar undoubtedly owes more to the American de-velopment of Transformational Grammar than to any other work. Their pervasive interest in this relationship and their con-sequent detailed analysis of ambiguity and hidden complexity have usefully been applied to stylistics by writers such as Richard Ohmann and J. P. Thorne. But in one respect Transformational Grammar diverts attention from matters of stylistic interest. Its starting point and end point are in the sentence, and the study of style goes beyond the sentence.

George Campbell's *Philosophy of Rhetoric* at the beginning of the nineteenth century suggested that 'Syntax regards only the composition of many words into one sentence; style, at the same time that it attends to this, regards further the composition of many sentences into one discourse', and again 'Where grammar ends, eloquence begins' or '... the grammarians' department bears much the same relation to the orator's, which the art of the mason bears to that of the architect'. More recently, in 1958, A. A. Hill suggested that stylistics 'concerns all those relations among linguistic entities which are statable, or may be statable, in terms of wider spans than those which fall within the limits of the sentence'. In 1952, Zellig Harris investigated the connectedness of sentences, naming his study 'discourse analysis'.

It is usual to include in discussions of style a study of structured tracts of language larger than a single sentence, though perhaps not all the architectonics of literature which interest the literary critic are properly called 'style', since the study of style works typically with short tracts of language studied closely. The links between sentences in connected discourse may be of as much stylistic interest as the links between clauses in a sentence. If sentence links sometimes cease to be of stylistic interest, it is because the link is so clearly marked and so inevitably determined that we feel its study has more in common with grammatical than stylistic ways of thought. For example, although the traditional sentence 'I shall go to town tomorrow' may theoretically have main stress on any of its words, the stress in particular instances will vary predictably if the sentence is used to answer questions beginning with *where, when, who* and so on; and to answer with main stress on *tomorrow* if the question is 'Who will go to town?', for example, would be as unacceptable as a departure from grammar within a sentence. The question and answer form a tract with related parts.

In writing, the paragraph, and in poetry the stanza, suggest divisions of language which transcend the limitations of the sentence, divisions too loose in organization to be brought within a rigorous discussion of grammar, though their management might find a place in a wider discussion of style. But even stylisticians are now less ready than Hill or even Campbell to find their chief work in these larger tracts outside the sentence. Hill had in mind the recurrent choices which mark an individual style, but these, though counted in a larger text, are usually identified with reference to small grammatical units. Stylisticians would however agree with Campbell and Hill that they are never in any way restricted to work within the sentence by the theory of their subject.

Outside grammatical theory as it is now understood, though within the sentence, is another concept, developed by eighteenth-century grammarians, Lowth and those who followed him, of the 'principal constructive parts' of a sentence. John Walker extended its application from written to spoken language, allowing parts corresponding with subject and predicate in a long one-clause sentence; in a two-clause sentence each clause would be a principal constructive part, and where there are more than two clauses a principal constructive part may include more than a single clause. If we analyse the sentence 'Everyone that speaks and reasons is a grammarian and a logician, though he may be utterly unacquainted with the rules of grammar and logic as they are delivered in books and systems', we first divide the sentence into two principal constructive parts, a main one, ending at the word 'logician', and a subordinate one. The subordinate member itself has a main clause ('though . . .') and a subordinate clause ('as . . .'). The possibility of talking of 'a main clause in a subordinate member', for example, seems to offer opportunities for subtle yet economical grammatical discussion of relevance to style, but the concept of 'principal constructive parts' proved to be unfruitful.

This was perhaps for two reasons. One is that the concept cuts across the hierarchical ordering of the ranks of grammar: sentence, clause, group, word and word element, each rank including the one below it. The other is that though the assumption that a well-constructed sentence will fall into two balancing parts fits the facts of periodic sentences in eighteenth-century literary English well enough, it does not apply to looser structures where the parts are less interdependent. Middle English religious prose often provides such tripartite structures as 'A lady was entirely beset by her foes, her land all laid waste, and she destitute, within an earthen castle', or (discussing three kinds of flatterers) 'The first is bad enough, the second is yet worse, the third is the worst of all'. Bacon retained this medieval pattern of threes in the structure of his thought and expression. The Trinity yielded but slowly to clockwork as a pattern for human thinking.

The existence of patterns of twos and threes is real enough, but it is not part of grammar. Like metrics, it is outside the orderly study of ordinary language. An interesting study of such patterns has been developed by an American writer on style, Winston Weathers, who outlines a 'rhetoric of the series', noting the varying stylistic effect as the number of items in a series is varied, as conjunctions are used or not and as parallelism is emphasized or not. A series of two items is assertive with a suggestion that no more need be said: 'Hear Lydiat's life, and Galileo's end.' A series of three items is reasonable, persuasive and representative: 'Those authors, therefore, are to be read at schools that supply most axioms of prudence, most principles of moral truth and most materials for conversation; and these purposes are best served by poets, orators and historians.' A series of four or more elements suggests a succession of events, a cumulation of detail: 'Toil, envy, want, the patron and the jail'. These are variations available within a single writer's style (my illustrations are all from Dr Johnson), though a writer may, of course, show habits of preference which mark 'the man'. So with the omission of connectives in a series to emphasize a profusion of detail or their inclusion to direct attention to each detail. In one book, Thackeray's *Vanity Fair*, I find 'was occupied, as usual, with his papers and tapes and statements of accounts', where each item is given weight, and 'Our good child ransacked all her drawers, cupboards, reticules and gimcrack boxes – passed in review all her gowns, fichus, tags, bobbins, laces, silk stockings, and fallals – selecting this thing and that and the other, to make a little heap for Rebecca', where, but for a momentary dwelling on unnamed items, the clothes tumble in a heap before the reader. Both profusion and contemplation are suggested in 'You may be sure that she showed Rebecca over every room of the house, and everything in every one of her drawers; and her books, and her piano, and her dresses, and all her necklaces, brooches, laces and gimcracks.'

A longer series emphasizes particularity and counters universality; in this it belongs with prose rather than poetry. Northrop Frye observes that the series is an expected element in a satire. On the other hand, Dylan Thomas in *Under Milk Wood* exploits its rhythmical possibilities and its suggestion of all the exciting variety of life: 'I am a draper mad with love. I love you more than all the flannelette and calico, candlewick, dimity, crash and merino, tussore, cretonne, crepon, muslin, poplin, ticking and twill in the whole Cloth Hall of the world.'

Since a series is normally a list of like items, the insertion of a disparate item is stylistically significant in Pope's 'Puffs, Powders, Patches, Bibles, Billet-doux' or Shirley Hazzard's 'a family Sunday of roast lamb and denunciation of Sir Stafford Cripps'. Items may also be arranged in ascending or descending order to achieve climax or bathos.

The rhetoric of the series allows us to look again at the Johnsonian couplet of a line with strong caesura followed by one with weak caesura. In

> Grief aids Disease, remember'd Folly stings
> And his last Sighs reproach the Faith of Kings

the two lines represent a (forceful) balance of two elements of which the first is itself a (forceful) balance of two elements so that the whole is also a (reasonable) series of three elements.

This chapter has necessarily been a very sketchy outline of English syntax with the merest hint of further patterns in the ordering of sentences and the management of series. It will nevertheless have been enough to show that much stylistic variation is possible within the limits of English syntax. Limits are, however, ultimately reached and may become cramping to the most strenuous thinkers and poets. Syntax controls an analysis of experience, and analysis itself is contrary to the unity and particularity of an experience, which a poet may want to capture. Even 'John runs' analyses into two elements, an actor and an action, what exists as a single event and is experienced as a single experience.

There is a rare figure of speech called 'hendiadys' (Greek for 'one thing by means of two'), the expression by means of coordinate groups of what is properly expressed in a single group. Francis Thompson's

> And with the sea-breeze hand in hand
> Came innocence and she

will illustrate this. 'She' and 'innocence' are not in reality separate, but are separated by a linguistic device. But all language is to some extent an inescapable exercise in hendiadys, analysis into subject and predicate, head and modifier, main and subordinate clauses, of what, in the words of traditional grammar, is 'a single thought' and relates to a single experience.

Professor Angus McIntosh, in a lecture reprinted in *Patterns of Language*, has described the very individual syntax of Gerard Manley Hopkins as an attempt to fight free of the linguistic fragmentation of unique experiences. Hopkins is found to avoid adverbs, relatively detached elements in a clause, in favour of adjective forms which reach ambiguously towards noun and verb, 'Some candle clear burns', or he seeks out participles which are ambiguously adjective and verb, 'meal-drift moulded ever and melted across skies', or the verbal noun blurring distinctions of subject and predicate 'Tall sun's tingeing, or treacherous the tainting of the earth's air'.

Hopkins reaches the edges of what is possible in English syntax. His preoccupation with what he called 'inscape', the individuating characteristics of processes and events, drew him away from analysis and classification. Yet language brings order into the succession of uniquely different moments in our lives only by distinguishing things, qualities, actions and kinds of action, and finding enough similarities between one event and another to describe them all with a manageable number of different words. The 'inscape', the uniqueness of a moment, is lost in generality, and must be in the end, though great poetry emerges from a refusal to accept the fact.

4. Vocabulary

When Marionetta, in Thomas Love Peacock's *Nightmare Abbey*, stumbles upon Mr Flosky (a thinly disguised S. T. Coleridge), and stammers 'I think, Mr Flosky – that is, I believe – that is, I fancy – that is, I imagine . . .', the poor girl is cut short with a little lecture on the various meanings of the words *think*, *believe*, *fancy* and *imagine*. Belief, says Mr Flosky, is a negation of thought, and the words *fancy* and *imagine* are different in a way he hopes some day to explain. Marionetta, very confused, unhappily calls such distinctions 'subtleties', to be accused of a 'vulgar error of the *reading public*, to whom an unusual collocation of words, involving a juxtaposition of antiperistatical ideas, immediately suggests the notion of hyperoxysophistical paradoxology'.

Perhaps only Peacock could have written this scene, but its undoubted individuality rests almost entirely on its use of generally available, if somewhat rare, words. The importance of words to style is unlikely to be underestimated; the opposite mistake of thinking that it is all that matters and that 'The fame and the girl and the money' await the man who will devote a few evenings to 'increasing his word-power' is much more likely. Of course 'the reader who has proceeded this far' (that faithful companion with whom an author can share his sorrow at the foolishness of less-informed minds) will know that there are other things to style than words, and indeed a study of vocabulary cannot be entirely separated from a study of sounds and syntax. The appeal of Peacock's phrase 'hyperoxysophistical paradoxology' is in part rhythmical.

Our study of words begins in syntax, with words as the units which make up a syntactic group and are themselves composed of smaller meaningful elements. Since the structure of words was more adequately studied in the past than the structure of syntactic groups, this time traditional terms, 'root', 'prefix', 'suffix' and 'compound' remain adequate. Modern linguists have added the term 'morpheme' for an element in word structure, sometimes defining it as the smallest element in language that is linked with a meaning. Perhaps it is enough here to say that we are aware of the composition of words, knowing that 'a bedraggled woman' is *be-draggle-d*, not *bed-raggle-d*, for instance. Morphemes may be further described as 'free' (able to form a word alone) or 'bound' (occuring only as part of a word). In *unlucky* the prefix *un-* and the suffix *-y* are bound morphemes, the root *-luck-* a free morpheme. Usually a word contains at least one free morpheme in its composition, unless it is a word of foreign origin, like *receive* or *iniquity*, and it is possible to argue that within English these foreign words should be considered single morphemes (as presumably *sputnik* is, though in Russian it consists of three morphemes, *s-put-nik*). Some exceptional words without a free morpheme are *dishevelled*, *disgruntled*, *unkempt* and *uncouth*, where the presence of the commonly detachable prefixes *dis-* and *un-* urges us to consider the rest of the word a separate morpheme, though it is not a word. The oddity of this group is noticed by some speakers and I have heard students play with a jocular *couth*. The *Observer* (14 April 1968) talks of 'a kempt baby' and in the same issue refers to 'forgettable' music to a musical, where we suspect a similar process of docking *un-* from *unforgettable*. Recently there have been moves to free the morpheme *flammable*, because *inflammable* has been interpreted as a negative. Those who erred are, if they are still with us, retrospectively justified, and smokers are wise to keep away from all undated texts on petrol drums.

The order of morphemes in a word is not subject to variation. *Upset* and *set-up* are entirely different sequences. Nor is a word interruptible; the sequence *absoballylutely* intentionally flouts normal rules. There is seldom ambiguity in the formation of words, though *undoable* can mean 'unable to be done' or 'able to be undone' or even 'unable to be undone'.

The stock of bound morphemes is only slowly altered by new additions. There has been the recent coinage of *mini-* and *maxi-* (which also become free morphemes as abbreviations for *miniskirt* and *maxiskirt*) and a recent extended use of *-wise* ('Saleswise he's a disaster'), standard in *otherwise* or *clockwise*, and a use of *-type* to coin or simply augment adjectives ('an E-type model', 'a modern-type style'). There appears to be an increase in the use of *-ness* among the young as familiarity with Latin becomes less common. In students' essays I meet *tenseness* for *tension*, *generousness* for *generosity* and even *trueness* for *truth*. Sometimes we may feel a stylistically valuable difference between a coinage in *-ness* and a standard abstract noun. *Sensitiveness* is perhaps not exactly replaced by *sensitivity*.

New compounds are continually made with the old stock of morphemes. *Output* and *feedback* are examples, one, as Margaret Schlauch has pointed out, in *The English Language in Modern Times* (Warsaw, 1959, p. 201), representing a British mode of prefixing a prepositional element to a verb, the other an American method of compounding, with a consequent American flavour stylewise.

Poets are of course coiners of new compounds. Most of the polysyllables in Keats's *Ode to a Nightingale* are coinages: *Lethe-wards*, *light-winged*, *deep-delved*, *purple-stained*, *spectre-thin*, *leaden-eyed*. These compounds remain 'nonce words', words made for a specific occasion. They are not, as the usual compounds of ordinary language are, sequences occurring together so frequently that they coalesce into a single word, as the elements of *headmaster* or *railwayman* have done. Poets who make compounds are not catching up with accepted ideas (except in E. E. Cummings's line 'The poorbuthonest working man') nor pointing the way to new ones. Compounding is a mode of thought in one kind of poetry, an intentional catching of the specific situation, and for this a specific vocabulary (which remains so) is appropriate. Scientists, too, are notable coiners of words, and again their coinages suggest a mode of thought rather than economy in many cases. *Tychopotamic* ('occurring by chance near a river') does not meet a common need, but scientific style leans to single-word classifications in its descriptions.

The word is perhaps the most difficult of all grammatical units to define, as all who try to make word-counts discover. Is *instead of* to be counted as one word or two? Did the student who consistently wrote *in particular* as *imparticular* commit more than a spelling mistake? If spelling dictates our decision, do we spell *plum tree* or *plum-tree* or *plumtree*? When I counted syllables per word in Pope and Keats, I counted such compounds as *light-winged* as single words. Is that correct procedure? Was I right earlier to hyphenate *golf-club* and *club-house*? Defoe wrote *nobody* as *No body*; today we would distinguish 'There was no body in the bathroom' from 'There was nobody in the bathroom', but some editors prefer *no one* to the hyphenated *no-one* (which makes a distinction from *no one* with equal emphasis, as in 'No one was better than another').

It seems to be true that speakers of a language, whether literate or not, can in general tell investigators where words begin and end. This is not the same as to say that we think in words. It is likely that many people think mainly in phrases, as we all do in all but strenuous conversations. 'Turned out nice again', 'We're none of us getting any younger', 'Well, I'll probably run into you again sometime soon', or 'Every teacher is a teacher of English' come ready made, and 'A chap at work was telling me the other day that fares are going up again', if not a single idiom, is pieced together out of two or three stereotyped parts. It is the educated writer who learns to think in words, weighing the contribution of each element in sequences which are tailored to the occasion, enormously multiplying possible combinations of items by working with smaller parts. He depends on an educated reader able to think in the same way.

The scholar goes even further in becoming a skilled writer or reader by understanding the parts of words. In English, since many words important in writing are of classical origin, this means understanding the classical elements in our vocabulary. Words such as *mordant* or *sympathy* are to the scholar as precise in meaning, as directly linked to elementary human experience and as clear in derivation as *biting* or *fellow feeling*. It is, admittedly, a principle of stylistics that what is not known to users of a language cannot be part of style, and etymology is part of what is not generally known, but some writers, in periods when a classical education has been general among the classes reading their books, have assumed a knowledge of classical languages, at least of Latin, and to read these writers properly we still have to meet this expectation. When Gray writes 'Purple tyrants vainly groan' or 'Where he points his purple spear' or 'the purple light of love', we should not imagine a glow of mauve, but the imperial crimson of Latin *purpureus*, a sense retained for educated readers in the idiom 'a purple patch', which comes from Horace.

One might be a useful citizen without understanding Gray's unusual Latinism, but it is introduced here as a colourful exemplification of a pervasive Latinity in eighteenth-century writing, prose as well as poetry. When Johnson writes 'The great contention of criticism is to find the faults of the moderns, and the beauties of the ancients', modern associations of the word *contention* help us less than the Latin word *contendo*. Johnson tells us what critics strive to do, without (in this word) judging them. Our current learned style was formed in eighteenth-century prose and we rely more often than we realize on similarly exact habits of reading. Once in an examination I invited students to 'discuss the process of word-borrowing with reference to English'. Almost without exception they described the foreign element in English saying nothing about how it got there. They regarded my words 'process of' as a meaningless enclitic (without meaning to be impolite).

Except when a writer and his contemporary readers share a background language, or a learned language is formed in that situation, etymological knowledge is as likely to impede as to aid understanding. When learning a foreign language, we may recognize words borrowed from our own, but this is not to know their current use in the other language. The Englishman who expects *smoking* and *tramway* to have their English meanings in French, or the Frenchman who expects *actual* or *eventual* to have in English the meaning of the French words of similar form, learns that the use of words is separable from their etymology. (A French visitor went shopping for 'a baby's brassière', but only once.) Eighteenth-century writers on language explained the misuse of language as a departure from etymology, and this influenced eighteenth-century practice, but when today Sir Ernest Gowers in the revised *Modern English Usage* affects to be puzzled by the etymologically malformed *subtopia*, our practice is cheerfully unaffected. A few words have remained partially affected by the older view, *aggravate* being a famous example, but this example really proves that use triumphs over etymology when the two conflict, and that etymology is of stylistic interest in this case only because it affects use, leading to a general and a special use of the word. To use such words against general current usage indicates a special style; *aggravate* in the sense 'make worse' suggests a careful and learned style, as Anthony Powell's use of *sympathetic* to mean 'congenial' suggests the usage of a literate class who read French and Italian. (I think Powell's [currently fashionable] use has this flavour, though Gissing anticipates it in *New Grub Street*: 'In Marian Yule they devined a sympathetic nature', where the context (Penguin edn, p. 70) indicates that 'congenial' is meant. Gissing seems to have been conscious of the origin of his use of the word, as earlier (p. 46) he has the same girl called '*simpatica* – as that ass Whelpdale would say'.)

Misconceptions about etymology may occasionally influence thinking, as in the Middle Ages the lodestone and the diamond were associated through a misunderstanding of the word *adamant*, but probably most misunderstandings have no such effect. Horne Tooke thought *wench* a past participle of *wink*, but presumably this followed rather than preceded his thoughts about wenches. It is sometimes a correct understanding of etymology that leads to more important misunderstandings, misunderstandings of the use of language. A very extensive knowledge of etymology among some speakers of New Guinea Pidgin English (those whose first language is English) becomes a social problem when these speakers find it difficult to realize that *bagarap* ('destroy') is an unanalysed morpheme to speakers with a different first language and that the stylistic flavour of the English elements 'bugger up' is irrelevant at least to these speakers.

The behaviour of taboo words in language is a particularly striking proof that the meaning of words does not inhere in them by nature or etymology. A friend's very small daughters were always reduced to giggles by the phrase *common market* because they once asked their mother what it meant and she answered 'I'll explain when you're older.'

Taboos in a language change, the genteelism of one generation becoming the vulgarity of another, or the good old straight-forward words of a past age coming back into favour until they lose their force again. Perhaps no part of the flavour of an older text is more difficult to recover than the degree of taboo which might attach to some of its words, to know, for instance, that *bother* is stronger in Trollope than it is now, or, conversely, when the beauties of the Middle English Fair Maid of Ribblesdale are described, to contemplate her 'tyttes' without a silly twentieth-century grin. Taboo depends entirely on current use. Etymology may reveal hidden taboo words in *orchid* or *partridge* without impairing their present innocence, and less innocent words may have more innocent origins. Even the topics to which taboo words attach are apt to change; once it was sex and now it is race. We shall probably live to see expurgated editions of *Othello* where the word *M..r* is avoided.

The search for euphemisms to avoid taboo words may promote a chronological succession of names for a single thing, resulting in a stylistically graded list of terms, becoming more genteel as they are newer. What in the good old forthright days was called *stool*, *privy*, or *jakes* was not so called by my parents. They were taught to say *W.C.* To me this seemed a little too forthright and I learned, presumably at school, to say *lavatory*. When my small son began kindergarten and was asked if he wanted the toilet, he failed to understand, and so I switched to *toilet* until he said 'Don't be silly – that's at the kindergarten.' I know a professor of history who calls it 'the ladies'. A euphemism is usually a stylistic variant of a more direct word, but the smallest room in the house, the loo or gents or dub or bog, seems to have no stylistically neutral name, only a constellation of stylistically marked variants. In 1962 a pottery manufacturer stated that in England 65 per cent of the people used *toilet*, 15 per cent *lavatory*, 14 per cent *bathroom*, 4 per cent *W.C.* and 2 per cent family names.

Throughout history there has been a desire to avoid naming the fearful and unpleasant. When I was a child at school in New Zealand at the time of the Napier earthquake, no child would pronounce the word *earthquake* and I remember that the rule was actually formulated 'If you talk about earthquakes, they'll come.' So it is that the ancient Indo-European word for 'bear', surviving in our word *arctic*, gave way to terms meaning 'the brown one' or 'the honey eater' in northern countries. So it is that Australian farmers do not talk of 'drought' but 'a dry spell', just as we all avoid talking of an economic 'depression', preferring 'recession'. When in early 1971 South Vietnamese troops withdrew from Laos, official United States comment avoided the word *retreat* or even *withdrawal* in favour of 'mobile manoeuvres' or, as General Westmoreland preferred, 'a readjustment of troops' with the object of 'getting into additional enemy logistic complexes' (*Guardian*, 19 March 1971).

Our examination of the composition and the use of words leads to a view that etymology is on safe ground while it merely indicates the structure and history of words and idioms, but that if the etymologist attempts to deduce the meaning of structures from the meaning of their component parts, he will often fail, since meaning is controlled by the use of language in situations, and when a sequence of morphemes or words becomes a single lexical item, its use and therefore its meaning may diverge from the uses and meanings of its component parts. An idiom 'to let the cat out of the bag' or a word 'broadcast' is not fully described when its parts are described. A German stylistician, Ludwig Reiners, once pointed out that the English word *self-conscious* and the German word *selbstbewusst* (meaning 'convinced of one's worth') are composed of elements with the same meaning. He thought the difference in use expressed a national difference, and so perhaps will Englishmen.

But while remembering that the meaning of words is socially defined and depends on the situations in which the words are used, we must not forget that the social situation itself sometimes demands a precise definition of words by artificial means, and, when this happens, etymology and precise attention to each separate word in a sequence becomes important. We have noticed, and will notice more fully in a later chapter, that etymology has its special and very important place in stylistics, because etymology as an analysis of the structure of language enters into a study of special varieties of language, especially scientific and administrative language and the language of carefully expository prose. Etymology as the history of words helps to define these same styles by defining an area of English vocabulary that derived from classical languages.

Even popular stylistics recognizes a category of 'big words' which corresponds generally to the part of our vocabulary which is derived from the classical languages. We need not be pedantic about origins, since though *ecclesiastical* from Latin is a big word, *church* from Greek is not, and a scholarly count of words by derivation may perhaps be less revealing stylistically than a more popular count of 'big words' if this could be made. Those who urge the use of 'plain English' would presumably accept *church* or *rock* or *very* and perhaps words more Latinate in form, if common, such as *except* or even words of pure Latin appearance like *extra* or *item* They will not, presumably, rule out the Greek *Idea*.

In early modern English, Latin words were sought by poets to give Virgilian dignity to common English. In prose they entered, it seems, with less welcome. Latin was inevitably the school for early vernacular writing and, when writers on learned subjects tell us that it would have been much easier to write their works directly in Latin, we need not disbelieve them. It was as difficult for a Tudor writer to translate his normally Latin thoughts into plain English as it is for a modern popularizer of scientific research to do much the same thing. The new Latin polysyllables which poured into English not only puzzled those who were meant to be instructed but also, as I. A. Gordon points out in

The Movement of English Prose, altered the rhythm of the English sentence. Later promoters of 'Saxon English' could bring forward both educational and rhetorical objections to Latin words in English. For them Dr Johnson became the villain in the history of English prose. Statistics do not confirm that Johnson's prose is inordinately Latinate, but his Latin words, which are sharp and precise in meaning, are driven home by a prominent rhythmical beat, controlled by balanced elements in his sentence structure. We notice his Latin words: 'When I had once addressed your Lordship in public, I had exhausted all the art of pleasing which a retired and uncourtly scholar can possess.' We less often notice that 'Saxon words' take on an increased vigour in the presence of these rhythms: 'I had done all that I could; and no man is well pleased to have his all neglected, be it ever so little.'

Johnson's balanced style and his Latinity recall the briefly fashionable Euphuistic style of the sixteenth century, and its antithetical rhythms echo back further still to Old English sermons, but neither its controlled utilitarian Latinity nor its rhythmical balance was counter to the trends of English prose in his time. The reassertion of balance in sentence structure was a necessary part of the evolution of a plain English style. When Joseph Glanvill revised his book *The Vanity of Dogmatizing* in 1665, replacing its 'dancing periods' with an 'unaffected eloquence' more in keeping with the linguistic ideals of the Royal Society, he changed the sentence 'we look with a superstitious reverence upon the accounts of praeterlapsed ages: and with a supercilious severity, on the more deserving products of our own' by altering the word *praeterlapsed* to *past*. This is not only a commendable gain in clarity for readers without Latin; it is also a change in the rhythm of the sentence, bringing out a balance in sound to reinforce the balance of ideas in 'past ages' and 'our own', where before we were distracted by a contrast between a learned word and little words that were lost in its reverberations. Writers were now to look more to the rhythm of sentences than to words and fine phrases. And the master of sentence rhythm was Johnson.

Self-conscious rhythms in prose are not without danger when they lack the intellectual clarity of Johnson's balancing Latinity. It is easy to yield to the style of Nietzsche's *Also Sprach Zarathustra*, but it is a style lulling critical thought. The early pages of D. H. Lawrence's *The Rainbow* are often praised out of context for their style, but there is a hint of self-indulgence in them, an incantatory singsong:

> The young corn waved and was silken, and the lustre slid along the limbs of the men who saw it. They took the udder of the cows, the cows yielded milk and pulse against the hands of the men; the pulse of the blood of the teats of the cows beat into the pulse of the hands of the men. They mounted their horses, and held life between the grip of their knees, they harnessed their horses at the wagon, and, with hand on the bridle rings, drew the heaving of the horses after their will.

Here syntax, rather than guiding the emphasis on words, is used to set up rhythms, and rhythm is not used to heighten the impact of carefully chosen words but is an end in itself. In a Johnsonian sentence – a well-known one will do – 'Whoever wishes to attain an English style, familiar but not coarse, and elegant but not ostentatious, must give his days and nights to the volumes of Addison', the small words marshall the words of precise meaning into emphatic peaks in the rhythm. Lawrence's unusual succession of qualifiers in 'the pulse of the blood of the teats of the cows', picked up and anticipated in other groups beginning with *of*, cannot be asked to do this, since the emphatic word might well be the vaguest word, the word *of* which occurs no less than ten times in the quoted lines. Moreover, where Johnson's syntax is periodic, allotting different weight to its clauses, Lawrence's is paratactic, a succession of items joined by *and* in which the mind is not required to find an order of importance. We are urged merely to sense a rhythm, a pulse (of nature) linking man and animal.

Lawrence's passage has been praised by F. R. Leavis, hardly a critic to be taken in by self-indulgent or mindless writing, and Leavis is right to point out that the passage works in the whole context of the novel, asserting only one of two themes, and

contrasting with the more fully developed theme represented by
the women in the story. But perhaps this is to apologize for a
kind of writing which is easily imitated by those less able to control
its hypnotic powers, and we have the uneasy feeling that Lawrence himself yields too fully to the mood of his subject, writing
as a poet rather than as a novelist, without the novelist's detachment and irony which is mindful of a total theme while developing each moment of it. We do not expect Dickens to become a
narrow patriot while describing Podsnap.

David Lodge mischievously inverts Lawrence's theme in *The
British Museum is Falling Down*, describing, instead of men in
touch with nature while women look to something more intellectual beyond the farm, an opposite situation of men at work
on their theses in the Reading Room of the British Museum while
wives at home look at the outward flowing traffic and vow that
their children will never be scholars. Here is the Reading Room:

... The dome looked down on the scholars, and the scholars looked
down on their books; and the scholars loved their books, stroking the
pages with soft pale fingers. The pages responded to the fingers' touch,
and yielded their knowledge gladly to the scholars, who collected it in
little boxes of file-cards ...

Again there is a soporific rhythm, but of course a parody cannot but be detached. Inevitably contrivance has to take the place
of yielding to a mood. Some of Lawrence's style is directly
imitated, notably the paratactic construction based on a repeated
and (except for one *who* which could perhaps have been *and
they*), but, though Lodge catches the rhythm well, his structure
does not match Lawrence's, even if the effect is the same. Lawrence uses many prepositional phrases as qualifiers, where nouns
are placed in an unemphatic position so that stresses are subdued
in a rhythmical flow of sound. Lodge achieves the same subdued
stress by a different device (also used by Lawrence), the frequent
repetition of nouns. In both text and parody the words of subdued emphasis sometimes have sexual undertones, more powerfully at work for being not too conspicuous and not too demanding of conscious analysis.

Lawrence was heir to a tradition which preserved Johnson's care for sentence rhythm but attacked the Latinity and the balance which associated it with precision of thought. The attack on artificial patterns of rhythm and on Latinity came early and especially in poetry. Like most stylistic revolutions, this one appealed to the people and to speech. Wordsworth was explicit: 'My purpose was to imitate, and, as far as is possible, to adopt the very language of men.' This is not an outright rejection of a special diction for poetry, but it is interesting to observe how much Wordsworth could achieve not only within the real language of men but even within the very commonest words, those already known to a very young child.

So far as I am aware, a book called *Words Your Children Use: A Survey of the Words Used by Children in Infants' Schools With the Resultant Graded Vocabulary*, compiled by R. P. A. Edwards and Vivian Gibbon (London, Burke, 1964), has not been used as an aid to Wordsworth studies, but it can be made to yield interesting information about his vocabulary, for example that all the words in

> The rainbow comes and goes
> And lovely is the rose

are in the vocabulary of a present-day English five-year-old child, and all except *lovely* and *rose* within his most-used 250 words. Yet I chose these lines not as the simplest that come to mind, but as Wordsworth at his most effective. Context helps to give them their power, admittedly, especially a contrast in rhythm with a long line preceding them, but the preceding lines too are simple:

> By night or day
> The things which I have seen I now can see no more

are also the words of a five-year-old, except for *which*. (*Which* comes a year later, but perhaps not as a relative pronoun.) Not all the 'Ode on Intimations of Immortality' is as simple as this, of course. The words are different in

> O joy! that in our embers
> Is something that doth live,
> That nature yet remembers
> What was so fugitive

but here I am pressing my point a little unfairly by choosing
lines which Peter Coveney in *The Image of Childhood* (Penguin
Books, 1967) has singled out as comparatively false in tone. In
fact, since I have begun to be honest, I confess I did look for
confirmation of a hunch that some of the most effective evocations
of a child's clear view of life would be expressed in words that
echo back to childhood, but I sought it in Blake and was disappointed. *Tiger* is learned early but *bright* is a seven-year-old's
word and *symmetry* an adult's word. I should have remembered
the message of my one-time compatriot Sylvia Ashton-Warner
that it is not the child's most frequently used words that mean
most to him, or discovered sooner Peter Coveney's observation
that though Blake associates innocence with the reality perceived
in poetry, he is not nostalgically identified with childhood.
Perhaps his vocabulary confirms this view. There is enough of
an adult standpoint to assert the strangeness of childhood in his
strangely articulate baby:

> My mother groan'd, my father wept.
> Into the dangerous world I leapt
> Helpless, naked, piping loud
> Like a fiend hid in a cloud.

Wordsworth, by finding the hidden poetic power in common
words, also gave new life to words derived from Latin, which
were now able to be effective not only when marshalled by
rhythmical devices into prominent positions, but by their un-
expectedness in a context normally without them. It is especially
for its most learned word that we remember

> No motion has she now, no force;
> She neither hears nor sees,
> Rolled round in earth's diurnal course,
> With rocks, and stones, and trees.

Within a text and within the language, Latin words took on a special flavour as they became stylistic alternatives to common English. The evolution of a plain style is also the evolution of a specially learned style. We shall notice in a later chapter the importance of Latin vocabulary in the developing language of science, but it also had general and even popular uses. If we clear our minds of Romanticism, we must observe that a popular or uneducated taste, far from preserving an ideal plain Saxon speech to inspire poets if it is not ruined by the spread of education, runs to an admiration of big words. It is an irritable admiration, plagued by an inability to understand and not inconsistent with a readiness to mock the 'jawbreakers' of scientists and the learned. At first the unfortunates who tried and failed to master learned words were mocked in the Dogberrys and Elbows of Shakespeare's stage, or in Sheridan's Mrs Malaprop, but the popular taste was soon to be put to literary use in a style which had it both ways, both using and mocking learned vocabulary and the sounding rhythms of a grand style. The resulting style is one that I. A. Gordon, in *The Movement of English Prose*, has called 'comic pomposity', and he finds it in the 'very fine writing' which Fielding promises and provides for the reader in *Joseph Andrews*, or in Smollett's description of spoons 'two of which were curtailed in the handles, and the other abridged in the lip'. The humour in this arises from a discrepancy between the grandeur of the style and the triviality of its occasion.

As Lamb's 'Dissertation upon Roast Pig' became for a century an inevitable text in schools, every ambitious schoolboy essayist's mouth watered at phrases like 'a premonitory moistening of the nether lip'. When Dickens added his mighty influence, comic pomposity became more or less obligatory in popular writing. It intrudes into memoirs and descriptive writing. It became almost a normal style in the first century of Australian and New Zealand popular literature, as though to write about these countries at all was something of a joke, but was justified, ultimately, in Joseph Furphy's *Such is Life*. It pervaded journalism until, to the astonishment of a modern reader, Jasper Milvain, in Gissing's *New Grub Street*, describes the writing of 'leaders' in 'the big dailies' as 'the kind of thing in which one makes a column out of what would fill six lines of respectable prose. You call a cigar a "convoluted weed", and so on, you know; that passes for facetiousness.'

Milvain and, even more, Gissing are beginning to rebel, and we have long had enough of the 'convoluted weed'. The danger now is in overlooking its triumphs. Australians do not properly appreciate Furphy and we forgive Dickens instead of understanding that comic pomposity was an important element in his success and in his permanent value. It was part of Mr Micawber's contemporary appeal, of course, and Micawber is still a good stylistic joke:

'Under the impression,' said Mr Micawber, 'that your peregrinations in this metropolis have not as yet been extensive, and that you might have some difficulty in penetrating the arcana of the modern Babylon in the direction of the City Road – in short,' said Mr Micawber in another burst of confidence, 'that you might lose yourself, – I shall be happy to call this evening, and install you in the knowledge of the nearest way.'

The contrast between the pompous style and the plain equivalent allows Dickens to mock the style as he uses it. It also allows a detachment of the author from his character, a detachment which reaches its maximum in:

Mr F.'s Aunt, who had eaten her pie with great solemnity, and who had been elaborating some grievous scheme of injury in her mind ... took the present opportunity of addressing the following Sibyllic apostrophe to the relict of her late nephew: 'Bring him for'ard, and I'll chuck him out o' winder!'

Mr F.'s Aunt, poor soul, is so far detached from writer and reader that a special term of Dickens criticism, 'flat character', is needed to describe her.

It seems possible that Dickens found himself, along with the potentialities of the comic pompous style, in *Martin Chuzzlewit*. Pecksniff and his family are introduced in an appropriate aura of pretentiousness and insincerity and the carefully inflated style of the opening becomes the style of the book. We could almost say that it is a book about fine words, the fine words which allow the fraudulent promotion of companies in England or new settlements in America, the fine words which provide the rhetoric of uninformed American patriotism and of Pecksniff's fraudulent piety. Certainly the book concerns appearances and the reality behind them, and the texture of the style as Pecksniff awaits the death of a wealthy relative 'whom, in his ample benevolence, he had made up his mind to forgive unconditionally' echoes a theme of which a deliberately hollow style is an essential part. Some adjustment had to be made for Tom Pinch; it is made too violently for a modern reader when it includes the sentimental apostrophe 'Blessings on thy simple heart, Tom Pinch, how proudly dost thou button up that scanty coat', but both the mockery and the detachment of the 'Pecksniff style' had to be broken. Both return in a new guise with Sarah Gamp, along with the versatile inflated style which gives the book, despite some faltering in the American part, its stylistic unity. We remember now the humanity and humour of Sarah Gamp but the comic inappropriateness of the inflated language in which 'this lady' and her lodgings are described was not lost on its first readers. If now our best and most serious writing would merely be the most natural way to describe the work of nurses, it is because Sarah Gamp has been laughed off the scene.

Wordsworth, who had not met Mr Micawber, was not thinking of learned or even pompous writing when he based his poetry 'as far as possible' on 'the very language of men'. In their context his words repudiate specifically a device which had become mechanically frequent in eighteenth-century poetry, the personification of abstract ideas. It is an embarrassment to admirers of Johnson to have to provide a deep grammar of the opening of 'The Vanity of Human Wishes':

> Let observation with extensive view
> Survey mankind from China to Peru

since *observation* is a nominalization of '(someone) observes' and *view* of '(someone) views', and both verbs mean much the same as *survey*, so that in deep grammar the meaning is something like 'someone observes with someone observes extensively observes

mankind extensively' (as Coleridge more or less pointed out).
Johnson gets away with it, perhaps, because *view* certainly and
survey probably are sufficiently unemphatic, and the length of
the (possibly deliberate) tautology is appropriate to a long steady
survey, but it is disturbing to find that fine-sounding lines can be
analysed to show an emptiness of content.

It would be a mistake, however, to conclude that all poetic
personifications of abstract ideas are empty, or even to agree
wholeheartedly that they do not belong to the 'very language of
men'. 'Time will tell' or 'Necessity is the mother of invention'
or a proverb recorded by Benjamin Franklin 'Pride breakfasted
with Plenty, dined with Poverty and supped with Infamy' show
popular use of such personification, even extended into allegory
in the last instance. In poetry as in proverbs, personification may
allow economical expression in a single clause of what in deep
grammar needs two or three clauses. 'Let not ambition mock
their useful toil' condenses 'Let not those who are ambitious
mock those who toil usefully'. There is some loss in the particularity which we currently seek in poetry, but the eighteenth
century looked rather for general truths, for 'images which find
a mirror in every mind'. Gray combined pictorial imagery with
abstract personification in his most memorable lines

> The paths of glory lead but to the grave . . .

but the picture is a general one. The pictorial or dramatic representation of abstract ideas in this line or in Johnson's 'And
Virtue guard thee to the throne of Truth' is not easily reduced,
without loss, to a set of underlying clauses. Even the forgotten
Langhorne enlivens a commonplace idea with 'And plant the
olive on Disorder's Grave'. The weakest use of the device is that
in which the abstraction is a redundant anticipation of the verb,
as in Shenstone's 'And Liberty unbars their prison door' which
reduces to 'someone is free causes someone is free'.

Personification has wider uses than to enliven abstract ideas.
In ordinary language (the kettle sings) and in literature, inani-
mate objects are sometimes talked of as if they were alive.
Dickens again comes to mind; what immediately comes to my

mind is the ferocious clock in *Little Dorrit*. When we refer to its context (Chapter 3) we find a whole constellation of such personifications as Arthur Clennam returns to the gloomy Sunday scene of his grimly religious childhood. There is the city 'in a penitential garb of soot', the ringing bell that 'abandoned hope' with 'a groan of despair', the tracts with a 'hiccupping reference as 2 Ep. Thes. c. iii. v.6 & 7', the mud that came with rain, though 'what the mud had been doing with itself or where it came from, who could say?', the lamps: 'one might have fancied them astonished at being suffered to introduce any show of brightness into such a scene', the 'wretched little bill FOUND DROWNED ... weeping on the wet wall' and finally the house which 'many years ago ... had had it in mind to slide down sideways' and was now 'leaning on gigantic crutches'. But when the house is reached, we have a kind of reverse figure or 'de-personification'. Jeremiah Flintwich, who opens the door, has a jaw not merely leathery but 'leathern' and 'he had a one-sided, crab-like way with him, as if his foundations had yielded at about the same time as those of the house'. There is more life in the 'hard-featured clock on the sideboard which [Arthur] used to see bending its figured brows upon him with a savage joy when he was behindhand in his lessons, and which when it was wound up once a week with an iron handle, used to sound as if it were growling in ferocious anticipation of the miseries into which it would bring him'. Life then ebbs again with his mother's 'glassy kiss'.

A reader following the story is unlikely to be consciously aware that so many instances of personification lie concealed in the details of its background description, but each one works to produce an unanalysed mood not easily described. Analysis shows that as each dead thing is animated and each living thing described in inanimate terms, the distinction blurs and a shadowy death-in-life or life-in-death takes its place. The surroundings are animate enough to add fierceness and gloom to the setting, but remain petrified in a dream-like half life. Since the dream and their life are Arthur's, we are strongly coloured with Arthur's mood. A similar dissolving of the boundary between animate and inanimate has been noticed by James Thorne in Donne's 'A Nocturnall Upon S. Lucies Day', where he finds in a cosmic and personal dissolution of death and life a 'sense of chaos and break-down of natural order'.

In his animation of the inanimate as in other ways, Dickens had followers who did not always share his complex purposes. We are now inclined to dismiss this style in adult writing as 'sentimentality' (a quality which has as strong a taboo for us as 'vulgarity' had for Dickens's contemporaries), but serious discussion of children's literature is still often impeded by a popular view that it consists of the adventures of Lenny Lamp and Clarence Clock. The style creeps into journalism sometimes; David Crystal and Derek Davy in *Investigating English Style* analyse a popular and a more serious newspaper account of weather forecasting, noting that where the more formal article refers to a 'computer, known as "Comet"', the popular one prefers 'Mr Comet – a £500,000 computer – joined the ranks of the Meteorological Office . . .' and tells us how 'he can come up with answers'. Perhaps a computer is a sufficiently heart-warming thing to allow a little sentimentality, but more likely the half-conscious point is the more than human cleverness of Mr Comet.

The transformational grammarian is ready to help in the understanding of personification, not only by analysing the formation of abstract nouns but also by devising rules to show how other personifications are grammatically deviant, that is, consciously used as figures of speech. For this the old concept of 'animate' and 'inanimate' nouns is revived and extended, e.g. to 'human' nouns, and 'selectional rules' are formed to forbid the coexistence of incompatible words in a sentence. For example, we would expect a grammar to generate 'The man frowns' but not 'The table frowns'. We make a rule that *frowns* is preceded by animate nouns (or, to rule out 'The cow frowns', human nouns). Now, what if I wanted to say 'The clock frowned on Arthur Clennam'? The answer is simple: I would say it, expecting you to perceive – though not necessarily very consciously – that I am using figurative language. The rule defines normal language and, by implication, figurative language. Perhaps in a poem, if a device is frequently used, it hardly seems deviant any longer but merely sets up a new grammar for the poem. Johnson's 'Reason frowns on War's unequal game' is hardly deviant in its context towards the end of 'The Vanity of Human Wishes'. But as it becomes less deviant, it becomes less striking and less forceful.

Some British grammarians deal with oddities like 'The table frowns' in a different way, in a separate lexical theory of 'collocation'. The idea behind collocation is simply that certain words tend to crop up in each other's company – *fish* with *chips*, for example. This is a freer theory than the selectional rules of transformational grammar. Perhaps this is useful. Is it absurd to ask how 'The monkey smiles' is dealt with in transformational grammar? Do we need a category 'human and simian subjects' or make a rule that rules for human nouns may sometimes apply to monkeys? The rules of collocation face no such difficulty. Words tend to occur together and it is for the statistician to define limits. *Smile*(s) is often preceded by *man* or *child*, infrequently by *monkey*, very rarely by *clock*.

Collocations need not be confined to a single sentence, though it is not quite clear how far apart words may be and still be said to collocate. My own feeling is that it would depend on the situation: in literature an alert reader may be aware of the echoes of words over a long span (noticing the word *wasp* just three times in Forster's *A Passage to India*, for instance), and the detection of compatible words in a whole text underlies much analysis of imagery in longer literary works. In *King Lear* words connected with animals collocate throughout the whole play, though it remains a theoretical problem how much an uninstructed reader can notice this, even unconsciously, and whether an instructed reading is a true reading of the author's text.

Carl Sandburg defined poetry as the union of hyacinths and biscuits, and we must agree that if one literary use of collocation depends on the compatibility of words, a coherent set of words relating to a particular activity or topic giving unity to a text, there is an opposite drive towards unusual collocations in the interests of variety. Pope's complaint about *breeze* and *trees* was about stereotyped collocations.

One way to unite incompatibles is simply to juxtapose them, making an ironic point of the contrast. Swift imagines ladies playing cards and prattling of his own death, and this is already enough to make a unified poem – though Swift goes further with words that collocate appropriately with both semantic areas: 'The Dean is dead, (*and what is Trumps?*)' or 'He lov'd the Dean (*I led a Heart*)'. Philip Larkin's 'Church Going' similarly allows a young man's colloquialisms (such as 'God knows') to take on significance in a setting suggesting different collocations.

A set of compatible words may, even without syntax, suggest a subject or scene. If the first vocabulary in a textbook of a foreign language lists words for *chalk, blackboard, table, desk, teacher, window, student, clock,* we can be pretty sure we are to be entertained with a description of a classroom. As prose, the passage will not be lively, except for the glow of a foreign language. This is because the words are so compatible that they merge into the expected details of a scene that is never really looked at. A more literary description, the opening of *Hard Times,* for example, will have some words that do not belong to such a well-defined set. There will be a little of the unexpected, something to catch our attention and make us really look at the scene.

One way is to combine two different sets of words: 'I was dug up from the ground; I was spun by no silkworm'. The first words suggest mining, the later words clothing. The groups mining and clothing intersect in one item, a suit of armour, and that is the answer to the Old English riddle that suggested my example. This is not an economical way to describe armour, but economy is not an absolute law of literary expression, and the description is more than just an equivalent for the word; it illuminates a concept from two angles so that we see it in 'a new light'.

Economy may be preserved if a single incompatible word replaces a colourless word in a description. 'The ship coursed the seas' is as economical as 'The ship sailed the seas'. It is a condensed riddle. The example is from T. E. Hulme, who points out that the metaphor brings a 'physical image' unlike the thought counter of ordinary language. Perhaps with Hulme's example in mind, Hugh Kenner in *The Poetry of Ezra Pound* analysed 'The ship ploughed the waves' in Aristotelian terms as a relation of four things, A is to B as C is to D, 'the ship does to the waves what a plough does to the ground', but Donald Davie, who, following Ernest Fenollosa, thinks of the transitive sentence as the type of poetic truth, protested that six things, these and the verbs *ploughing* and *sailing* are related.

Neither view is quite satisfactory because the metaphor 'The ship ploughed the waves' is a more vigorous poetic device than the simile 'The ship sailed the waves as a plough ploughs the ground', though both link words from different sets. If, as James Thorne thinks, the important effects in poetry relate to its deep grammar, it is a little lame to reduce the metaphor and simile to the same deep grammar. In metaphor the effect is concentrated, and this is important if the implied set (the new set) of words reinforces the main set representing literal meaning. Keats's 'leaden-eyed despairs' introduces with *lead-* a hint of *heavy*, *dark* and other appropriate words, and the addition of *eye-* suggesting 'heavy eyes' echoes *dull*, *drowsy* and *opiate* of the opening lines. All this could not easily be spelt out in similes. In the metaphor the elements are not merely added together but fused together. We are reminded of Coleridge's distinction between fancy and imagination, and are tempted to suggest that whereas the underlying clauses are added together by normal syntactic processes in the simile, they are *multiplied* by a special poetic syntactic process, a transcendent grammar of the imagination, in the metaphor.

Not all metaphors have the same underlying form as 'The ship ploughed the waves'. 'He was a tower of strength' seems to fuse 'he was strong' and 'A tower is strong'. Different again is the description of a camel as 'the ship of the desert'. Here a metaphorical element 'ship' is explained by its literal association with the desert. It is a principle used in word formation, e.g. *airship* or *sandyacht*. Similarly in Old English poetry the sea was called 'the gannet's bath' or the 'whale road'. In these cases (called 'kennings' in Old English), one element (*desert, whale, gannet*) collocated with the main words in the context, while the other, the head word, is intrusive.

Kennings are also found in Old Norse poetry, where a man is a 'tree of battle' and a lady a 'tree of rings'. The Norse taste in ornament ran to intricacy, and kennings were elaborated by replacing one of the elements by another kenning. Winter was called 'the snake's sorrow' and a snake was called 'thong of the footpath', so that winter became 'the sorrow of the thong of the footpath', linking words from three different sets.

A word is metaphorical only when it has both literal and figurative meaning together. A metaphor cannot therefore exist without a context. Say the word *fire* alone and you might start a stampede or get shot, but 'the fire in your eyes' masks out these irrelevant applications and associations of the word *fire*, to bring a small number of appropriate associations into focus. A metaphor must, however, also retain some implication of different contexts from the one in which it occurs. The word *arrive* was once a sailor's term and meant 'reach the shore'. When it was first used in another context, both 'shore' and the literal destination must have been in mind at once and there was a double underlying meaning. 'He arrived home' meant 'He reached home as a sailor reaches the shore'. The sailor's meaning is now forgotten, so that *arrive* is no longer a metaphor.

Even words of more obvious origin lose metaphorical power; 'the goals of our study', 'a field of study', 'to throw light on a subject' – all these are dead metaphors. Perhaps better, sleeping metaphors, ready to wake up irritably if some unwary writer tries 'to throw light on the goals of this field'. The three concealed metaphors, *light*, *goals* and *field* suddenly produce a normal collocational set and 'conjure up' irrelevant visions of a nocturnal football practice. In the facetious 'I put my foot down with a firm hand' we have an even more dangerous situation where the collocating words *foot* and *hand* form a nonsense shadow-sentence.

The danger of mixed metaphors is often mentioned, though Shakespeare's 'take arms against a sea of troubles' seems satisfactory enough, perhaps because the futility of a literal action of this kind (if we are right to think of it) is not inappropriate to the context. The real danger is in forgetting the literal meaning in metaphors (as a left-wing journalist did when Italian submarines were sinking ships helping Spain and he urged Britain to 'sweep the mad dogs from the sea') or forgetting the metaphorical meaning that lurks in many words normally taken literally (as a politician did when he wanted to develop 'a virgin land, pregnant with possibilities'). The hidden metaphorical meaning is the usual danger in scientific writing, where intentional metaphor is rare; especially as educated readers are likely to be fleetingly aware of the derivation and hidden metaphorical meaning in Latin elements in vocabulary, and to become irritated if a shadowy play of intrusive meanings blurs the argument: 'The judicial reader will be struck by several salient features in the major lines of advance in this rapidly expanding field, where several workers have responded to fruitful aspects of the challenge laid down by pioneer accounts of the area . . .'

Conversely a metaphor or a simile becomes a thing of beauty if it can be made to reinforce a writer's theme and purpose. Chaucer recalls his reader, if not his monk, to a sense of Christian duty in the lines (in modernized spelling):

> Men might his bridle hear
> Jingle in a whistling wind as clear
> And eke as loud as doth the chapel bell . . .

5. Context

It is not difficult to think of a thousand different ways an announcer might say 'Now Smith hits the ball'. Being an announcer, he might pause after any word or not at all. These five possibilities exist for each of three positions of *now*, giving fifteen variants. Each might have falling or excitedly rising tone, or a falling-rising 'interrupted tone', bringing us to forty-five variants. In every case any of four words might be stressed (180 variants). Any sentence might be fast or slow, loud or soft, and (to take us well past the thousand variants) pronounced laughingly or not. In addition, the original sentence may be turned to a passive including or omitting 'by Smith', or prefixed with 'It is' (It is Smith that hits the ball now; It is the ball that Smith now hits) or the sentence may begin 'What Smith does now' or 'now does' or 'What is now hit' or 'What Smith now hits (or hits now)', and these new sentences themselves may each have over a thousand varieties. Then all the sentences could be further varied by a number of voice qualities.

In practice an announcer need not waver among several thousand possibilities, because a situation narrows down the possibilities. Excited tones will not come to a commentator if the match is very dull (though some announcers improve on reality a little). There is even a literary theory that a writer's choice of words is limited by his context to one, *le mot juste*, or the exact word. The suggestion that context is entirely explanatory of style in this way is probably too extreme. Stylistics is not to that extent an exact science, but a theory of style is clearly incomplete without some attempt to describe the situation or context in which language is used.

We are back with Mr Appleby in the club-house, with the

vertical glint of light on bottles and good English worsted elbows
resting on the bar. We are back, too, with the problem we raised,
a little artificially it may have seemed, with the dying sounds of
Mr Plumtree's pronunciation of the word *runs*. That problem
was solved by describing the sound as a 'particular pronunciation'
of a more generalized element in the structure of English, the 'z'
sound, or, more technically, the phoneme /z/. But if we try to
describe the situation or setting in which the sound was made,
we find an inexhaustible wealth of detail if we are to count the
bottles on the shelf and particularize each floating mote of dust
in the air. Can we find a way to describe the situation too as a
'particular realization' of 'generalized elements', or must we
merely multiply the thousand variants of a sentence by a thousand
possible situations, and the infinite number of sentences in
English by the infinite number of situations in which they may
be found, to be left with what mathematicians call a transfinite
number of unclassifiable speech acts?

This time no formal theory has been established to guide us.
To those who told J. R. Firth that no linguistic event is exactly
repeated, he answered 'Come, come!', but this, like Johnson's
practical refutation of Berkeley's idealism by kicking a stone,
merely avoids the idea behind the problem. To adapt Aldous
Huxley, we might reply that when Firth uttered his second
'come', a little more of Queensland had been covered by prickly
pear. We must escape from the actual situation to a scheme or
formal account of situation, just as grammar rests on abstracting
from particular utterances in all their variety a formal scheme of
language.

Some formal specification of situations is, we find, if we think
about it, not outside our experience. A rather elaborate and
detailed example is provided by the printed text of a play, including its stage directions. Each production of the play will vary
within prescribed limits and these limits, the text itself, will define
all authentic performances of the play. The written text of an
actor's lines is one part of a wider prescription including scenery,
movements and gestures which must be present if we are to count
the performance as a genuine performance of 'the play'. Much,

of course, is not specified, allowing actors their individual 'style' in the lines and producers their individual style in the setting. Burton and Gielgud may differ even when both are Hamlet, but each must say Hamlet's lines; ingenuity in dress and details of setting does not destroy authenticity, but the play, to be authentic, must be set in Denmark in a castle where there are ghosts.

Dramatists vary in the detail with which they specify the performance of their plays. Shaw is much more specific in his stage directions than Shakespeare. A point of some interest in the theory of dramatic art arises with those details which are not specified but may be taken to be implied. Shakespeare did not specify that his plays were to be performed on an Elizabethan stage, but he clearly had such a stage in mind. Is a present-day performance more authentic if a reconstructed Elizabethan stage is used? Such surroundings are perhaps distracting to a modern playgoer in a way they were not in Shakespeare's time, so that it could be argued that what Shakespeare had in mind was an unobtrusive stage – that is, one familiar to his audiences. A producer does, however, need to interpret stage directions, where they occur, in the light of scholarly knowledge of the theatre contemporary with the play, even if there is an element of 'situational translation' in his adaptation to the later stage.

A play is a very detailed and rather special example of a 'form' uniting many specific situations (in this case the performances of the play). But 'all the world's a stage' and our ordinary experience also provides 'forms' of situations, more abstract than the specifically designed situations of a play and not necessarily with an accompanying linguistic component as there is in a play. We talk as if 'the 8.15 a.m. train to London' is the same train every day even though different carriages, guard, engine and passengers may make it up on different occasions. We understand a teacher's claim to have taught the fourth form for twenty years, even though no fourth former is yet twenty years old. We think no ill of a housewife who 'eagerly awaits the postman'.

The most general statements in grammar (in its wide sense to include all schematic description of language) have been made by reducing the rich variety of all speech sounds to a manageable set of pairs of 'distinctive features' (voiced – unvoiced, nasal – oral, and so on) which can be used to identify the phonemes of any given language. Can we similarly reduce the setting or context of language, the infinite variety of situations in which it is used, to a general characterization of all speech situations, to describe the essential situation of language?

It is easy to think of three basic categories to begin with, since all language involves a speaker, a hearer and the linguistic code itself. In literary study, these categories may become complex as the speaker is multiplied into an initiator of language and an assumed voice, as when Shakespeare speaks through the mouth of Hamlet or a poet re-enacts a mood in tranquillity, and the hearer is similarly multiplied as Hamlet speaks to Horatio but also to a theatre audience and the poet appears to commune with himself but sells his poem. Nevertheless it seems that in its most abstract and basic form the situation of any sample of language must involve at least one speaker (or writer) intending to communicate, one or more hearers (or readers) and perceptible linguistic activity which links them. It must involve further some sort of circumstances or surroundings shared or partly shared by speaker and hearer. These circumstances may be relevant to the understanding of the language, and may also influence its form. It is, for example, because your circumstances and mine are only in a most general way shared that I write instead of speaking to you. This formal difference brings another one: in speech, but not normally in writing, speaker and hearer may at any time exchange roles, at the invitation of the speaker, if he asks a question, or on the initiative of the hearer who varies his responsive 'Yes' or 'I see' with a 'Well . . .', or otherwise signals his intention to speak. Writing, lacking this aid and interruption, must cultivate continuity, whereas the dynamic of speech is exchange. Writing can therefore be planned in a way that speech normally cannot; Syme in *The Man Who was Thursday* prepared a dialogue of forty-three questions and answers leading inexorably to a challenge, but forgot that one cannot prepare both sides of a dialogue.

Our model is not yet complete because the immediate situation in which speech takes place, or, more obviously, the very generalized situation in which writers communicate with readers, is not the only relevant situation for the understanding of language. Communication presupposes earlier experiences shared by speaker and hearer. One such experience which must be shared is, obviously, experience of the language used. You and I communicate only because we both have experience of the English language. But along with this there is another kind of shared experience, an experience of the same or similar past situations which provides the 'content' of language. When at the beginning of this book I mentioned the loquat tree outside my window in Adelaide, you would not, unless you are among the small group of possible readers who have visited my house in Adelaide, see quite the picture I saw out of my window. Even so, I rely on your previous experience of other loquat trees, or, if you have not seen loquats, I am satisfied if you understand 'some kind of tree known to the writer'. If you are unfamiliar with trees of any kind, communication becomes more difficult, since the use of language depends on some sharing of experience, both of the language used and what is talked about. It is a philosophical problem whether some very basic concepts of space and time or of deep grammatical structure are innate and not based on past experience, but certainly most of the detail of language links the situation in which language is used with other situations experienced by the speaker and hearer, and assumes some matching or essential similarity in the experience of the two. The shared experience of a particular community or group can be referred to as a 'culture' (in the anthropologist's sense), but there seems to be no current general term for all the background situations relevant to a particular speech situation or text (though the 'meaning' of language comes near to describing them) and so I will adapt a term from medieval logic and call them, or their generalization into a single 'content of discourse', the 'supposed situation'.

If a supposed situation is extensively developed in a coherent way, it acts in the way that circumstances act in shorter speeches, to provide a context for each of its component details. This is the basis of fiction; a world is built up in words and this world becomes the context in which each sentence has its meaning. The words 'pretty dear' mean little in isolation, but when Mrs Moore says these words to a wasp in *A Passage to India*, they are read with echoes from a debate between two Christian clergymen about which of God's creatures might enter heaven, where wasps were specifically excluded, and echoes of a Hindu mystic who tried to love a wasp . . . But, you protest, these things come later in the book! So they do, but a supposed situation differs from circumstances in becoming a timeless artifact, a shaped world, analysed and yet contemplated as a whole. Literary criticism is a discussion of a second reading of a text, where all is relevant – but your point is a good one: criticism should know when it is based on a second reading and have a theory to support its practice. And we should all notice that not only fiction has this quality of supposed situations; historical writing and the scientific report also arrange selected experience into a timeless artifact. Historical writing at least follows the order of events as a rule, unlike the scientist's report, which ends with the 'conclusion' the scientist usually begins by seeking, but both give shape to what are 'really' unformulated events. This need not dismay us, for language cannot be said to deceive us if we understand its nature.

We must add one detail to a description of the speech act. True language, as opposed to a parrot's talk, is a human activity and an instrument of human purpose. The intention to communicate or engage with another person appears to be basic to language. There is some difficulty in accommodating intentions in a theory, or at least in naming them, since purposes and intentions do not appear to be accessible to scientific observation. Intention is, however, subject to specific variation which is sometimes observable in resulting linguistic forms (though not, as we shall see later, in a completely matching way), so that statements, questions or commands, reflections of differing intentions in a speaker, are necessarily part of a theory of grammar. Other variations in intention, such as irony, have no corresponding indication in the grammatical form of language but are of considerable interest to the student of style. It clearly would not do to 'explain' these effects by referring to an unobservable 'intention', but if we can detect them by observing language in its situation, the word 'intention' may serve to sum up what we observe, as it does in ordinary language. It is a quick way to tell American visitors how to recognize subject and object in Cowper's words inscribed on the Boadicea statue at the northern approach to Westminster Bridge:

> Regions Caesar never knew
> Thy posterity shall sway.

We may now turn Mr Appleby and Mr Plumtree into manageably abstract figures. The essential elements of the club-house situation were that two English speakers exchanged roles of speaker and hearer, using audible language, in circumstances relevant to this conversation only in the essential way that it brought the two men together and in the accidental way that a pattern of wet rings on the counter provided an opening topic. The words 'Makes a neat figure eight' are incomplete without the wet rings, which are, in a way, the 'subject' of the sentence. Similarly the 'it' of the answer 'It does' refers to the pattern of wet rings. The words are not wholly explained by reference to the immediate circumstances, however, since Mr Appleby has linked an immediate perception of the wet rings with past experiences of a written symbol, using language to interpret a present experience by linking it with past experience. When conversation resumed with talk of the school sports, immediate circumstances ceased to be important and a new situation was supposed. Both men knew 'the school' (as the definite article indicates) and had seen boys running and jumping hurdles, so that the 'supposed situation' of school sports was easily recalled, or, more exactly, elements of such situations were recalled and arranged into a particular pattern communicated from speaker to hearer. In the first remark about the sports, Mr Appleby's 'willingness to communicate' was more important than a desire to communicate a particular supposed circumstance, since the remark was essentially sociable rather than informative. Mr Plumtree's reply was more concerned with information.

Both sociability and communication have obvious utilitarian justification. There seems to be less usefulness in Mr Appleby's remark about a 'neat figure eight', though, in fact, it brought the men closer together than the polite remarks about the sports. Mr Appleby was a little off guard, perhaps, almost musing aloud, putting a thought into words and publishing the words. Why did he publish them? This is a basic problem in literary discussions, but perhaps not one that can be solved. Men delight in finding pattern in experience and some men delight in communicating their awareness of such patterns in words.

Can these words, like other published words, be fully studied by the normal procedures of linguistics? Nothing in the theory seems to prevent it, yet the linguist's too hasty assumption of omnicompetence lands him in a dilemma. If literature is entirely composed of ordinary language, its language does not define it, and its essence is completely inaccessible to linguists. If, on the other hand, its language does define it, then literature is a special use of language and a linguist's ordinary methods may not be appropriate unless he proves them so or adapts them to his special task. Mr Appleby's simple words mislead us now, since literature normally works with much more complex language than a musing remark in a bar, and this added complexity of language and supposed situation, as much as its playful or aesthetic intention, defines it. Whether the situational patterns of character and plot are within the scope of linguistics is doubtful, though they resemble on a large scale the patterns of noun and verb, and Ernest Fenollosa, Donald Davie and others have seen 'plot' in a sentence. Davie cites Pope's 'The rights a court attack'd, a Poet sav'd'. But the syntax of literary plots awaits its Chomsky.

If the literary stylistician lets such uncertainties prompt a unilateral declaration of independence from linguistics, he must look to a dilemma of his own. If his study is of an uncharted, special and complex use of language, he remains nevertheless a specialist within a wider linguistics. If, appalled at this, he decides that literature is not a kind of language after all, he relinquishes the language and style of literary texts to the linguists.

Attempts at an absolute separation of language and literature lead to absurdities of this kind, and we should rather look for the kind of overlap which takes place and attempt to make it as profitable as we can. We can distinguish the linguist when he studies etymology or the literary man when he studies literary biography, but the two move closer together when interest centres on texts. Even here the linguist may analyse grammar with only occasional glances towards the critic who has listed traditional patterns of deviation, and the literary critic may analyse metre and diction with only occasional glances towards the linguist who can tell him the pronunciation and meaning of older words or disturb him with theories of stress and the timing of stresses in English, but it is never quite certain that a technique developed by one side will be quite useless to the other while a study centres on a text.

For example, a quite complex theoretical analysis of the *style indirect libre* in novels appears to be quite outside ordinary language. It rests on the 'double speaker' of literature, the author who tells a story but also gives words to his characters in dialogue. Sometimes the author appears to address us directly but uses words appropriate to a character in his novel. An example is this remark of George Meredith's in the tenth chapter of *The Egoist*: 'Marriage has been known to have such an effect on the most faithful of women that a great passion fades to naught in their volatile bosoms when they have taken a husband.' In isolation it is an odd remark, but in the context Sir Willoughby Patterne is scheming to marry off Laetitia Dale to a friend, and we glean from Meredith's remark that Sir Willoughby has a momentary concern that Laetitia's devotion to himself could be affected.

Such ambiguously direct and reported speech would seem at first to have no place in ordinary language or in the procedures of ordinary linguistics, but when I was recently checking the currency of the word *boongary* in Australia for the *Oxford English Dictionary*, and could not find evidence that it was still a current word, I came across it in a book published in 1967, first in the quotation 'They were secured upon information by the natives that a tree-climbing kangaroo, which they called "Boongary" existed in the scrubs of that region', and then a little further down the page in the sentence 'The flesh of the Boongary was greatly valued as food by the natives.' Is the second quotation an English use of the word *boongary*? I think not on this much evidence and in this text, but it must then be a kind of *style indirect libre* and the literary concept helps in explaining a lexicographical problem. Many words pass from one language to another, and some become permanent, by just such a process, and further thought suggests that not infrequently in conversation we talk of someone and his interests in the sort of words he would use himself. In writing, quotation marks may indicate these uses.

It is easy enough to find examples where linguistic ideas are of service to literature. After all, linguists are often given 'ancillary status' by literary people, who might be presumed to be men of enough classical background to use the word etymologically. But if *style indirect libre* might interest linguists as I have suggested, this is a cooperative rather than an ancillary service. If we accepted Donald Davie's suggestion of using the concepts 'noun', 'verb' and 'clause' in relation to plots, we would acknowledge a cooperative influence the other way. Perhaps there are parallels; the difference between the plot of a Chekhov and a Maupassant short story is something like the difference between an imperfective and a perfective verb; the gloomy stories in which characters have no control over their fate, Arthur Morrison's *A Child of the Jago*, for instance, resemble impersonal verbs – but probably this is little more than fanciful metaphor to describe impressions. Work is needed to see whether a plot of a certain type is expressed in grammar of a matching type, and further independent work in clarifying concepts for describing both plots and grammar may have to precede study of the relation between fine texture and total effect in literature.

If linguistics is represented by Mr Plumtree's 'John runs' and literature by Mr Appleby's 'Makes a neat figure eight', it might seem that where the grammarian studies a pattern in language, literature rests on a pattern in experience, which language conveys.

But linguistics does not end with grammar and there is argument about the essence of literature. The two studies come together in their ultimate interest, the understanding of language. It is good method in linguistics to delay reference to meaning and content for as long as possible while patterns are thoroughly studied in grammar and vocabulary, just as a boy keeps a kite flying as long as he can, but linguistic discussions must ultimately return to meaning as a kite has its home on the ground. The meaning of language itself can be studied abstractly as a pattern of component elements, so that *boy*, for example, is analysed as 'human, male, not adult', but ultimately this study too comes to earth as a complex of intentions, references and effects, of human behaviour in human situations. Meaning is always more than pure reference, though in certain kinds of language, such as scientific texts, meaning other than the referential may become minimal.

The urban guerrilla warfare between linguists and literary men – that two-culture myth within the humanities – has its origin in university politics, not in the nature of the subjects. The linguist and the critic remain different people, or different sides of a writer on literary texts, but the relationship is not necessarily one of rivalry. The linguist attempts to explain as much of style as he can without giving up the rigour of his methods. If he falls short of complete description, he must give up part of the total complexity of the text to preserve his description. The literary critic, working with the same material, has different priorities. He too will analyse as much as he can of the language of his author, but if this description is inadequate, he must go beyond it, abandoning the rigour of his description to preserve his text. Thus the better the grammarian and the better the critic, the closer the two come together as the grammarian reaches up towards the whole text in all its subtlety and the critic reaches down deeper into the nature of the linguistic patterns that make the work of literary art.

The literary man begins with understanding, which is the ultimate aim of the linguist; the linguist begins with the patterns that complete the analysis of literature. The literary man is free to come straight to the interpretation of a text, but he cannot, without analysis of demonstrable patterns, persuade himself or others that his interpretation is the right one. The grammarian, further from ultimate truth, works on firmer ground.

The grammarian's world is a sunny one where understanding is assumed, or misunderstanding, if it arises, has clear edges and is without embarrassment to the users of language. The grammarian is aware that the words 'Time flies' can be answered with 'I can't; they fly too fast', or that 'What's for dinner, mother?', if pronounced with a pause at the comma and a rise in pitch to begin the upward-curving pronunciation of the word *mother*, takes on a lugubrious meaning. He knows that in a long and useful life he will never arrive at a single meaning for 'Flying planes can be dangerous'. But nobody misinterprets any of these sentences in any real context. In the real-life jungle of misunderstandings, outlines are less clear and misunderstandings more various. There is always someone who says something to someone somewhere, and none of these variables can be neglected, because all affect the understanding of what is said.

It is useful to distinguish between 'understanding', the ultimate purpose of communication, and 'arrival at a meaning', which resembles 'understanding' but, particularly in a discussion of poetry perhaps, can be distinguished from it. Understanding is occasionally less than arriving at a meaning. Children may be said to 'understand' the nursery rhyme 'Hey Diddle Diddle' if they recognize the normal words in it and enjoy hearing and chanting it, though they could hardly be said to 'know what it means' in a full referential sense. (Does anyone?) Probably some effects in poetry are so complex that their meaning is not reached in all its complexity by most people who enjoy the poems and may be said to understand them. No poet would welcome an approach to poetry which sees it all as a warm, mushy, indefinite feeling promoted by soporific word-patterns, but neither does a poet profit from an opposite fault in readers so anxious to get at literal meaning first that the receptive alertness required for poetry is destroyed. One poet even tells us that 'a poem should not mean but be', but this was in a poem.

If understanding is sometimes less than a full extraction of referential meaning in words, it is also frequently more. I recall with embarrassment an occasion on a bus in Tours when a large healthy-looking man informed me that he was a *mutilé de guerre*. I understood his words, but thought he was making conversation in a rather odd way, failing to realize that in France one may be expected to surrender one's seat to a man who was once injured in war. I did not understand the situation, and if he wore a badge or if the seat was labelled, I did not know what to look for. Anyone who has been in a foreign country or has talked to foreign visitors in his own will know that much misunderstanding arises from unfamiliar patterns not in language but in culture, in the understanding of situations that accompany the use of language. Teachers of English as a Second Language explain to Asian students in English-speaking countries that Europeans talk at mealtimes, and to European hostesses that many Asians do not.

With less embarrassment, I have misunderstood situations in my own country. My friendly Australian doctor greets me when I go to see him with the standard Australian greeting 'How are you?' Momentarily in the ambiguous situation of a doctor's rooms, I wonder whether to say 'Fine, thanks', before explaining why I am far enough from 'fine' to need to consult him. In this case we make a joke of it, for little misunderstandings are not necessarily a mark of inefficiency in language. They have friendly or 'phatic' uses. Perhaps I should in this case decide that I extracted too much meaning from the words, more than the doctor intended. My rapid 'arrival at a meaning' impeded understanding, which in this case was both more and less than meaning.

The minimum 'living unit' of language, as of literature, is not a word or a grammatical pattern of words but an act of speech, in which a speaker with his own background of experience, interests and place in society, wishing to ask, command, advise or otherwise influence an audience, or establish a friendly relation with it, chooses, in particular circumstances which are fully understood only in relation to other circumstances, that is culturally, a specific linguistic 'wording', which itself, as speech proceeds, becomes a context, and utters his words to one or more hearers, some of whom are perhaps not participants in the exchange, who have their own partially different backgrounds of experience. To understand is to apprehend this situation.

Theoretically complete understanding of a stretch of language would require complete control of all these elements in all their detail by both speaker and hearer, but only a theologian need contemplate a concept of understanding as complete as this. We may instead suppose 'sufficient understanding' if relevant details in the situation are controlled. Even 'sufficient understanding' is a theorist's fiction rather than a construct from experience (unfortunately), but it is approached when people know each other very well or when a conventional message is given in a stereotyped situation. For conventional messages (as a railway guard's 'Tickets please'), sufficient control of context on the part of hearers is often aided by a uniform. Linguistic as well as sartorial uniforms have in the past distinguished gentleman from churl in ways relevant to the understanding of language, and even now 'received pronunciation' will help its user to obtain credit when ordering goods by telephone.

Because the living situation of language is complex, it is tempting to omit part of it in describing the understanding of language or literature. It is, for example, easy to assume that we understand language, as distinct from knowing its meaning, if we arrive at a speaker's intention, which will include the transmission of a meaning but also include awareness of relevant circumstances. Words imprecise in cognitive meaning or reference reveal in a situation precise intentions. 'Put it down there' may be a precise command as someone brings a box into a storeroom. It is true that if I had known the intention of the man in Tours or my doctor, and if European hostesses knew that the reticence of Asian students indicates no dissatisfaction with European cooking, misunderstanding would be rarer, but it is dangerous to yield entirely to the temptation to equate awareness of a speaker's intention with understanding. An intention can only be deduced by a hearer or reader from language and situation, and it cannot simply be assumed that intentions are always fully known to a speaker himself, even when it is not his intention to conceal his intention. How are we to interpret the unintentional joke or witticism? These are sometimes, but not always, embarrassing to a speaker; a good lecturer, finding he has accidentally made a good joke, knows how to pass it off as an intentional effect.

In literary criticism the problem of intention is important enough to have a special name. Writers who think it idle to attempt to arrive at a poet's or author's intentions call the attempt 'the intentional fallacy'. The question is important, since much literary biography presumably rests on a belief that a knowledge of authors and the formative influences in their work controls our assumptions about their intentions and consequently our understanding of their work. In reality, it may be doubted whether we would understand Shakespeare better if we knew as much about his life as we do of Wordsworth's, though students of Old English would probably welcome information, if it could be provided, about the intentions of the unknown writer of the poem editorially called 'Wulf and Eadwacer', interpreted by naughty Victorians as a song of illicit love, but in our more moral age thought to be perhaps simply a marital poem. In this case, however, and perhaps in most cases where biographies are usefully used, what we especially lack is knowledge of the situation described in the poem and the situation of its intended readers, especially their expectations and conventions of interpreting their literature.

If intention is not to be the criterion for understanding a poem, should a poet read reviews of his own poetry to find out what it means? If he disagrees with a consensus of critics, who is right? Might a poem have different valid meanings for different people? Does a poet discover his complex intention only by writing, discovering it in the poem as other readers do? Perhaps not surprisingly, poets are seldom willing to answer questions about the meaning of their poetry or their intention in writing it, though A. D. Hope in an essay in *The Cave and the Spring* (Adelaide, 1965) compares interpretations of his poem 'Imperial Adam' by three critics with his intentions in writing it.

Hope does not assume that a poem is defined by a writer's intention but he specifically rejects an opposing view that a poem is whatever it means to its reader. A search for the key to understanding in the effect that language has on the hearer or reader also has its dangers and a name. Literary critics who reject it call it 'the affective fallacy'. The effect that language has on a reader is scarcely more observable than the intentions of its author. A. E. Housman claimed that remembering a line of Milton brought a perceptible gooseflesh to his skin, enough to be dangerous while he shaved, but, thinking this a good way to get a better shave from an electric razor, I have found that Milton has no such effect for me at the hour at which custom demands that I shave, though there are effects in Old English poetry that can make me feel roughly groomed when taking classes later in the day. The consensus of readers through the ages conveniently marks a corpus of classics but does not tell us the qualities that make them classics. Where there is less agreement, we are left to wonder who is right, or is a text to be understood in many valid ways? When an author is neglected by one age and acclaimed by another, as Donne has been, which age is right, and was Donne the same poet in the eighteenth century as he is now?

Poetry has been variously called 'expressive' and 'emotive', one term emphasizing the writer, the other the reader. Horace thought that poetry should be 'useful and pleasant' and periods where classicism has been dominant have been aware of the reader and the public. Romantic critics, often poets themselves, are more interested in the writer, but the bard or seer has divine inspiration, and since Shelley's time has been an acknowledged legislator for his age, so that readers are not disregarded. Pleasure and persuasiveness were long thought the end of poetry and both are judged by the reader's response.

In our time, linguists and literary critics alike have moved away from a preoccupation with the intentions of speakers and writers and the responses of hearers and readers to a study of the utterance or text itself. Linguists have been less doggedly linguistic than many of the critics, because at least an influential group among the linguists has added to a study of the linguistic code an interest in the situations in which language is used. This is, however, only recently a widespread interest, and for much of the twentieth century it is true to say that context and meaning, both in linguistics and in the discussion of poetry, have been comparatively neglected during a time of preoccupation with linguistic form. We have discovered a 'textual fallacy' but left it unnamed.

All that can be discovered about a situation – speaker, hearer, circumstances and text – is relevant to understanding. Our lack of knowledge of the author of 'The Dream of the Rood', or even whether there was one author or two, is a limitation of our understanding of the poem just as the missing beginning and end of 'The Battle of Maldon' is a limitation of our full understanding of that text. We know too little about Old English writers, circumstances and audiences to undervalue a knowledge of situations in assessing literature. To deduce a different world from texts is an exercise in sympathy which is one of the values of learning to read older literature, but the attempt acknowledges the importance of the world as well as the texts.

Something of the situation of older literature, beyond what is directly described, can be deduced from texts because stylistic choices are governed by situations and the text thus implies the situation which moulded it. It would be wrong to assume an exact correlation between situation and style (that would be 'a situational fallacy') and certainly much correlation that exists is yet to be worked out, but that situation is to some extent inferred from the words is evident from the opening lines of a play or from the ease with which we could agree on situations to attach to 'Say ninety-nine' or 'No Smoking – Fasten Safety Belts' or 'Going, going, gone' or '. . . four, three, two, one, zero' or 'Cheers' or 'One owner, low mileage, £1,000 o.n.o.'. If all language specified situation as readily as these items, situation could be ignored as redundant or subsumed under meaning, and stylistics could ignore it or become an exact science of the contextual determination of linguistic choices; but texts are seldom so specific of situation, as we saw with 'Put it down there' (which would be quite specific if it was an order to a general to put down a rebellion in an indicated territory). There is stylistic choice where text is partially determined by situation or situation is uncertainly implied by text, so that we commend the appropriateness of language or understand an ironical implication.

Our abstract analysis of situation isolates elements which occur in all situations, but it provides a basis for studying variations in situation if we treat the elements, speaker, hearer, language and circumstance, as variables. At the same time, it will provide a basis for a general theory of linguistic variation, showing that differences among languages and within them are not accidental but arise from the nature of the speech situation itself.

Since speaker and hearer may exchange roles, we may assume that every person who uses language has a dual capacity and acquires a dual competence, a receptive competence, or ability to understand language, and a productive competence, or ability to speak or write it. The two are separable since it is possible to understand language we could not produce, and indeed this is normal in early life, since all of us presumably began to understand words before we produced any, though we produced phonetic sounds before either competence developed. Experience of language moulded our babbling and we imitated the speech we heard, accommodating our productive skill gradually to our receptive competence. Such imitations are theoretically unlikely to be absolutely exact, and understanding and communication do not depend on absolute conformity, so that a language, existing only in a tradition of imitations of remembered auditory experience, naturally drifts from generation to generation, or from place to place if communities become separated. This natural tendency of language to change and diversify was particularly noticed in nineteenth-century language study, with its dominating interest in comparative philology.

On the other hand, speakers constantly adapt their linguistic habits to ensure understanding and acceptance, approximating their productive competence to their receptive experience, so that sustained communication promotes linguistic uniformity among speakers. People vary in adaptability; Defoe when touring Somerset marvelled at a boy who read in a Bible before him 'I have put off my coat; how shall I put it on? I have washed my feet; how shall I defile them?' and pronounced aloud 'Chav a doffed my coot; how shall I don't? Chav a washed my feet; how shall I moil 'em?' Defoe knew that this simultaneous translation did not show lack of intelligence in the 'dextrous Dunce'. Most of us find it easier to adapt, and such standardization is, as much as change, a natural process in all languages, given by the theory of the speech situation. There has been in the history of languages rather more natural unification of dialects in this way than nineteenth-century students of change in language usually conceded.

Comparative philology depended on purifying part of the total truth about change, stability and adaptation in language. Reversing the message of Biblical linguistics, which saw an original and natural unity of language artificially disrupted by the imperfections of man, the nineteenth-century historian came to think of standardization as an artificial interference with the natural process of linguistic change, and the decay of dialects was regretted almost as the levelling of villages by motorways is deplored now. We can hardly think of a preservation of dialects as anything other than artificial, but the power of the view of language which isolated change and diversity as its most important themes proved to be impressive. Nineteenth-century philology brought an immense increase in our understanding of language, and we will begin our investigation of the stylistic implications of situation by taking its fiction of pure change seriously.

Change is constant though hardly observed by the users of language. It cannot be abrupt since there is always communication between generations, perhaps more in the past than now. A five-year-old can converse with an eighty-five-year-old, though a dozen such conversations take us back to Anglo-Saxon. We can imagine each speaker connected with all his ancestors by a single line of imperceptible change. If the line is long enough, it reaches back to languages unintelligible to the present speaker, and from a hypothetical starting point modern speakers of languages as diverse as Gaelic and Hindi may trace their linguistic ancestry. An original language or a number of original languages have fragmented in a slow-motion disruption of Babel to produce the multifarious languages and dialects of today.

It is assumed that while speakers of the dialects as they form have no contact with outsiders, any dialect might introduce and preserve any sporadic change so that any degree of differentiation is possible. An interesting task remaining for present-day comparative philology is to examine this assumption. Is there perhaps some pattern in the changes in particular languages and groups of languages? Germanic languages have tended to modify vowels in syllables preceding a syllable containing *i*. Some think the change had already occurred in the original unified Germanic language and was reflected in spelling only when a loss of final syllables made the vowel difference significant, but it is at least possible that it represents a direction of change that was merely potential in the common language, that, for example, it results from a developing pattern of initial stress which concentrated tense pronunciations of vowels early in the word. There is some indication that Armenian, with later stress in the word, shows a tendency to move earlier vowels away from such pronunciation, and though it is difficult to accumulate enough evidence to define a law, it seems that what appears to be a special change in Germanic languages may result from a more general principle of change. Even the Rotuman language of the Pacific shows a relation of stress and vowel sounds recalling the Germanic ones.

If sound changes are not arbitrary and sporadic but are adjustments to deep-seated changes in the pattern of a language, it is even theoretically possible that some day changes in the most general patterns of language will be linked with changes in the social situation in which it is used, as was suggested early in the history of comparative philology by Jakob Grimm, who thought that the consonant changes he described were related to the heroic vigour of the people who spoke the language. Such intrusions of stylistic evaluation into comparative philology have been rare.

Less speculatively, time and change enter stylistic discussion in a study of the contacts between older and newer phases of a language. Essentially each successive state of a language dis-appears with a new generation and is not available as a stylistic choice, but some modification must be made to this absolute statement. For one thing, small but perceptible differences in the

language of older and younger generations coexist. At present
the pronunciation of *cloth*, *loss* or *off* with the vowel of *claw* is a
somewhat 'old-fashioned' but still an acceptable pronunciation.
Even more dating is the use of slang, since this changes rapidly,
and a well-meaning parent attempting sociable informality
with his sons and daughters risks many a stylistic infelicity.
More importantly, writing preserves older stages of a language
as part of the receptive competence of later generations.
This competence is imperfect; we all know the wry bewilderment
which some of Shakespeare's puns and wordplay can bring to a
modern reader, who senses that a joke is afoot without knowing
what it is. It is like the bracketed (laughter) in the less obviously
funny Parliamentary reports. But with the artificial aid of scholarship, our receptive competence as readers of Shakespeare is
cultivated, and even Anglo-Saxon lives as a receptive competence
for those who study English at university, though it has ceased to
be within the productive competence of anyone.

Auden uses some of the syntax and metre of Old English in his
poem 'The Wanderer', but to notice this is 'literary etymology',
a study of the sources of the poem, rather than part of a modern
reading. It is doubtful whether the young Auden expected batteries
of scholars to trace his debt to the Old English *Wanderer*, the
Middle English *Sawles Warde* and (I suspect, from its reference
to an avalanche driving a man from his home) the opening of the
Icelandic *Hrafnkels Saga*. For most modern readers the poem
must be primarily an exciting new experiment in verse. A 'period'
style can be cultivated with the expectation that the reader will
recognize it only if the style is a recent one, as in Thackeray's
Henry Esmond or John Fowles's *The French Lieutenant's Woman*.
And even *Henry Esmond* is less appreciated as we become less
certain which details represented an older style when it was
written.

A writer sometimes borrows details of older language with the
full intention that they be recognized as archaisms. Spenser
borrowed words and phrases from Chaucer in conscious cultivation of an old-world style. The practice has never gone unchal-
lenged. Spenser's contemporary, Thomas Wilson, remarked that

'Phauorinus the Philosopher ... did hit a yong man ouer the Thumbes very handsomely for vsing of ouer olde and ouer strange wordes', and in 1713 the *Guardian* in a mock recipe for an epic compared 'darkening it up and down with Old English' to the practice of a painter who 'made his daubings to be thought original by setting them in the smoke'. On the other hand, only a couple of generations ago Sir Walter Raleigh, who thought common language could not keep a school for style, commended the use of archaisms.

We no longer like archaisms. A disadvantage of their use is that they quickly become hackneyed. Fresh ones cannot be easily introduced since, though the archaism by definition is not current, it is necessary for communication that it be known. Archaisms tend therefore to have special uses, in poetry or (like *albeit*) in formal style. Since Sir Walter Scott's *Ivanhoe*, they have had a special usefulness in the dialogue of historical fiction, to bring a flavour of a past period without an authentic reconstruction of a language no longer intelligible.

Styles have their own history, a history of fashions in language with the occasional preservation of a passing fashion into a longer life. As religious uniforms have preserved the medieval wimple and the late nineteenth-century bonnet, so religious prose long retained the idiom, already tinged with archaism in its time, of the Authorized Version, and Boy Scouts preserve Kiplingesque Anglo-Indianisms when talking to Arkela. Strangest of all, a German polemical fashion of the 1840s was given permanence by Marx and Engels, and, reinforced by Lenin, joined inept translations of words like *comrade* in English to ensure that fears of a 'red menace' in English-speaking countries would always carry a sense of unreality.

Change in language, which is different in different places, brings about geographical diversity if the communication which regulates and standardizes language is infrequent. Dialects naturally occupy an area, not a line, but like the phases of a language in time, they tend to merge into one another without abrupt transition, unless communication is completely impeded, by a geographical obstacle perhaps. The boundaries of dialects, like the names of periods (Old English or Elizabethan English, etc.), are assigned by scholars for convenience and do not necessarily represent sharply defined realities. We can imagine the dialects and phases of a language in a three-dimensional space within which we may isolate larger or smaller zones and give them names, 'Northern Middle English', 'Early Fourteenth-century Kentish dialect' or 'Eighteenth-century Scots English' for instance. In the modern period, new areas in North America, South Africa and Australasia are less diversified but not without some variation within their boundaries as well as variation from the source language in England.

It is not easy to divide the concept 'dialect' from the wider concept 'a language'. In practice the criterion is based on the speech situation; if two speakers are unable to understand one another, they speak different languages. But modifications to this definition are necessary; a chain of mutually intelligible dialects in a large country may include mutually unintelligible dialects at the extremities and conversely, as in Scandinavia, political divisions may give varieties the benefit of the doubt and the status of languages.

Separate languages are only marginally of interest for the study of style (except for that branch of stylistics, which there is not space to pursue here, which assesses the stylistic potential of various languages, examining whether French is really a logical language or Italian a musical one, or whether Jespersen was right in thinking that languages which, like English, have lost most of their grammatical inflections have 'progressed' more than languages like the one that was first sung, with seven cases in its nouns, from a sputnik). John Gower wrote in English, French and Latin, but that reflects a special situation in medieval England. Samuel Beckett or Julien Green write equally naturally in English and French, but for different audiences. Milton's Latin, Greek and Italian poems are the exercises of a scholar. Today, so far has the England of Gower receded, even the foreign quotations which lent colour and wit to older writing are frowned on by a wider reading public too busy to acquire French and Latin.

Dialects have more obvious stylistic relevance. They are not outside our receptive competence, and much information in speech situations is unintentionally conveyed by an accent. Some dialects, like Irish English, have wide appeal and give rise to regional varieties of our literature: 'Good evening kindly, stranger, it's a wild night, God help you, to be out in the rain falling.' (Synge.)

The literary use of dialect need not in theory be more accurate than the Middle English of *Ivanhoe*, but in practice a writer will be conscious of 'native speakers' and will deviate from fact only by purifying and condensing the more widely intelligible features which give a dialect its identity, to produce a self-consciously local idiom. It will normally be felt by author and reader alike against a background of standard English. A writer may use dialects not his own, as Chaucer does in *The Reeve's Tale*, or may bring several dialects together as Shakespeare does in *Henry V*, Act III, Scene 2, and Furphy does in several passages in *Such is Life*.

There may be some deviation from probability in deciding whether or not to use dialect for the speech of a particular character. On linguistic, but not literary, grounds, Nellie Dean in *Wuthering Heights* ought to speak dialect, as I. A. Gordon has pointed out, but she tells the story and is in part the author's voice, and dialect would be obtrusive in her speech where it is not in Joseph's.

Traditionally dialect has been used for minor and especially comic characters. Even Dickens gives his heroines, however deprived in other material ways, the outward marks of a superior education in English. He had a more important motive than linguistic accuracy; he wanted to convince middle-class readers that Rosa Dartle's consoling view of the poor, 'that, when they suffer, they don't feel', was mistaken, and he was perhaps wise to appeal to his readers in their own dialect, a standard one implying universal truths and sentiments. Male characters, less delicate in the Victorian view, might be allowed a little heart-warming dialect. Even so, it is not easy to imagine a tragic hero speaking dialect in the days before Sean O'Casey. Macbeth could perhaps have a Scottish accent, though the text does not provide it, but Scots has long had the status of an independent literary language. It was not too difficult for Scott to allow the Deans family to 'speak the Doric' in *The Heart of Midlothian*, but Hareton Earnshaw in *Wuthering Heights* was given dialect as part of his degradation.

The novel, less universal than tragedy, allowed earlier experiment with the serious use of regional English. (There is a very good note on this subject in Q. D. Leavis's Penguin edition of *Silas Marner*.) Scott had set a precedent for English writers. Mrs Gaskell, whose husband the Rev. William Gaskell is remembered for his philological studies of Lancashire speech, used dialect, toned down to encourage sympathy rather than humorous effect, in *Mary Barton* in 1848. George Eliot's *Scenes from Clerical Life* uses dialect for comic characters in the conventional way, but Adam Bede is allowed his natural tongue. It is of course again a literary impression of dialect, avoiding dialect words that would not be understood, but an excellent impression of dialect can be given with very few strange words.

In *Silas Marner* there are perhaps not above half a dozen words unknown to the general reader. There is *mushed* 'subdued, depressed, crushed'; Mr Macey observed that 'Folks as had the devil to back 'em were not likely to be so mushed' as poor Silas was. The word has no exact standard equivalent and is therefore not easily exactly defined, but it is reasonably intelligible in its context, as are *springe* 'active, supple' – 'The Squire's pretty springe considering his weight'; *piert* 'brisk, lively, cheerful, in good health' – 'more pleasanter looksed when he's piert and merry'; *moithered* 'broken into small flakes', hence 'bewildered' – 'You'll happen to be a bit moithered with it while it's so little' ('it' was the baby, Eppie) and *colly* 'dirt(y) from coal dust' – (the coal hole) 'was enough to colly him all over, so as he must be new washed and dressed'.

Except for these words, which could not easily be replaced by standard ones, the effect of dialect is gained by ordinary English with minor indications of dialect pronunciation. George Eliot's accurate observation went beyond the merely lexical and phonetic.

She was aware of the loose trains of thought in those unused to the discipline of written language; questioned about the ownership of a cow, Mr Macey replies, 'Ask them as have been to school at Tarley: they've learnt pernouncing; that's come up since my day'. There is poetic flavour in the local syntax of a description of pups: 'They *will* worry and gnaw – worry and gnaw they will, if it was one's Sunday cap as hung anywhere so as they could drag it.'

An interest in dialects developed in both literature and philology as railways and the beginnings of modern communication were lessening the linguistic importance of geographical separation. Linguistic distances, measured by a speaker's opportunities for contact with other speakers, were diminishing. The growing cities merged speakers from different rural areas into wider speech communities, so that there was a falling away of country words and of dialect forms and pronunciations not generally understood, or likely to attract mockery. The process recalls the 'composite photographs' which were to be devised by Francis Galton at the end of the century to give precison to the concept 'a family likeness'. For these, portraits of several members of a family were superimposed on a single photographic plate. Individual traits disappeared or were faint; those which recurred in several members of a family were strongly reinforced.

As the nineteenth century progressed, more people went to school and to varying extents adjusted their language to the dialect which had begun as that of the South East Midland and London area, had become adopted by the court to become the King's or Queen's English, and had become the language of administration. We remember the adoption of English in the law courts as a triumph of English over French, but it was also a triumph of London English over other regional dialects. The administrative and upper-class language based on London became partly dissociated from place to become a 'standard' for literature, government, the church and education.

Thomas Hardy, who had seen railways enter 'Wessex' when he was still a boy, is not merely evading dialect words ('those terrible marks of the beast to the truly genteel', as they are called in *The Mayor of Casterbridge*) when in *Tess of the D'Urbervilles* he gives his heroine standard speech. He is quite explicit about the social change that was taking place:

Mrs Durbeyfield habitually spoke the dialect; her daughter, who had passed the Sixth Standard in the National School under a London-trained mistress, spoke two languages, the dialect at home, more or less; ordinary English abroad and to persons of quality.

Tess is somewhere between the little 'pernouncing at Tarley' and the respectable education in English and modern languages acquired by the Brangwen girls in Lawrence's *The Rainbow* and *Women in Love*. She has enough education to separate her from the country but not enough to give her a place in the town. It was enough to make her rural surroundings uncongenial and even hostile. Vernon Lee, with both the insight and the erratic judgement that surprise her modern readers, condemns Hardy's description of countryside, preferring the neatly arranged landscapes of R. L. Stevenson. The landscape, she complains, is allowed to dominate Tess. More ready to see passages in context, we recognize this as Hardy's strength. *Tess of the D'Urbervilles*, like *Jude the Obscure*, is a tragedy of one who finds nowhere to belong.

Why should Hardly feel so strongly about education that the integrity of *Jude the Obscure* is endangered by its bitterness of feeling? His own education was a good one by almost any standards – but the one exception, based on Oxford and Cambridge, was the dominating one in the literary world he had reached. Hardy's uncertainty of style is well documented. He cannot write prose as Congreve can. There is in his writing the pervasive unease of a man who cannot trust his natural spoken idiom to give him fluency. There is a tendency to the over-literary which we find for similar reasons (though it bothered them less) in Australian writers in the nineteenth century. For instance both Henry Handel Richardson and Marcus Clarke use the quaint inversion of subject and verb to indicate a conditional clause ('Did he do so-and-so' for 'If he did so-and-so'). Even the earlier American writers were unable to trust their ear in 'speech-based prose'. A related uncertainty perhaps even now explains the magnitude of the gulf between certain kinds of American academic writing and plain ordinary speech.

Two opposite modern tendencies may give American writers confidence. One, which officially excludes them, is the development of a concept of Commonwealth Literature, with its accompanying tolerance of regional variation and multiple standards; the other is the partial dissolution of boundaries between English and American literature. Librarians who separate the two wonder where to put Eliot or Auden, or even Henry James. Hemingway, certainly an American writer, could hardly be ignored in a history of English literature and Poe even has his strange but secure place in European literature.

Commonwealth literature itself widens rather than reverses the trend towards a standard language and literature. Its writers never achieve that single-minded absorption with the outlook of a single locality that allowed Wells to confine a 'war of the worlds' to an area fully mapped by the London Underground 'Diagram of lines'. They write with a complex sense of audience, contriving to make the local generally intelligible, so that each subliterature is accessible to readers of the others, since each has an awareness, whether it is in the forefront of writers' minds or not, of a standard English which is the tradition of British literature. Overseas literature in English therefore gives the general reader of English some of the advantages of bilingualism.

Yet, though this sharpens our sympathetic awareness of other places and cultures, perhaps ultimately we remain tourists when local themes are treated in local language, unless a writer of the stature of Patrick White or William Faulkner uses the local to reach themes of universal importance. I suppose I respond to an idiom like 'not for the Lough Nahanagan and it filled with gold' as to a colourful street market in a Mexican town with no sense that it could be part of my life. I suppose others take a similarly detached pleasure in Frank Sargeson's shy laconic style, which for a New Zealander catches the essence of ordinary speech:

I wished I'd gone to the beach because the sun was real hot and there wasn't a cloud. It had been a dry spring and everybody said it was going to be a hot summer. There was the yarn they always say about how the Maoris had said so. Though it was getting a bit late in the day to go off to the beach so I played penny catches with Fanny, but the ball kept on banging into the washing and in the end Mrs Clegg went crook, though she needn't have done because her clothes weren't as clean as all that.

Overseas varieties of English have now more literary importance than true dialect, but true dialect has not disappeared from literature in our century. Its use for 'comic effect' in texts peppered with such respellings as *woz* (how did the authors themselves pronounce *was*?) has mercifully disappeared, even in Australia, where the English literary 'low dialect' mixed with some local words used to be humbly accepted as Australian English by readers of C. J. Dennis. There is perhaps a hint of the same tradition in the more complex 'Strine'. In England, Shaw used dialect for 'low characters' in several plays, but seriously examined the social problem of dialect in *Pygmalion*. H. G. Wells also notes the social significance of dialect as Archie Garvell attacks Ernest Ponderevo in the opening chapter of *Tono Bungay*:

> 'He drops his aitches like anything.'
> 'No E doesn't,' said I in the heat of the moment.
> 'There you go,' he cried, 'E, he says, E! E! E!'

In the eighteenth century Thomas Sheridan would have abolished dialects by an ambitious programme of elocution and so abolished social classes, or, as he preferred to put it in his flamboyant Irish style, banish the Giant Corruption with his hundred hands from the land. But such a programme would need to re-educate Garvell as well as Ponderevo, since the optional suppression of *h* in unstressed pronouns is standard.

A language has its major variations in three dimensions, two of place and one of time. It is uncertain whether theory ought to allow for a fourth dialectal dimension of social class. In some countries at some times class has been as divisive as geography. In England regional variation becomes less as the social scale is mounted, so that a combined diagram of regional and class variation at a given time would have a more or less conical shape with the Queen's English at the apex. Since the centre of influence in a language is not usually at the exact geographical centre of a country, the cone will be somewhat skew, perhaps with 'foothills' representing local centres of influence. A point on the outside of the cone below the apex would represent a form of speech locally considered 'good' or 'upper-class' but in a wider setting given a lower or regional status.

While a social or class dimension might have practical value in a particular linguistic discussion (it has been used in descriptions of Jamaican English, for example) it is not clear how far it is a theoretically necessary dimension of language. I am aware that my own background prompts me to underestimate its importance. In Australia there is some tendency for a pronunciation closer to the British to correlate with length of schooling, but little other discernible linguistic indication of social class. In Australia, as in England, the children of professional people often have a wider experience of life and language, and one better adapted to the school situation, than the children of manual workers, but it is uncertain how far this is a genuine difference in language and how far a difference in command over language.

A full study of social class and the English language by someone more alert to the nuances of the subject than I am would be a very useful linguistic, literary and educational project, but at present I will assume that 'class dialects' can be analysed into a selection from other varieties, including polite language, educated language, literary language and the elimination, by means of special schools, of what is local in speech. In a wide sense of the term, recalled by the children's chant 'Tinker, tailor, soldier, sailor, rich man, poor man, beggar man, thief', class merges with occupation; historically the duke and the zoo-keeper differ in their professions. Above all, class language links with a language of administration and government and higher education, and this, rather than such relics as U and non-U, is the real 'language of the ruling class' in the modern world.

Whatever dimensions of variation we assume for the situations in which living language is found, we may claim (to review our progress this far) no more than to set up guide-lines to describe an unimaginably diverse human experience. Our material is an infinity of possible linguistic forms multiplied by an infinity of possible situations. Both the language and its situation can be described only by generalizing, by finding a common form in diverse instances of linguistic activity. We begin to study the situation with a very general pattern; speaker, hearer and language. The speaker perhaps brings an innate competence or capacity for language, at least a predisposition to analyse experience into component elements, like the 'things' and 'actions' represented in a general way by the nouns and verbs of most languages, though even this much is difficult to prove. He perhaps brings also a desire to seek and impart information and to influence the behaviour of others, so that questions, statements and commands are, it seems, found in all languages. His desire to share experience is not always utilitarian, and literature especially may reveal a delight in contemplation, though this is not confined to literature nor necessarily its essence. The speaker and his hearer use language in particular circumstances, which may influence the form of the language, and add a linguistic context to the situation as they proceed, especially in the longer texts of written language. Because most of the detail of language is not innate but an agreed set of arbitrary symbols learned by each successive generation, language is subject to change and to regional and social variation. Except perhaps for variations relating to social class, these varieties are usually given rather than deliberately cultivated. We are now ready to go on to describe more closely those more purposeful variations which, instead of dividing some speakers from others, extend the linguistic range of individual speakers.

6. Register

How small can a dialect be? Scholars sometimes find it convenient to talk of large dialect areas like North American English, at other times specifying Canadian English or subdividing further, finding local variations within a district or town. Ultimately we come down to the speech of one individual speaker and call his speech an 'idiolect'.

This concept is easy to understand and has become popular, but it is more theoretical and abstract than is always supposed, since it usually represents only the productive competence of a speaker, and the speaker is only part of a minimum speech situation. Nevertheless, the concept 'idiolect' is useful to separate the major linguistic dimensions determined by time and place from another kind of variation, variation in technicality, in formality or in choice of speech or writing. Time and place separate idiolects; these other varieties are found within an idiolect.

In one case, when we compare dialects, we normally compare entirely different linguistic situations; speaker, hearer and circumstances all differ between one dialect and another. In the other case, in studying the variations available to a given speaker, or different 'registers' as they are conveniently called, we compare partially overlapping situations. Usually we identify registers by taking the speaker as the invariable element in overlapping situations, and discussing how he adjusts his language to a situation. It would be possible to do otherwise, to see technicality for instance from a hearer's point of view, imagining perhaps a school class remaining in a classroom to be visited by a succession of teachers of various subjects, but the children do not always find out *why* different teachers speak in different languages. Explanations seem to centre on the speaker who makes linguistic choices in response to or in relation to situations.

The difference between dialect and register is not absolute. There are a number of links between the two. Tess's 'two languages' represent that contact of dialects which alone brings dialect into a discussion of style. But the role of dialect in this case is changed (we are reminded of the 'rank-shift' of grammar); Tess's home dialect becomes her informal or intimate language, while 'ordinary English' for 'persons of quality' and strangers becomes her polite and formal language. This is not an accidental link either, since informal language varies locally more than formal language does, and dialect words added to a formal standard language sometimes retain a homely flavour. In Latin, *popina* ('tavern') is an Oscan variant of the Roman *coquina* ('kitchen').

If a dialect may sometimes function as a register, it is also true that register sometimes acts, as dialect does, to divide speakers as well as speech. This is especially true of technicality which could in these cases perhaps be taken to form special 'dialects of one register' within a community. A sailor's English might represent such a 'dialect'. It is also true that register enters into the formation and definition of dialects and of historical phases of a language. Local occupations may help to mould a dialect and contemporary industry colour the idiom of an age. Middle English is in part feudal and early mercantile English with a greater interest in sheep than we have now, just as part of what is special about Australian English is the language of the woolshed and shearing. If we could assess how much and how subtly historical change in a language is a response to social, economic and intellectual history, we could be more illuminating than we are about theories of 'progress in language'.

Nevertheless, though any variety might be adopted by a sufficiently versatile speaker for a special purpose such as play-acting, imposture or teaching Old English, some varieties are obviously more arbitrary than others and arise from limited contact among groups of speakers, while the others are useful and necessary and are maintained by the purposeful activity of speakers. In English the trend has been away from arbitrary variation towards useful variety and it is perhaps in this that we should look for 'progress' in our language.

Since situations appear to be infinitely various, some linguists have hesitated to embark on a systematic study of the situations which mould the various registers of English. But we may deal again only with an abstract situation, and deal with situation at all only as it affects the form of language. If a conversation begins in a teashop and is continued during a walk through a park but these surroundings have no observable effect on the language used, then teashop and park are linguistically irrelevant and all we need specify is a situation bringing the participants together. Dryden makes his *Essay of Dramatic Poesy* more interesting by setting a conversation about drama in a boat on the Thames, but it is not written in a nautical register. Even when Crites, discussing a superficial writer during this conversation, suddenly makes a point by saying 'these swallows which we see before us on the Thames are the just resemblance of his wit: you may observe how near the water they stoop, how many proffers they make to dip, and yet how seldom they touch it; and when they do 'tis but the surface', we need add no details not provided by the text.

Literary relevance is in any case wider than linguistic relevance, in setting as in phonetics. Just as the coming together of particular phonetic sounds in a word, considered arbitrary by the linguist, may have special onomatopoeic effect in a poem, so a linguistically arbitrary setting, such as the weather, may be contrived for effect in literature. In poetry, such effect might almost become the substance of the poem:

> This ae nighte, this ae nighte,
> *Every nighte and alle*
> Fire and sleet and candle-lighte
> *And Christe receive thy saule.*

In this case, admittedly, the suggestion of surrounding storm is an accidental one, since the author must have written 'fleet', meaning 'a floor', 'a room' or 'a fireplace', but the wide acceptance of the version with 'sleet' confirms that in situation, as in sounds and grammar and vocabulary, literature has its 'extended schemes'. We understand them better by seeing that they deviate from the normal relations of language to its situation.

Since in ordinary language a speaker's choices may be governed by any of the three main elements in the situation, that is by his own role, by the number and status of his hearers, or by the particular circumstances which direct him to speak or write, we have three main ranges of variation in register according to which of these elements is dominant. The first defines a range of technicality, the second a range of formality and the third determines whether speaker and hearer are within audible range or whether some other kind of message must be sent. A 'variety' can be identified by more than one range of variation at a time: a legal document is formal, technical and written; a conversation between scientists might be informal, technical and spoken. These ranges, like the time-scale or dialect areas, can be infinitely subdivided. Technical English includes as subvarieties the language of chemistry, botany, or linguistics. (In practice, subdivisions cease to be very interesting or useful when nothing varies but a few technical terms.) Conversely, broad categories such as 'urban' and 'rural', children's and adult English, are sometimes useful.

Though we must avoid the mistake of thinking of varieties as isolated little boxes of language, it is not necessary to suppose that a three-dimensional model for variations in register has the kind of reality that it seems to have in a model of variations in time and place. It is pretty certain that a linear arrangement of technicalities is not possible, for instance, as those who try to devise ideal library classifications discover. The subject Linguistics, for example, might plausibly be related to Psychology, Anthropology, Philosophy, Literature and Education at least, but can only relate immediately to two of these in a linear classification. Its position between Social and Physical Sciences in the Dewey system is probably the best one, but it separates a Spanish dictionary from Spanish Literature. It seems fruitless to try to count the dimensions of knowledge. We merely observe that what

I have called a 'range' may have more than one dimension, just as the range 'regional dialect' has more than one dimension.

Technicality is illustrated by the man who changes his language, along with this clothes, when he leaves home to go to the lab. It is language with a proper social setting; its use outside that setting is condemned as 'talking shop' if the hearer shares the technicality, or pedantry or jargon if he does not. Among the registers, technicality is least easily defined without reference to other at least potential situations and is the most likely to divide users of a language (at least in societies where no strong formality marks social classes). It therefore most resembles dialect. In some technicalities a protective obscurity is deliberately sought; a reference in the early nineteenth-century underworld to 'three peters cracked and frisked' was not meant to be as lucid to chance overhearers as 'three chests broken and robbed'. In some languages, men and women have different forms of speech, and there are at least traces of this in English. Nevertheless, in all these cases, we have varieties potentially and usefully available to speakers in all regions. Even the men's language of the fifteenth-century *Paston Letters* (marked by a stronger influence of Latin and the language of the law) is now available to women who want it. The range of variation defined by the social role of the speaker reflects occupations and preoccupations first and only incidentally distinguishes special people.

Social changes have sometimes separated technicalities but more often brought them together. When factories took spinning and weaving from the home, once-common craft terms became less widely known, until now English speakers are sometimes uncertain of the past tense of the once everyday verbs *spin* and *weave*, so that a minor result of the Industrial Revolution will perhaps be to hasten the addition of these two verbs to the 'weak' class (with past tense in -*ed*). On the other hand, education and the unifying influence of science tend to bring technicalities together and make them widely available. When leisure increases, older crafts are revived as hobbies or readers acquire the language of other lives through books. Democratic philosophy promotes the

s.–9

public discussion of administration in all its branches, and newspapers and broadcasting make this possible.

In any case a man may change his job or use the language of another man's job. A New Zealand academic claimed to be able to get timber when it was in short supply by phoning not for 'fifty running feet' but 'a fifty-foot run', the builders' idiom. Occupations link producers and consumers, and the consumer is likely to consume some of the language with the product. Moreover some occupations with a special language of their own bring no profit and so must be combined with others. An electrician who is also a keen stamp-collector has two special interests more easily distinguished by the economist than by the linguist. Occupation merges into a defined interest and its subject matter.

Subject matter alone does not prescribe a special language or register. This book, after all, attempts to separate a subject matter assumed not to be the speciality of its readers from the special language in which it is professionally discussed. True technical language is the language of specialists addressing other specialists. Of course a special subject always makes a special language more likely, and popularizers do not always avoid technical terms. Theirs is a modified technical language, often introducing special terminology in quotation marks, because they have to talk about the language of their special subject before using it. This language is, in any case, part of what the general reader wants to know about, and is to some extent necessary to introduce the distinctions made by specialists. What is lost in popularization is the brevity of the specialist, and therefore, in a book of practicable length, much of his detail and the qualifications he would make.

When technical language becomes so widely known that it is accessible to everyone, it ceases to be technicality and becomes part of the general language. The language of Christianity in medieval Europe, or the language of communism in the Soviet Union now, hardly represent technical languages. A student of Middle English, whatever his own religion, must master medieval Christianity not as a technicality but as a mode of thought before he can understand the literature of the time. The language of literary criticism designed for readers rather than writers and the language of journalism are, in a strict definition, perhaps hardly technical languages either, because both are designed to reach the general reader. On the other hand, the critic draws on technical knowledge and the journalist discusses politics, economics and other technical subjects, so that both are exercises in the modified technicality of the popularizer.

The language of a special occupation may be marked by a special pronunciation, the intonation of a clergyman being an example, or by subtleties of syntax beyond what formal written language provides, legal documents being this time an example, but the formal linguistic distinguishing marks of technical languages are especially found in their vocabulary, both in a tendency to abbreviation and in the development of special vocabularies.

There is a law of language which states that frequently used words tend to be short. Now, since a technical writer is normally restricted to a narrowed subject matter, the frequency of words relevant to his subject will be greater in his text or in his conversation than in the general language. Some of his words will become redundant, that is, entirely predictable from their restricted context. An electrician asking which of three wires is 'the earth' clearly means 'the earth(ed) wire' or 'the wire connected with the earth', but hardly needs to spell it out. As frequently used words are shortened and phrases are shortened by the omission of redundant words, abbreviation is a natural result of the technical situation. The electrician understands *shorted*, students (in Adelaide) call a tutorial class in economics 'an eco. tut.' and we glimpse something of a medieval huntsman's professional language in *Sir Gawain and the Green Knight* in a line praising the deer killed by Sir Bertilak's hunters, which may be literally translated 'Two fingers they found in the meanest of all', that is, in the worst of the deer the fat was thick enough to be measured by the breadth of two fingers.

In the special vocabulary of technical registers two contrary tendencies are found. One is a specialization of vocabulary so that distinctions neglected in non-technical language can be made. An example of this is the linguist's distinction between a phoneme and an allophone. Both are sound-units used in language, but the phoneme is a sound-unit considered as an an element in the pattern of language, used to make meaningful distinctions, while an allophone is a particular variant of a phoneme, usually in a particular phonetic environment. In the word *tall*, /t/ is sounded through rounded lips but in *teeth* it is not. The difference in sound is small and is not one that our language trains us to detect, but it is a difference. The rounded and spread allophones both represent the phoneme /t/. A less modern but not basically different set of distinctive terms is the farmer's *ewe*, *ram*, *wether*, *hogget* instead of the townsman's less precise *sheep*.

The opposite tendency in technical language is towards general terms to represent more inclusive concepts than those of ordinary language. A zoologist not only multiplies names for what a plain man calls collectively *shellfish* (sometimes specifying oysters), but also gathers up shellfish with slugs and snails into a wider concept of *molluscs*. The farmer distinguishes two-tooths from older sheep but also gathers sheep, cows and horses into a concept *livestock* or briefly *stock*. The linguist not only distinguishes words from morphemes, but also gathers up morphemes, words and fixed idiomatic sequences like *instead of* or *mother of pearl* into a wider category *lexical item*. Both the more general and the more particular concepts of technical thinking multiply vocabulary, and this, reinforced by its tendency towards ellipsis and abbreviation, makes technical language inevitably somewhat esoteric, an accident not always regretted or combated by those who cultivate it.

There is something of the initiation ceremony in the training of apprentices and scientists. The magic of secret names is powerful. The student of geometry is never to *draw* anything; he may *describe* circles, *construct* a triangle, *produce* its sides and *drop* a perpendicular, so that geometry is in part the learning of new collocations of words special to the subject. The student goes on to chemistry and learns to discuss milky limewater in terms of a *white precipitate* or interesting cracklings as *decrepitation*. It is all linked with training in precision of thought and care about language, and I know I am grateful for such stylistic training as I had in school labs and, even more strikingly later, in university lectures on palaeontology, a rigorous training in describing spiral staircases without waving your hands, since it includes a description in words of all the possible shapes of fossil shells.

Even where a science merely replaces a common word with a special one with no gain in exactness of meaning, the term is not necessarily without usefulness. Part of the function of technical language is to announce a specific technical intention. If we *describe* a circle, we intend to talk about it exactly and logically. In common language a preoccupation of a speaker may be less apparent and this is a source of ambiguity in the use of language. When in Sterne's *Tristram Shandy* the Widow Wadman asked Uncle Toby where he had been wounded, her words immediately suggested to him his favourite topic of military topography and he happily embarked on diagrams of fortifications and battle plans. But the widow's mind ran to marriage and she intended the words in a more medical sense. She understood in general that Uncle Toby had been wounded in the groin and her plans for marriage awaited more precise information.

Technical language, when it is used, does not always specify a technicality without ambiguity. A style using many passive constructions may be administrative or scientific. The word *cell* may indicate a technical discussion of biology, politics, electricity or prison administration. In each of these cases, the word *cell* would have different collocations and the larger set consisting of a word and the words collocating with it in a text is more specific of the special interests which restrict the interpretation of the text.

Even common words in unusual collocation may define a technical style. Mr Derek Davy has pointed out to me that only in stockmarket reports would the inanimate noun *tin* be subject of the verb *suffered*. Hoping to confirm this usage by a random reference to *The Times* (2 July 1971), I immediately discovered that on that day the breweries 'came alive with a start'. One 'soared' and others 'moved up hopefully' and they were still 'active' some days afterwards. In this improbable world, lead may be buoyant and oil firm, but steel may sag badly as the day goes on.

Linguists are interested in correlating definable linguistic forms with definable situations, the more narrowly the better. This has been the aim of dialect study. When Shakespeare uses the word *dwindle*, apparently not common before he used it, we want to know whether it is specifically a Warwickshire word. Similarly the isolation of special elements in a register will not always be an exhaustive description of actual texts but will isolate the criteria which allow us to place them. Technical language will in practice be mingled with less specific language, sometimes making a common word its own, as chemists use *flask*, sometimes borrowing from other technicalities, as phoneticians use *acoustic* in a sense developed in physics, sometimes borrowing with a change in meaning, as *transformation*, from mathematics, is redefined in linguistics.

Most interesting linguistically are the styles which are marked by a number of specific 'features' and at the same time are specific to a narrowly defined situation, especially when the situation is defined with reference to a very small segment of one range of variation. An example of such a style is a written account without comment of a game of chess. Very likely such a description will begin with the statement 'P—K4' and, with this notation established, further text is entirely determined by the progress of the game. Conversely the text would unambiguously imply the situation 'a game of chess' and every relevant detail of the game would be reflected in the text.

Chess cannot stand for all games because it is made up of a limited number of possible moves and *how* the moves are made is irrelevant. Left-handedness makes a difference in many games but not in chess. A formulaic description of a tennis-match would not completely report the match because tennis is not ultimately analysable into a specific number of moves. There is style in both chess and tennis, but the style in chess is entirely in combining elementary moves; in tennis, style enters into making the moves as well. One backhand shot will differ from another. The language of tennis is therefore less stereotyped than the language of chess. It has its specific formulae – any text containing all the items *love–fifteen*, *seeded player*, *volley*, *serve*, *court*, *game*, *set and match* is pretty certain to be about tennis – but the reporter of a tennis-match will want to say something of how the basic 'moves' were performed, and stereotoyped terms are less readily available for this. Tennis commentary will contain more ordinary language than a report on a game of chess.

If 'language is a game', it is more like tennis than chess, and perhaps most like backyard ping-pong on a small and uneven table where special rules have to be made to deal with the unpredictable. It is really not a game at all but a serious activity which must continually adjust to new situations and say new things about the old, and the last details of its rules are never established.

There are outside the language of games a few cases of very specific varieties of language, the recipe language of cookery or the language of a knitting pattern, for instance, and these already indicate the differences between language and chess or even tennis. Most recipes will use established ingredients combined by established processes, and most knitting patterns will use established stitches in established ways, but either may conceivably add a new element, ingredient or stitch, and a new way of combining elements, and if this happens we still have a recipe or a knitting pattern. But to introduce a new move into chess is to invent a new game, as a new game, rugby, was invented by a boy who picked up a football.

The language of chess, reflecting the very specific and finite analysis of the game itself, is therefore unusual among special languages. In most cases both situation and language are adaptable and neither is entirely predictable from the other. In many cases possibilities in a linguistic response to a given situation are very wide. Two men in a bar may talk of many things, though some rules of politeness and acceptable topics exert their influence. In some groups one is expected to discuss sport or last night's television, in other groups, any topic but these. Usually 'shop' is avoided; Mr Appleby, you probably do not recall, was an architect, but the only relevance of this was that he did not discuss architecture. Polite inquiries about family and shared friends are often acceptable in informal conversation, and Mr Appleby skilfully combined the topic of sport with polite inquiry when he mentioned Mr Plumtree's son's prowess at the school sports. But these constraints operate weakly, and it is open to any conversationalist to be original if he will. The remark 'Makes a neat figure eight' does not automatically arise from a club-house situation.

The literary critic, if he does not play chess, knit or specialize in those modern French novels that devote two hundred pages to a close study of two wet rings on a bar counter, will be ready for a more interesting turn in the argument. He is least interested in the explanatory successes of stylistics with chess notation and most interested in styles where choice is freest. This is indeed the most lively study of style, but we know when choice is free only if we know when it is determined. Part of an author's freedom, moreover, arises from an unexpected use of expected styles, the use in another context of terms usually found only in restricted situations. Even the language of knitting can make poetry; 'sleep that knits up the ravelled sleeve of care' depends first on the ordinary domestic associations of the language to give exactness of feeling and idea to the metaphorical use.

More elaborately, Pope, in the *Guardian* (1713), used a recipe style in his directions for composing an epic:

For a Tempest. Take Eurus, Zephyr, Auster and Boreas, and cast them together in one verse. Add to these of rain, lightning and of thunder, (the loudest you can) quantum sufficit. Mix your clouds and billows well together till they foam, and thicken your description here and there with a quicksand. Brew your tempest well in your head before you set it a-blowing.

The style sinks the sublime in the mundane, and its suggestion of cookery – or possibly pharmacy – with its fixed ingredients must have given readers before Coleridge some idea of the limitations of 'fancy' where we might expect 'imagination'.

A particularly interesting use of a pervasive style is seen in the often discussed opening of *Bleak House*:

London. Michaelmas term lately over, and the Lord Chancellor sitting in Lincoln's Inn Hall. Implacable November weather. As much mud in the streets, as if the waters had but newly retired from the face of the earth, and it would not be wonderful to meet a Megalosaurus, forty feet long or so, waddling like an elephantine lizard up Holborn Hill. Smoke lowering down from the chimney pots, making a soft black drizzle, with flakes of soot in it as big as full-grown snow-flakes – gone into mourning, one might imagine, for the death of the sun. Dogs, indistinguishable in mire. Horses, scarcely better; splashed to their very blinkers. Foot passengers, jostling one another's umbrellas, in a general infection of ill-temper, and losing their foothold at street-corners, where tens of thousands of other foot passengers have been slipping and sliding since day broke (if this day ever broke) adding new deposits to the crust upon crust of mud, sticking at those points tenaciously to the pavement, and accumulating at compound interest.

What exactly is the effect here? Readers will perhaps agree that the style is marked by these characteristics: the passage describes a scene of activity, filling in enough background information to provide a setting and taking some care to make the scene interesting. Though this is a written text, we have the impression of someone speaking, an unbroken monologue marked by fluency and a number of 'long intonation patterns', but with a variety of sound effects (the lowered tone of a parenthesis, the suspended voice at a dash or the single-word tone units like 'London' or 'Dogs'). Grammatical links (connectives) are comparatively few or simple and there is some use of lists ('Dogs ... Horses ... Foot passengers'). Incomplete or 'minor' sentences are frequent (in fact no sentence has a 'main verb'). There is some repetition. There are many adverbials (adjuncts) to indicate time, place or direction of motion (some but not all of these become minor sentences). There are many modifiers and qualifiers but they are not clustered in complex groups. There are a number of expected collocations ('one might imagine', 'the face of the earth', 'day broke'). There are few learned words, apart from those necessary to the subject matter ('Lord Chancellor', 'Michaelmas term').

Now, I based this list, apart from its bracketed commentary, not on the text itself but on a very careful description in Crystal and Davy's *Investigating English Style* of 'the language of unscripted commentary', the professional language of radio announcers, whether describing a cricket match or a state funeral. The radio commentator is an institutionalized version of someone standing at a window describing a scene to someone who cannot see it. Dickens has imagined the essence of this situation, and even attracted the standard charge against radio commentators, of making events seem more interesting than they are, since Gissing thought 'this darkness visible makes one rather cheerful than otherwise'.

If my radio parallel is unsatisfactory, it is because it gives too little attention to metaphor. The 'few learned words' included the striking *megalosaurus*, reinforced by the phrase 'waddling like an elephantine lizard', and even if *infection* and *tenaciously* count as ordinary language, *compound interest* is figurative and the snowflakes in mourning will recall the personifications of *Little Dorrit*. Of course Dickens's passage is far from 'unscripted' and we marvel at the general impression of unrehearsed comment rather than the carefully planned effects. If the megalosaurus, compound interest and the snowflakes (and perhaps the word *infection*) 'stand out' it is because they are meant to. They make a pattern on another level, a thematic pattern of unwieldy monsters arising out of corruption, of money and of death, and these are the hidden pattern, now made visible, in London and the law.

Technicality, like dialect, can be used selectively to give a flavour to literary writing without an attempt at a full-scale reproduction of a technical register. Dryden justified the use of sea-terms in poetry, 'the terms of Art in every Tongue bearing more of the Idiom of it than any other words', in the preface to *Annus Mirabilis*, but the poem itself uses very few such terms even at its most technical:

> The distance judg'd for shot of every size,
> The Linstocks touch, the pond'rous ball expires:
> The vig'rous Sea-man every port-hole plies,
> And adds his heart to every Gun he fires.

The language of the sea has been a favourite technicality for novelists from Smollett onwards, perhaps because it is a plain man's technicality, close to ordinary language. Bookish technicalities are less suitable and give an oddity of flavour to much Science Fiction, especially as they are often combined with a tough laconic style of American popular fiction: 'Get back in there', he snapped, 'It's the Chi-phenomenon!' An exception must be made of C. M. Kornbluth's story 'The Altar at Midnight', which imagines a popular idiom developed among 'spacers' (the men who man spaceships):

> 'You get something every trip, hah?'
> 'Shoot. You call a trip a shoot.'

The spacer explains to his interlocutor that when 'you spend so much time outside in a suit', you may 'lose your point' and not know which way the 'can' (spaceship) is. The spacers bear marks of their trade in small burst bloodvessels called 'redlines' and may also suffer from 'Bowman head', named after the inventor of the 'Bowman drive'. Linguistically all this seems entirely plausible.

Occasionally it is uncertain whether a writer is using a word in a specialized sense or not. Some have enjoyed Milton's use of the word *conclave* in *Paradise Lost*, I, 795 to describe the assembly of hell, since it is a term of the Catholic church, but in the same poem (II, 391) he calls the same assembly a 'synod', so that it seems that rhythm rather than technical connotation has governed his choices.

Technical terms, like dialect words, may pass into the general language. When this happens, a word used by a restricted group of people in a restricted situation becomes used more widely by more people and the reference will tend to be less concentrated or precise. We say that a word usually widens its meaning when it becomes a general word. We see this strikingly with a fashionable word like *allergic* but it is also true of more stable words like *insanity*, once a legal and medical term, but now capable of loose or metaphoric use as well. Even technical mannerisms have their wider influence; a radio announcer's habit of stressing prepositions has become more widely noticeable. Perhaps the reason *for* this mannerism *in* radio announcements, is that the announcer has in *front* of him a sequence *of* words which he must pronounce, but they are other people's words which do not engage his mind and he is not much aware of the total and orderly meaning *of* them. In other people, the acquired habit promotes as well as reflects an inattention to syntactic meaning.

At particular times particular technicalities are particularly influential. In Shakespeare's English the upper-class pursuit of hawking was a source of metaphor and of words (*lure* is an example). Later, astronomy and then biology had their day; later still we reacted to psychology. During the war, stay-at-homes waged a 'blitz' on the office in-tray and now small Americans learn early to count down to zero.

Our age is not hierarchical in its thinking, and as meanings widen they tend to become diffuse. It is for us an effort of the imagination to recover medieval modes of thought where a word could have two integrated 'special meanings' or sets of connotations at once. 'Love sacred and profane' retains this way of thought, revived in the students' slogan 'Make love not war', where *love* seems to have two sets of meanings at once, each a highly integrated concept. In Old English literature, heroic and Christian modes of thought seem to have interfused, keeping enough of their separate identities to make difficulties for modern scholars. Some see 'monkish interpolations' in whatever is not heroic; others justify the witticism that 'every new window opened on the Middle Ages proves to be a stained glass one'. Chivalry itself is a complex alloy of the Christian and the military, later applied to love as well.

We have inherited along with many relics of the age of faith and chivalry a more analytical tradition which grew up especially in the thirteenth century among the scholastic philosophers. This tradition has become the tradition of modern science.

If general literature finds little use for systematic technicality, scientific literature has come to cultivate it almost exclusively. Yet if scientists are distinguished from technicians by their ability to use language, it is not in the technicality of their language that the distinction lies. The Royal Society scientists, Boyle, Hooke or Newton, wrote good prose of their time in personal styles. The baroque richness of Hooke contrasts with the classical chill of Newton, but both tell us sometimes how they felt when experiments proved interesting.

But science must be 'invariant to all observers' and experiments, not experimenters, were the centre of interest. This encouraged an impersonal style, that is, in relation to the general language, a third-person style. If the scientist must mention himself, he calls himself 'the present writer', but he is seldom present at all.

The passive voice, with elimination of the active subject, was favoured by the demand for impersonality, but it proved to have a more important use. Active subjects in the general language are very often animate nouns, and the active sentence carries a suggestion of an actor initiating an action. In the history of physics the problem of 'action at a distance' became a central one in discussions of gravitation. As the new and related science of electricity and magnetism developed, the causes of the phenomena observed were unknown and it was an embarrassment even to find a subject for an active sentence. Something deflects a needle. What deflects it? A needle is deflected. That is all we know.

Faraday has been praised for stating no more than he knew, and it is in Faraday that we feel that a style depending on a frequent use of the passive voice reaches full development. The history of science, even more essentially than the history of literature, is in an important sense a history of style.

The impersonality of modern science rests not only on a frequent use of the passive but also on a frequent use of abstract nouns formed from verbs and adjectives (examples are the words *use* and *impersonality* in this sentence). To use such words requires even more stylistic skill than to use passives, since whereas a passive deletes an active subject from an underlying complete statement, an abstract noun may omit a subject and up to two objects (direct and indirect). The sentence 'Mr Brown teaches John chemistry' is more explicit than the abstract *education*, but educationists have to bear in mind that their subject is 'someone teaching someone something' and that the organization and training of the teaching profession, classroom method, child psychology and the curriculum are a unity, not merely a chance constellation of related topics. Could a committee of highly paid academics spend an afternoon discussing the purpose of examinations without asking themselves 'What do we examine?'

Traditionally we have learned to ask such questions by writing Latin prose, more recently by training in transformations and deep grammar. Classical Latin, as taught in schools, favours concrete expression. This is not quite true of Cicero; and early Christianity, with its influx of Greek philosophical terms, finally changed an earlier peasant concreteness of thought. The scholastics added Arabic terms and made new abstract terms, not worrying too much about hybrids (like the word *grammar*, or, in the scientific language which continues the tradition, *television*). The scientists have developed the medieval tradition, encouraging relatively simple sentence structure but complex word formation. As science came to be written in vernacular languages, the medieval technical vocabulary was grafted on to the grammatical framework of these languages, sometimes unchanged (as the medieval scientific term *impetus* is unchanged in form or medieval scientific meaning), more often adapted to the orthography of the receiving language. The power to go on making new terms was taken over with the stock and goodwill, so that all Latin words became potentially English. Boswell, while touring the Hebrides with Johnson, coined a word *equitation*, but was surprised to find that the Earl of Pembroke had hit on the same word. In fact the *Oxford English Dictionary* records the word from 1562, but the creative process is in this case more important than the first use of the word, since its users did not learn it, as they learned common words, in contexts, but formed it when it was needed from the Latin word-building stock. Scientific words are often formed and interpreted in this way. We do not hear *pyrolytic* or *tychopotamic* often enough to learn their use as we learn the use of *fire* or *river*; to try to remember such terms without knowledge of their formation would be a time-wasting and insecure way to learn them.

The language of medieval science and speculative thought was current throughout Europe and was adopted into European vernaculars as these came to be used for science. Thus the scientific varieties of modern languages are unusual among varieties within the several languages in remaining partially international. A highly technical document in English is from one point of view a scientific variety of English, but from another, an English variety of scientific writing. It could be thought of as very bad medieval Latin. To translate it is to change its regional 'errors' into those of another region, so that it is easily translated and may even be translated by machine. In such texts, common vernacular words even come to be avoided; it has been pointed out that a foreign reader of technical English might have more difficulty with the word *tumbler* than with the standard sequence 'a cylindrical glass vessel of 7 cm in diameter and 10 cm deep'.

The classical basis of learned vocabulary has not gone un-challenged, but even those who tried to avoid Latin word forms could not avoid their underlying pattern of thought. Reginald Pecock in the fifteenth century wrote *endal* instead of *final* and *inleding* instead of *introduction*, but these are still the international concepts with merely a little extra phonetic deviation in the component parts. The same is true of German learned vocabulary.

Some sciences are less classical than others in their vocabulary. Physics drew on Latin and the biologists responded to a developing interest in Greek, but geomorphologists, who might be expected to be both widely travelled and down to earth, drew on commoner words, either from an exciting array of exotic languages or from their own. So we have *pahoehoe* and *aa* from Hawaiian, *geyser* from Icelandic, *kopje* from Dutch, *moraine* from French, *loess* from German, *volcano* from Italian, *yardang* from Turkish or *corrie* from Gaelic. At the same time we have *rock*, which has long been English.

Of these words, perhaps the most difficult for a student to learn is *rock*, because a geologist uses the term more widely than other people. How soft can rock be and still be rock? In ordinary language there is an indeterminate zone between soft rock and hard clay. The geologist solves problems of definition by calling both of them rock, and includes sand as well. Hardness is not a defining characteristic of rock for him.

Ordinary language acquires emotive overtones. Rock is not merely geological material but a symbol of steadfastness. The words *progressive* and *regressive* are geometrically simple in basic meaning but each acquires a different cloud of overtones in ordinary use until 'linear movement in or away from a direction faced' becomes a very inadequate description of all the meanings of the two words. Even in Marxist writing, where the word *progressive* is used against the background of a scientific theory which conceives history as an onward movement which may be aided or opposed, the word may have a few uncontrolled overtones. Science therefore cultivates an insulation of its vocabulary from the associations of common use.

One method of achieving such insulation is to promote an artificially acute attention to the composition of words and phrases, defining exactly the use of the suffixes *-ide*, *-ite* and *-ate* in chemistry, for instance, or avoiding in medical language a popular use of *get better* which can have a total meaning, 'recover', different from its analysed meaning 'improve'. Another method is to rely on definitions, ignoring those common uses (as of the word *allergic*) which transgress this boundary.

It remains something of a nuisance to scientists if popular use of their terms is indefinite. Biologists are secretly glad that you are unlikely to call your pony *Equus caballus* and technicians suppress a thought that we are all bio-degradable. Statisticians probably wish you had never picked up the word *average* (and might wish my use of *probably* had some supporting numbers with it). The difficult words for scientists in training are *base*, *salt*, *weight*, *work*, *fish* and phrases and compounds based on common words, the musician's *white noise* or the engineer's *feedback*.

We shall in a moment meet a particularly irritating example of this tendency of general language to bring irrelevant and distracting associations to technical terms, when I come to seek a name for the next kind of variation under the general heading of register. We are now leaving the discussion of technicality, relating to the

social role and qualifications of the speaker or writer, to investigate the ways in which a speaker or writer adjusts to his hearer or
reading public. Our association, dear reader, has now reached
a point where it seems appropriate to murmur 'Let's talk about
you.'

The trouble is – who the dickens *are* you? The general reader?
An identikit face stares glumly. 'Will interest workers in related
fields . . .' I imagine men with aching backs, looking up irritably.
'Will find its place in schools . . .' A clearer picture now, of a
cluster of pretty schoolgirls; I frame some sentences in a fatherly-
flirtatious manner and meet the steely gaze of a professor from
the related fields. You laugh, you girls, but it is a serious problem;
perhaps, sir, the most important problem in writing, this problem
of imagining an appropriate audience.

That language changes with audience was well observed in the
Guardian, 18 August 1713:

> My lord Froth has been so educated in punctilio, that he governs
> himself by a ceremonial in all the ordinary occurrences of life. He meas-
> ures out his bow to the degree of the person he converses with. I have
> seen him in every inclination of the body, from a familiar nod to the
> low stoop in the salutation sign. I remember five of us, who were
> acquainted with one another, met together one morning at his lodgings,
> when a wag of the company was saying, it would be worth while to
> observe how he would distinguish us at his first entrance. Accordingly
> he no sooner came into the room, but casting his eye about, 'My lord
> such a one, says he, your most humble servant. Sir Richard your
> humble servant. Your servant Mr Ironside. Mr Ducker how do you
> do? Ha! Frank, are you there?'

In our time, Martin Joos, in his *The Five Clocks* (a highly
recommended short book which shows that a stylistician may also
be a stylist), also isolates five degrees of ceremony in language,
but five is an arbitrary number of steps to cut in a gradation from
slang to ceremony. Joos calls his steps 'styles', but since the
adaptation of language to a hearer is only a part of what we are
calling 'style' in this book, we need another word. Usage allows
two choices, and neither is good.

We may use the word *tone*, and that risks confusion with the other technical meaning of *tone* to refer to the pitch of the voice, the basis of intonation. The two are admittedly not quite unrelated. When Hazlitt remarks that 'Reading the finest passage in Milton's *Paradise Lost* in a false tone, will make it seem insipid and absurd' he probably refers to a tone of the voice, but one which suggests insufficient formality. In a more extended use, we could comment on the *tone* of Empson's discussion of *Paradise Lost*, when he calls Eve 'a social climber trying to angle an invite to Heaven'.

Our other choice is to avoid the ambiguous word *tone* and talk of 'degrees of formality'. This too is ambiguous if we use the adjective *formal* because this word has a technical meaning within linguistics as an adjective from *form*. 'The formal situation' could, then, mean 'the situation considered as an abstract scheme' or 'a situation requiring some ceremony'.

Crystal and Davy avoid both words and use *status* to describe a dimension of variation which includes formality, but for our present purpose this word perhaps suggests too exclusively variations relating to social position. We adjust to an audience not only according to social status but according to how well we know our hearers and whether we address one person or several. J. R. Firth had a promising term, *tact*, but probably had a wider meaning in mind, as he describes tact as 'that complex of manners which determines the use of fitting forms of language as functional elements of a social situation'. This would perhaps include technicality, but, again, variation according to audience is not entirely separable from this other variation, since the nature of the audience will determine whether or not technicalities are used. No term is finally satisfactory. I shall use either *formality* and its adjective *formal* or *tone* for the range of variation reflecting adjustments to an audience, hoping that the words will not be ambiguous in context.

An intimate situation is reflected in language by a relaxed pronunciation, marked in English by assimilations (for example, 'ap my house ing Kent') and reduced forms (for example 'n' for 'and'), and by less carefully precise grammar than that of formal writing. The often debated 'It's me' is often justified by the need for an emphatic pronoun in English as in French ('c'est moi'), but its survival may also relate to its use in friendly and relaxed situations. Some languages such as Malay have special intimate forms of pronouns, and older English, like other European languages, distinguished an intimate second person singular pronoun (*thou*) from a more formal *you*. Angus McIntosh has studied the use of *thou* and *you* in *As You like It*, and in Middle English literature the intricacies of *thou* and *you* must be noted by careful students if the tone of dialogue is to be understood. The demonstrative pronoun *this*, suggesting closeness of speaker and subject, is more informal than *that*. A popular writer might use 'this word' or 'a word of this kind' where a more formal writer would use 'that word' or 'a word of that kind'. Both in English and French, informal spoken grammar is indicated by a summarizing pronoun as in 'A friend of mine, he was telling me ...' or 'L'oiseau, il vole'. This informal usage is noted by F. von Wartburg, who also remarks on the informal use of locally valid prepositions with place names. In England newcomers learn when to say 'up' or 'down' to Oxford; in Adelaide a local use of 'down the Mount' replaces 'to (the town of) Mt Gambier' in informal speech.

Special forms of personal names (first names or pet names or the more formal Mr or Dr) are important in controlling tone when a distinction between intimate and formal second-person pronouns is lacking, as it is in English. In literature an author's relation with his characters is controlled by his decision to talk of Mr Plumtree or Charles Plumtree or Charlie Plumtree. It is typical of V. S. Naipaul's ironical humour in writing of his Trinidadian characters that he refers to Mr Biswas with the formal 'Mr' even when recalling his adventures as a baby.

In vocabulary, any risk may be taken in informal styles for colourful effect, if a shared background makes the message intelligible. The resulting neologisms may be nonce words or they might find imitators, but the colour which justifies such ventures soon fades and they are usually abandoned when the novelty wears off. Intimate language requires a loose-leaf dictionary.

The word 'slang' is usually used to describe ephemeral additions to intimate vocabulary. In its proliferation of words slang resembles technical vocabulary, but its purpose is different. It is not designed to make fine cognitive distinctions. It would be idle to try to define how *batty*, *nutty*, *dotty* and similar terms vary from *silly*; fashion demands that new terms replace old, and for some concepts (drink, women – or men – money, intellectual inadequacy, for instance) a battery of terms is necessary if any are to have enough freshness to give colour to intimate language.

Because a trade or profession defines an intimate social group, there will often be a slang vocabulary associated with a particular occupation, so that some kinds of slang are defined both by their informality and their association with an occupational group. They form a composite register of informal technicality, defined by two ranges of variation, just as Old West Saxon, for instance, is defined both by age and place, but their informality rather than their technicality marks them as slang. Such occupational slang may pass into general colloquial use, as a number of sea terms (*on deck*, *ship-shape*, *learn the run of the ropes*) have become general colloquial English. These borrowed terms have some usefulness in their accuracy of reference; terms which remain special to a group are often more humorous than useful. They may be institutionalized shared jokes, like the British railwayman's *gnat's blood* 'tea from a railway refreshment room', *daylight saving* 'failure of electric circuit in a coach', *liquid sunshine* 'rain', *Rip Van Winkle money* 'money earned asleep while returning to a depot' or *genial menial* 'happy shed labourer'. One wonders how generally current some of these items are. They are reported by Frank McKenna in a History Workshop Pamphlet from Ruskin College, Oxford, along with items more likely to be used unselfconsciously: *Bible* 'railway book of rules', *boomerang* 'return ticket', and perhaps *miner's friend* 'a Royal Scots class locomotive, heavy on coal', *do-it-yourself kit* 'a steam locomotive' (after Diesels were introduced), *navvy's wedding cake* 'bread and butter pudding' or *birth control hours* 'a midnight to 5 a.m. shift'.

Slang is intimate language but its intimacy once it becomes current is a group intimacy, and an individual may use current slang to disguise his private feelings. Shirley Hazzard, a novelist who is often acute in her observations about language, traces in *The Bay of Noon* a friendship which fails to become intimate and specifically notes the defensive use of slang expressions like 'keel over' or 'press on regardless' as an indication that the intimacy is not real. I have had teachers dispute my use of the description 'intimate language' for slang, because, they say, the greatest obstacle to any real intimacy, of the kind that might encourage self-awareness and development, in the friendships formed among their pupils, is the more or less obligatory use of slang in their social group. They are right; real intimacy needs no special language because the deepest private needs are also the most universal. Poetry resembles slang in its creativeness but is at the opposite pole from the mindless repetition of words that happen to be fashionable. Slang may even have its usefulness among children as a protection, so that they can begin to learn social behaviour without staking too much of themselves at once. These are problems of adolescent spoken style which should be studied by a wise and kindly educationist.

It seems theoretically likely that texts could be arranged in a single linear sequence according to their degree of formality, but that the situations in which they occur could not, since the same linguistic forms may indicate an increase in the number of hearers, an approach to a stranger of unknown background and interests, respect for a known hearer of high status or deference to an important topic of discussion. Politeness, however, can be separated from formality within language, since it is possible to have language which is both polite and informal, as in 'I say, Jim, you wouldn't have such a thing as a spanner handy, would you?', and conversely one can use very formal language to be cheeky, as every schoolboy knows. In some languages politeness is marked by special grammatical forms, especially in pronouns, so that its relevance to general linguistics is not in doubt, but it is not certain how politeness should be fitted into a theory of linguistic variety. Should we link polite forms with class dialect, note them as an extra dimension of formality in language or take them as marks of a 'polite intention', making politeness a special

s.–10

function of language, on a level with asking questions or issuing commands, and noting that polite language usually (though not always) makes use of language marked by its high degree of formality? This problem must be left to the sociologists of language, especially those specializing in languages with developed 'polite forms'.

We have noticed in passing that subject matter has some relevance to the degree of formality in language, as it has to the degree of technicality. It is possible to be intimate with an audience and yet respectful to a subject and so use formal language; conversely it is possible to be flippant about a serious subject, without necessarily coming closer to an audience, in informal language. But just as subject matter does not inevitably prescribe technicality, it does not prescribe a level of formality either, and again the popularizer may be instanced as proof. A book 'without tears' usually avoids solemnity as it avoids unfamiliar technicality, though to be successful it must avoid facetiousness as it avoids inanity.

In a spoken situation the audience is given, but in writing, an audience must be imagined and is to some extent chosen. To write technically is to choose a learned audience; to adopt a friendly style is to write for friends, but with a risk, if your ideas are not congenial to a particular reader, of antagonizing him much more than a more respectful approach would do. He may have been schooled in British railway carriages to freeze at an affable approach from uncongenial strangers. There is also a danger of seeming to write for a coterie if anything excludes some readers. No one is more a stranger than a stranger among his friends.

There is a more interesting problem. Does the adoption of a particular 'tone' or degree of friendliness carry theoretical or philosophical implications? If I talk lightly on a religious topic, does this already commit me to a definable religious outlook? Recent British philosophy has very often been written in a gentlemanly conversational or casual style; does this already commit the writers to a standpoint about the seriousness of life and action very different from that in the philosophy of Marx or Aquinas?

Even more complex is the problem of intimacy in poetry. Poets very often deal in intimate self-revelation, though we do not often feel we know poets well. This is because the poet is separable from the 'I' of his poem and the reader is separable from the 'you' of the poem. But, within the poem, the 'I' may speak with great intimacy to the 'you'. This is seldom achieved by using the slang and colloquialism of familiar speech, but goes deeper than these forms, which are always partly protective of the inner self. Often very simple language is used, words learned early in life, rich in associations. Intimacy is controlled by pronouns, the use of first and second person rather than the third person of science.

Donne was a master of the poetic use of pronouns, often emphasizing them by placing them in rhyming position, and he explored the possibilities of the pronoun with an ingenuity that remains surprising. 'The Legacy' contains the puzzling couplet:

> Though I be dead, which sent me, I should be
> Mine own executor and legacy.

In an earlier couplet, the words 'I die as often as from thee I go' give us a clue. It is a conventional enough statement that the 'I' of the poem ceases to be when his lady is not near. But we must suppose that Donne explores the implications of this conceit with more than usual consistency. If his existence is dependent on his lady, his lady is not fully distinguishable from his own being and might equally well be called 'I'. The two separate persons are confused in an entity called interchangeably 'you' and 'I'. A less ingenious (partial) statement of the difficult couplet might rest on the literal statements 'I am (figuratively) dead', 'You sent me (away)', 'You shall be my executor' and 'I shall be your legacy'. The second item is perhaps alternatively – or as well – 'I sent myself (to you)'.

Later in the poem the same assumption of an interchangeability of pronouns explains:

> I heard me say: 'Tell her anon,
> That my self' (that is you, not I)
> 'Did kill me'; and when I felt me die,

> I bid me send my heart, when I was gone;
> But I alas could there find none.
> When I had ripp'd me, and search'd where hearts did lie;
> It kill'd me again, that I who still was true
> In life, in my last will should cozen you.

The last two lines of the poem are:

> I meant to send this heart instead of mine:
> But oh, no man could hold it, for 'twas thine.

I assume that the parenthetical 'that is you, not I' is to be taken literally and represents a beginning of a polarization of the composite self into the two component selves. She has killed him. He continues to play with the interchangeable pronoun (the lady is to send her heart) but he finds her heart untrue, so that the legacy, their combined heart, or love, is a defective one. In the final couplet the pronouns have literal meaning; the two hearts are now quite separated.

At the opposite extreme of intimacy, Auden's 'Wanderer' uses only third-person pronouns, and few pronouns at all. The effect is of lonely remoteness. In the Old English model for this poem, person is less consistent. The poem begins in the third person but changes to a first person. Critics are uncertain whether to assume a dialogue or a monologue with a commentary. Marshall McLuhan has suggested that in general medieval writers, unable to imagine consistently a single audience, failed to achieve unity of tone. To prove or refute this would require much research, but one advantage of learning to read the literature of another time or place is to enter into different values, and different ideals of unity or different kinds of organization in a literary work may once have prevailed. The Old English *Dream of the Rood* has such a marked break in tone after seventy-eight lines that some scholars assume an unfinished poem continued by a lesser writer. Yet it is possible to see in the existing text a controlled development of mood, from the rich excitement of a vision to the drab monotony of life without it, so that a longing for death, with its renewed vision of the cross, is unusually plausible.

Sociological studies of literature are particularly concerned with audience and the social history of the reading public. Levin L. Schücking in *The Sociology of Literary Taste* or Q. D. Leavis in *Fiction and the Reading Public* are well aware that the linguistic situation, speaker, hearer and circumstances, is relevant to literature as to other language. George Gissing's *New Grub Street* gives us many an insight into the force an audience exerts on a writer. In the thirty-third chapter, Whelpdale explains the motive for a new magazine: 'I would have the paper address itself to the quarter-educated; that is to say, the great new generation that is being turned out by the Board Schools, the young men and women who can just read but are incapable of sustained attention.' The fare for this audience was to be 'frothy chit-chat', 'two inches at most'. How far papers such as George Newnes's *Tit-Bits* and Alfred Harmsworth's *Answers* responded to such an audience and how far they created it, and the political motives which lead writers to favour or oppose the cultivation of such fragmentary attention to the written word, provide complex questions for the literary sociologist to answer.

Such special forms of writing as technical books or children's literature remind us that an author may choose an audience. He may also create one. The element of fiction seen in the poet's 'you' sometimes extends to the real reader. Probably you do not work on a sheepfarm, and neither do I, but (except that the convention is rather dated) I could write a little poem about shepherds and shepherdesses, pretending that I am myself a shepherd writing for other shepherds and shepherdesses. Historically the sheep industry has especially attracted poets, so that we call such poetry 'pastoral', but William Empson has usefully extended the term (in *Some Versions of Pastoral*) to any literature in which writers and readers take on fictitious roles. A writer in Los Angeles writing cowboy stories for other residents along the motorways or a Sydney flatdweller writing about the bush for other urban Australians is writing pastorals. Empson brings *Alice in Wonderland* into the group, as it is ostensibly written for children but with a richer appeal to adults. The style of pastoral is more influenced by its real audience than its supposed one.

Shakespeare's Corin in *As You Like It* speaks as a real shepherd, but it is Silvius who represents the pastoral style.

The theme of the foregoing pages is that language is a product not of speakers alone, but of speakers in relation with hearers. We must now add that the forms of language are a response to a combination of speaker and audience in particular circumstances. Circumstances, apart from sometimes providing topics of discussion, affect language in several ways.

First, some linguistic forms are tied to the situation of their birth by grammatical indications of time and place. Words like *here* and *there* or the pronouns are chosen according to the situation in which they are used. In writing we usually assume that such words relate to the writer's situation. A nineteenth-century novelist mentioning 'a room furnished in a modern taste' clearly refers to a style modern to him, not to us. Sometimes the situation enters in another way, by providing the unspecified subject of a predicate, as when 'Nice dog' means '(You have) a nice dog' or '(You are) a nice dog' or '(That is) a nice dog' according to whether one addresses a dog or his owner or someone else. Some linguistic forms, for example 'American Airlines carry more passengers than any other airline in the world', are comparatively free of context. A passage long enough to provide its own (linguistic) context is especially likely to be free of situation, though it is a matter for debate how far the circumstances in which a literary work is composed are relevant to its appreciation.

Situation is relevant to language in a second way, in the appropriateness of the tone or length of what is said to circumstances. A compliment is too hesitant or too glib; a report of a witty remark ends with a stammering 'I wish you'd been there.'

Thirdly, language proceeds through a cooperation of speaker and hearer in a situation. Even when making no real statements, a hearer is not inert. He acknowledges that he hears and understands by various devices, by saying 'Yes', 'No', 'I see' or 'M'm'. You can make a list of such devices by listening to the uninteresting end of a telephone conversation and you can convince yourself of their necessity by the simple experiment of withholding all such signals when someone speaks to you on the phone and measuring how soon you get back an anxious 'Are you there?'

If the hearer of a first utterance replies more fully, to participate in a conversation, both participants influence the direction of the discourse, perhaps arriving at truths neither would reach alone (the theory of the seminar). This active interchange between one mind and another is missing in writing, though it can be imitated in dialogue:

BEATRICE: I wonder that you will still be talking, Signor Benedick; nobody marks you.
BENEDICK: What, my dear Lady Disdain! Are you yet living?
BEATRICE: Is it possible disdain should die while she hath such meet food to feed it as Signor Benedick?

For that matter, the dialogue in Harold Pinter's plays, if we acknowledge its truth to life, reminds us that a mutually adjusting mechanism of progress is not universal in conversations. Nevertheless, conversation, by its very nature, is likely to have it where writing, by its nature, normally lacks it.

Because speech is closely associated with its situation, because the speaker can continually gauge his communication by the audible and visible responses of his hearer and because the interchange between two or more participants in a conversation provides a dynamic for its progress, speech would appear to be in every way a subtler and richer means of communication than writing, but a fourth characteristic of the speech situation is a limitation: it is confined to a single occasion, a single place and a single moment of time. 'Speech writes itself on air', as A. M. Bell put it, 'and is gone.'

This limitation is overcome only by accepting other limitations. Two separate situations may be bridged by using a messenger, but the two separate 'births' of the utterance will not be identical. Subtlety of tone is lost and the original situation is only reconstructed (and then only partially) by linguistic elaboration in the message. If the sender of the message said 'this dog', the messenger would have to say 'the dog with him' or 'the dog with me' or 'a passing dog' or whatever specific description accorded with fact. On the other hand, repetitions, hesitations and cancellations made in the original giving of the message might be eliminated in the delivery, so that the more elaborate delivered message need not be less concise.

A messenger links two situations, but a more ambitious wish is to transcend situation altogether and achieve permanence and universality in language. One way is to make language memorable and this is done by weaving those specific details of pronunciation and rhythm which are especially likely to become altered as messages are delivered into memorable patterns of alliteration and rhyme. Proverbs and nursery rhymes are such 'emancipated utterances', freed from specific situations and given, if not permanent life, perpetual rebirth. They are an extended version of the idiom or 'emancipated partial utterance'.

Not even those who make a living out of language are exempt from the threat of automation, and a new device, arising out of memorial art, provided an automatic and deathless messenger. Writing was invented. Not all linguists have accommodated themselves to this change yet, and sometimes, like Mark Antony, have scolded the messenger while overlooking the value of the message. The medium is not the message. Writing is, of course, a reflection of speech and implies its own translation back into speech, since even such 'pure' writing as an unpunctuated legal document can be read aloud. Writing is not itself a variety of language. But we distinguish writing (the messenger) from written language (the message). We do this in practice whenever we accept a phonetic transcript as a sample of spoken language or read to a class a passage of Johnson to illustrate the style of written language.

The written message makes use of a visible medium so that it appears that written language is itself visible and spoken language is alone audible; but writers believe this at their peril. Rather the writer should think of himself as the initiator of a receptive experience of speech in his readers. These readers, if competent and adequately helped, will have the experience of having 'heard' a message with those tonal qualities necessary to the control of emphasis and grammatical meaning. A good writer can be read only one way; he chooses unambiguous rhythms, those that can be intelligently read only with the desired intonation. It is the hardest part of writing to learn and teach, and the justification for fussing about the placing of *only* and the avoidance of 'fused participles' and rhythmically awkward complex nominal groups.

As a small concession, the writer may remember that the act of writing itself creates a new situation shared by writer and reader, sometimes with some shared assumptions as clues to intended meaning. While it is true that a question in an application form for service with the U.S. Government, 'Do you favour the overthrow of the government by force, sedition or violence?', is tonally ambiguous, it is difficult to believe that a candidate who answered 'Violence' was seriously misled by the question in this context. The contexts of writing have their own variation, leading to a range of styles which form the subject matter of rhetoric.

It is difficult to describe the distinguishing characteristics of written language because the less important ones are obvious and the more important ones subtle. It is obvious that a visible system of spelling and punctuation replaces (or, better, represents) the phonetic substance of the basic language, and it is also well known that some linguistic forms are 'to be seen and not heard', as J. R. Firth put it. We rarely say, though we often read, 'Received the amount shown above' or such 'written words' as *woe*, *fleet* (adjective), *slay*, *chide*, *weep*, *delve*, *swift* or *bide*. These literary words were listed by Logan Pearsall Smith, but several of them have a surer place in newspaper headlines than in literature now. Conversely, other words occur almost exclusively in speech, so that all lexicographers know the difficulty of finding written documentation for the early use and history of slang words or even, sometimes, deciding how to spell them. Again, just as some speech is unprintable without loss because it depends on affective intonation, so, though more rarely, some writing is unspeakable because it depends on printing devices unrelated to pronunciation. 'Trust Him and He will comfort you' loses its religious specification when spoken, and the sentence in a radio announcer's notes 'These speakers are all most interesting' may be ambiguous when read out. The occasional spoken use of the words 'quote . . . unquote' or 'and I quote' tries to make good one deficiency in spoken language. Absolute differences between speech and writing are, however, comparatively trivial, and the important linguistic differences ensuing when writing is added to a spoken language are those which, while theoretically able to occur in both speech and written language, arise especially from the detachment of writing from the immediate environment of its production.

Writing, like a human messenger, does not convey exactly the voice of the sender, and perhaps neglects important tonal indications of how the message is to be taken; writing must therefore cultivate rhythms and connectives which indicate to a trained reader the appropriate emphasis to be given to items in the text. The writer must also elaborate his message to describe relevant details of the context in which it is issued. Except in private letters, guarded by social taboos against reading other people's correspondence, writing communicates not once but many times, reaching many people, friend and stranger alike, so that it is normally formal rather than intimate. The interchange of speech is missing in writing, nor are any regulatory assenting, protesting or inquiring noises available to the writer, at least until he reads reviews. The writer must anticipate his reader's difficulties and objections and take his interest on trust, or play as best he can the role of stranger-reader as he checks his work. The writer has to provide continuity in an unaccompanied monologue. He converses alone in an empty room. A playwright or writer of dialogue in a novel simulates an exchange of language, but the continuity still depends on one issuing mind. An argument may be presented in dialogue, as in Plato, and all argumentative and scientific writing perhaps assumes a dual role in the writer, who is both advocate and critic of the ideas he expresses. There is a dramatic interchange in every sentence containing a concessive clause. It is a purer form of fiction where there is a pretence of arriving by argument and experiment at the conclusion which in real life the investigator began by hoping to prove. It is a lone game of chess in which one always lets oneself win.

The greater, or at least tidier, complexity of written language, made necessary by the loss of the subtler phonetic details of speech and by the absence of a hearer's responses, is made possible by the visible permanence of writing. Like proverbs, writing has, if not immortality, continual rebirth, and it reaches not only other places but other times. It makes sense of talking to oneself in a diary or a shopping list, and, most importantly of all, it functions, as C. F. Hockett has pointed out, as an external immediate memory. A pencil in hand helps us to work out complicated sums on paper, and helps us in a similar way as a thought is pinned on paper to be slowly shaped and reshaped, elaborated without slipping from the thinker's grasp, left and returned to. It similarly helps the reader ('I think I should understand that better', Alice said very politely, 'if I had it written down: but I'm afraid I can't quite follow it as you say it.')

The written message is explicit, typically with subject and predicate as a minimum utterance since surroundings cannot provide an understood subject, and often hypotactic in structure since surroundings, though not the centre of interest, need to be explicitly described as subordinate details. The written sentence is composed with a balance and rhythm designed to control a reader's intonation, and continuity is supplied by a careful attention to connectives, conjunctions and words and devices which link sentences, which, along with proper attention to the arrangement of the details of an argument, and further hypotactic elaboration to concede and qualify, compensates for the physical absence of the questioning or helping hearer. The visible objectivity of writing, stripped of intonation, emphasizes the word rather than the group, and good writers learn to use words rather than formulas.

These are the qualities of written language, but none of them is confined to writing. Speech may be hypotactic, connected and careful of words, and writing may be without these qualities. This has theoretical importance in literary criticism; the association of formulas with speech has been so well recognized recently that 'oral formulaic' has itself become a formula, and since it is a written one, it may remind us that formulas are not so absolutely confined to speech that their presence proves a spoken origin for a text. Cowper's 'John Gilpin' is full of formulas. All that can be said is that formulas are more typical of speech than of writing, just as hypotaxis, connectedness and a careful choice of individual words are more typical of writing than of speech.

Writing, like a musical score, is not valuable only to record with some loss an individual performance; it initiates experience of a complexity and deftness of touch impossible without it. It is writing that has trained an extended and coherent habit of thought and has aided the development of science and philosophy. This importance of writing is not seriously challenged by other and more recent artificial extensions of language. The telephone retains the advantage of a speaker's response, or at least that part of it which does not depend on facial expression and gesture, but it is only filtered speech artificially extended in range. The radio provides mechanized oratory and the film mechanized drama, both deprived of the power of adjusting to the response of an audience. Film has permanence, but not the immediate permanence of writing which allows referring back and stopping to think, the essential conditions of analytical and complex thought. Television combines the advantages of radio and film but adds nothing to the sum. There are of course enormous possibilities to be discovered in film and television, but increasingly the competition is seen to be less with language than with the visual arts.

A writer transcends one element in the speech situation, the particularity of surroundings in the normal speech act. He does not, if he publishes his work, transcend the other basic element, the necessity of an audience. This need is transcended in a special (somewhat inaccessible and marginal) form of language, syntactically at the opposite pole from written language, described by the psychologist L. S. Vygotsky as 'inner speech'. In this the 'speaker' is his own hearer; apparently, though there is no observable sound or writing, using linguistic forms. It seems to make sense to say 'I think in English', though this English is not easily observed and differs syntactically from both spoken and written English. Inner speech has no need for expressed subjects and becomes a chain of predicates linked by private associations. Bloom's internal monologue in *Ulysses*, though an artifact, has been widely accepted as a plausible approximation to inner speech and will have to serve as a sample of it, though it is of course also a controlled part of James Joyce's complex communication with his reader. We see a transition from author's narration via reported speech to an inner train of thought in

> Mr Bloom put his head out of the window.
> – The grand canal, he said.
> Gasworks. Whooping cough they say it cures. Good job Milly never got it. Poor children! Doubles them up black and blue in convulsions. Shame really. Got off lightly with illnesses compared. Only measles. Flaxseed tea. Scarlatina, influenza epidemics. Canvassing for death. Don't miss this chance . . .

The tags of cliché which come inappropriately to Bloom's mind contrast with the literary tags which intrude into the fleeting thoughts of Stephen Dedalus, so that Joyce has not only captured a flavour of the elusive 'inner speech' but begins to explore the stylistic variants of the inner train of thought to add a new dimension to characterization in the novel.

'Inner speech', because it fuses speaker and hearer and because it is inaccessible to observation, is an atypical use of language. The linguistic situation that we can observe links a speaker or writer with other people through audible or visible language. It is on the basis of this essential situation that we have defined an idiolect (the observable language of a single speaker or writer) within the language community by relating it to a particular place and time, and have then gone on to find within the idiolect three major kinds of variation, in technicality, in formality and in the choice of speech or writing. Technicality relates to the occupation or special interest shared by a speaker or writer and his audience; the level of formality is adjusted to the status, familiarity and size of the audience and also to subject matter; the choice of writing rather than speech normally results from the separation of writer and reader in place or time, and leads, despite an obvious omission of some of the living quality of speech, to new functions for language and new linguistic forms to develop them. These major variations within a speaker's or writer's language are not overlooked by students of style, but they are too general, and perhaps too obvious, to lead us directly to the uses of language that have interested most writers on the subject. There are other and finer adjustments of language to situation, less easy to fit into a tidy theoretical pattern, yet perhaps capable of some methodical description. As we go on to look at some of these in a new chapter, we will come a little closer to the kind of stylistics that has traditionally interested literary writers.

7. Specific Functions of Language

Perhaps you would unthinkingly agree that anyone who asks a question wants to know something, but would you continue to agree after reading these questions:

Why is a raven like a writing desk?

Would some nice little boy like to set the table?

Where are the snows of yesteryear?

How far was Wordsworth successful in using 'language really used by men'?

Is whispering nothing?

Wilt thou have this woman to thy wedded wife?

Grammatically these are all questions indistinguishable in form from 'Where did you leave the keys?', but they differ in their *intention*. Grammatically 'I wonder if you could tell me where to find the keys' is not a question though it is spoken by someone who wants to know something and in its intention resembles 'Where are the keys?' Intentions are not observable and are easily misunderstood, but language functions efficiently only if, from a complex of grammatical hints and surrounding circumstances along with general cultural assumptions, hearers deduce the intentions of speakers with reasonable accuracy. An account of linguistic variation would be incomplete without some attempt to deal with the shadowy problem of intention. To centre interest in the language itself, we may say that language has several different *specific functions* within its situation.

'Specific function' labels a third level in the adjustment of language to its situation, and since it is the level where we find the most frequent and most conscious variation, it comes closest to what is commonly thought of as style. At the first level a writer's dialect and historical period are almost entirely determined for him. Even the degree of technicality and of formality or the choice of speech or writing are largely determined by circumstances and tend to be stable throughout a work. Some might argue that these first- and second-level variations are so much determined by circumstances that they are not strictly style at all, though it would be agreed that they need to be described first if only to separate the freer choices left to a writer.

The third-level 'specific functions' of language are sometimes marked by grammatical forms, sometimes understood from the situation in which the language is used. The general purpose of language is to modify the present experience of its users by relating it to past experience. A speaker's experience is communicated to a hearer (the didactic or declarative function of language) or the speaker seeks to augment his own experience by drawing on that of the hearer (the interrogative function) or the speaker endeavours to direct the behaviour of the hearer in a situation (the imperative function).

These three functions are marked by special indicative, interrogative and imperative forms of the clause, though function and grammatical form do not always exactly coincide. 'I wonder if you could tell me the time' is grammatically a statement but has interrogative function (with a dimension of politeness), and 'I know a little boy who always sets the table for his mother' is a statement best interpreted as a command. 'I wonder if some nice boy would like to set the table' is really a command but pretends to be a question of the kind that pretends to be a statement.

Statements, commands and questions are not confined to any particular occupational variety of language, but they are sometimes institutionalized as important tasks within occupations. A lecturer is a professional maker of statements, an examiner is an asker of questions, a commander commands. Special languages may apply to these tasks. An examiner, however staunch a defender of survivals of the dual number on other occasions, will often, for clarity, in an examination paper label three alternatives (his word) 'Either ... or ... or ...' The examiner has his formulas; *Punch* once made use of one of them to rewrite Wordsworth's well-known apostrophe:

> O cuckoo, shall I call thee bird
> Or but a wandering voice?
> State the alternative preferred;
> Give reasons for your choice.

Lecturing, examining and commanding are some of the aspects of a teacher's work; it is the task of educational theory to assess the relative importance of each. The linguist will note that the wider category 'occupational language of teachers' will include sub-categories according to its special functions, didactic, exploratory or relating to classroom control.

In the same way, sermons, prayers and theological treatises will appear as special forms of religious language. The sermon will include moral statements and will be based on a controlling moral statement or text. Chaucer's *The Pardoner's Tale* with its text 'The love of money is the source of evil' will serve as an example, though in this case there are many extra subtleties arising from the situation in which the whole sermon is delivered. The sermon will also contain a little story, or exemplum, ostensibly factual but in its function a statement implying a command. Prayers are linguistically a special form of polite command, or request, addressed to a Deity, and a theological treatise is more purely factual, yet with an ultimate moral purpose or justification which links it with command. It is for literary theorists to decide how far all literature is tinged with an ultimate moral purpose, whether it is all, as Shaw thought, statement ultimately justified as command; and different ages have given different answers to this question. In our age the word 'moral' is rather out of date but we can reframe the question by asking whether advertising differs from other arts only in its more trivial purpose and its frequent indifference to truth. Is an Oxfam advertisement to be classified with *Oliver Twist*? And as the moral becomes subtler and less obtrusive, does it at any point disappear entirely?

If special functions appear in a technical context, the statement may be elaborated into a report, paper, monograph, lecture or accountant's balance sheet. In logic, it becomes the proposition. The question may be elaborated into a statement of a problem, an examination paper or (with supplied answers) a catechism. A command may be elaborated into a recipe, a prescription or a law. In contexts varying in their formality, a statement may be an oracle or an opinion, a question may be a motion at a meeting, a question in parliament or an 'innocent question', a command may be elaborated into an oration or a pep-talk. According to whether it is written or spoken a statement may appear in a newspaper or radio news, a sporting page or radio commentary, or (in legal contexts) take the form of an oath or an affidavit. A questioning situation may take the form of a written examination or a viva; a command may appear as a will or regulations or as the verbal commands of the parade ground.

If negation is taken to be a special function of language, it marks a special relation between a speaker and the content of his language, since a 'supposed situation' is called to mind and cancelled. All other possibilities are by implication weakly asserted. A negative statement can therefore be used to assert a corresponding positive one. Snorri Sturluson in the prose *Edda* tells us of a giant that he was 'not little', and we understand that he was big. But this is Icelandic understatement because, taken literally, 'not little' includes a neutral size as well as 'big', and, unless opposites are, like *open* and *shut*, separated by no neutral zone, the negative statement is always an understatement or weaker assertion. In a combination of two negatives, as in 'not unlikely', there is a double weakening of a kind congenial to cautious academic writers. In substandard speech, however, double negatives often reinforce a strongly negative colour in an assertion. 'I don't want nothing from nobody' is a threefold declaration of independence, not a logical see-saw. Even speech that is less substandard may contain double negatives with the effect of simple negation. 'I don't know as it won't rain' or 'I wouldn't be surprised if it didn't rain' are ways of predicting rain. In the *Volsunga Saga*, Sinfjotli having found a poisonous snake in the meal he used to bake bread remarked (in literal translation), 'I am not without suspicion that there was not something alive in the meal.'

A special use of a series of negatives in a description is seen in the Old English poem *The Phoenix*, where paradise is described by cataloguing all the varieties of harsh weather which never come there. It is effective, perhaps as snow outside may enhance the warmth of a winter fire. Max Beerbohm uses a catalogue of negative descriptions in another way to describe in what ways Zuleika Dobson 'was not strictly beautiful'. Her eyes 'a trifle large', her mouth 'a mere replica of Cupid's bow' and 'no waist to speak of' are among the defects which make up this wittily seductive portrait.

Negation is freely combined with the indicative, interrogative and imperative functions of language, though these functions do not combine readily with each other. It seems that a clause cannot at the same time be a command and a question in function or in form, though it might combine imperative function with interrogative form ('Would you mind paying attention?') or interrogative function with imperative form ('Tell me what's the matter'). A question may exceptionally contain a statement, or imply one, and then we call it a 'loaded question'. If someone, for example, asks 'Is communism likely to destroy freedom in Australia?', he implies that communism is opposed to freedom and that Australia is free. The question 'Have you been using the good towels to clean your shoes again?' is not easily answered briefly and directly by the permanently innocent. But where such a mixture of functions is exceptional among indicative, interrogative and imperative functions, it is normal for negation. A negative finite clause must also be indicative, interrogative or imperative.

A positive question sometimes functions as a negative statement. 'Did this in Caesar seem ambitious?' is equivalent to 'This in Caesar did not seem ambitious.' Conversely a negative question 'Are there no prisons?' represents a positive statement 'There are prisons.' Such questions are called 'rhetorical questions'.

A 'rhetorical command' is also possible, formally indistinguishable from other commands, but used where obedience is inevitable or, if we include Donne's 'Go, and catch a falling star', impossible. Usually a natural force is addressed so that in literature the figure is a variety of apostrophe and has links with personification. The issuing of the command seems to imply permission or approval, and this may be explicit: 'Blow, northern wind, send thou me my sweeting', but the acceptance is rueful when W. S. Gilbert tells the world to roll on despite his private woes and notes that 'it rolls on'. More complex ironies are found when a winter wind is told to blow because it is less unkind than man's ingratitude or when Lear tells the tempest to rage because it was given no kingdom. Ultimately rhetorical commands are statements disguised as commands, 'the wind blows', 'the storm is raging', but the stylistic overtones so dominate the simple statement that literal meaning is in this case a very small part of a total effect.

The commonest use of the indicative clause is to make a statement, which may be true or untrue. This function of language is uppermost in the mind of a scholar at his desk and so it has had due recognition in accounts of language, even seeming to be its prime purpose. Literary writers have not insisted that statements be true, since they may agree with the bishop who said of *Gulliver's Travels*: 'I personally believe this book to be a pack of lies' and still wish to discuss it. But a pack of lies is still a pack of statements.

Modern philosophers, notably J. L. Austin, have reminded us that is it not accurate to suggest that the indicative sentence always makes a statement. Austin has discussed in detail another function of the indicative, its 'performative' use. When a properly constituted chairman says 'I declare this meeting open' or a properly ordained clergyman says 'I name this child Tristram', we cannot meaningfully question the truth of what is said, though if we are unsure of the speaker's qualifications we could wonder about its validity. A performative utterance has validity if the speaker's social position entitles him to make it; it is therefore often part of an occupational language. No special linguistic form (except perhaps the adverb *hereby*) marks a performative function, though it can be said that they usually contain a first-person non-continuous present indicative verb. Thus 'I promise' may be performative but 'he promises' or 'I promised' can only be statements.

Because performatives are usually part of set ritual, they offer exceptionally little possibility of stylistic variation. H. G. Wells varied a report of a wedding ceremony by writing its words as 'Wis ring ivy wed', but such a deformation would pass unnoticed at an actual wedding and merely indicates how stereotyped the formula has become. Muriel Spark goes further in *The Ballad of Peckham Rye*, allowing the ritual question 'Wilt thou have this woman to thy wedded wife?' to receive the unexpected answer 'No, to be quite frank, I won't', a clever exploitation of the normally total lack of choice in this exchange.

A performative utterance, depending for its validity on the social role of its speaker, has some resemblance on a smaller scale to an occupational variety of language. Similarly informality in language has its less extended parallel in greetings, solicitous inquiries about health or comments about the weather, designed more to put a hearer at ease than to convey information. No special grammatical form marks this 'phatic' use of language either, though some lexical items, greetings especially and words such as *please* and *thankyou*, normally have phatic function. It is perhaps no accident that the phatic function of language has no special form to mark it. Suppose it did have one, say a verbal prefix *fa-*. Then a desire to communicate a genuine concern about a friend's wife's health could be seen to be genuine from its form 'I hope your wife is well', possibly a very impolite remark if it ought not to concern the speaker deeply. On the other hand a polite formula in the hypothetical language would be 'I fa-hope your wife is well,' but this would explicitly mean 'I express a routine concern but I don't really care.' This also is impolite. Therefore phatic language has no formal mark, but it is usually understood clearly enough from context, unless the context itself is ambiguous, as it is when my friendly doctor greets me with 'How are you?'

The usefulness of phatic language is to assert one's belonging to a community. In a foreign country we are less distressed by an inability to satisfy wants than by the sense of strangeness and stupidity that comes from being unable to make any contact with people near us. Even managing to buy a box of matches in the

s.–11

language of another country brings a human contact worth far more than the matches, though only with people in our home region can we achieve through language a sense of total belonging. All language has some phatic purpose in this wide sense, but we use the term especially for language in which the dominant function is to promote social cohesion.

Greetings represent a typical instance of phatic language. These very often take the form of an inquiry about the hearer's health and well-being (e.g., with descending formality, 'How do you do?', 'How are you?', 'How's it going?', 'How's she going?') or announce a speaker's presence (colloquial French *suis-la*, pronounced as though *chui-la*) or his awareness of a hearer (Maori *tena koe* and variants, literally 'there you are'), or use special otherwise meaningless words (*Hello* or informal Italian *ciao*) or preserve a religious flavour (southern German *Grüss Gott*) or simply wish the hearer well (*Good day* and variants). The religious flavour is (historically) in English *good-bye* as in *Adieu* or *Adios*. Alternatively a hope to see the hearer again is expressed in *Au Revoir* and its equivalents in German, Italian, Russian and other languages, or the informal 'See you later' or 'Be seeing you'. A special written form of greeting is the Christmas card.

There is a negative counterpart of the friendly phatic intention of language in jeering and sneering, where the intention is this time less to convey information than to exclude. Among children this intention may be manifested in special intonation. Occasionally among good friends abusive language is used with friendly intention. A rather more complex intention, where a desire both to wound and to caress compete, may lead to teasing.

In literature, phatic uses of language may be relevant, since writers, though seldom beginning a book with *Hello* (as I have done, but only with quotation marks round it to ward off the steely-eyed professor), usually have among their complex purposes a need to belong, if not to the whole community, at least to some congenial part of it, sometimes, to gain plausibility, placed among an enlightened posterity. A writer may be friendly or may even tease, but, outside private letters, he cannot perhaps sneer. If this seems contrary to experience, reflect that when you read a sneering book with enjoyment, you almost certainly take the sneers to be directed at someone else so that you are in friendly phatic collusion with the writer.

It may seem that a study of phatic language would solve many of the problems of psychiatry. If everyone cultivated friendly language and avoided sneers, how happy we should be. Undoubtedly the role of language in promoting our sense of identity and belonging needs study, but no simple panacea is likely. A friendly intention is not enough; an implicit phatic component of language is not always understood. Cultural differences intrude. I once heard two Mexican guides off duty discussing a tourist at the pyramids of Teotihuacan who said to his guide 'I think we've seen this bunch of rocks. Where's there a bar?' It is very possible that his intention was friendly, that he offered the guide a drink instead of work, but he had convinced the guide of his shallowness, for Mexicans, though lighthearted people, take their history seriously. It is a lucky person whose intentions are always understood.

A phatic function may be added to a statement by a tag question with falling intonation. 'The sea is rough today' in a letter might be a pure statement; to a fellow-passenger on a ship 'The sea's rough today, isn't it?' is phatic. In many languages a single formula, like the French *n'est-ce pas*, is available to give a phatic function to statements.

Questions and commands may be phatic in function. 'How are you?' is a phatic question; 'Never mind' or (historically) 'Farewell' are phatic commands. Phatic questions may be ambiguous in that they are sometimes taken to be real questions. Even outside a doctor's surgery 'How are you?' sometimes invites a medical summary. A home dressmaker once showed my mother a dress she had made, holding it up with a triumphant 'What's wrong with that?' Unfortunately my mother, a trained dressmaker, understood it as a genuine question and pointed out a few mistakes. Situations like that are difficult to manage from there on.

If we give the name 'phatic language' to all language which is designed more to accommodate and acknowledge a hearer than to carry a message, we may separate from greetings and other purely sociable and friendly linguistic devices for achieving social camaraderie a more utilitarian strain of phatic language which aids communication by ensuring a listener's attention. 'Mr Chairman, Ladies and Gentlemen' at the beginning of a speech calls the audience to order and indicates that a speech is to begin. In New Zealand I used to begin university lectures with 'Ladies and Gentlemen' and I continue this practice in Australia, where I suspect the students think it rather formal, but all it actually means (if the meaning of language is its use) is 'All right, shut up now – I'm ready to start.'

Oral literature, or the written ballads, romances and other styles developed immediately from it, very often begins with a formula to command the attention of an audience, 'O, listen, listen, ladies gay', or in *Beowulf* the briefer 'Hwæt!' Phatic language of the kind that helps an audience to apprehend a message continues through an oral style, or one based on oral style, in 'fillers' or little tags which do not add materially to a narrative but dilute it to allow a hearer or reader to rest between more meaningful words. A fair lady becomes 'the fairest lady for the nonce that might go on body and bones' in *Sir Orfeo* and the fair maid of Ribblesdale is 'the fairest one that ever was made of blood and bone' (an exercise now in the suppression of irrelevant horticultural associations).

Beginners in Middle English often have difficulty with these 'fillers'. Used to a closer written style and working hard and closely at a text as a beginner must, they feel dissatisfied at finding that a qualifier in a noun group merely tells us that a person is 'alive' or 'in clothing' and that an adjunct merely means 'without doubt'. Yet in their speech the device is familiar. Phrases like 'what you might call' or 'I suppose' or 'you know' abound. Even in formal writing, not every word advances meaning. In my style, a sentence 'The word *hello* is used as a greeting' would not be unusual, but the first two words in it add nothing to the meaning already shown by italics. They are meant to help the reader and the flow of communication. A last revision of a written text may need to add many of these helping redundancies.

A phatic intention, with its concern for the hearer or reader, encourages a diffusion of style, but circumstances apart from the hearer sometimes make a counterdemand for brevity. A telegram may stand as a type of economical language. 'Arriving Saturday – Bill' would never do as a letter but is an acceptable telegram. Technical examples of abbreviation are the formulae of mathematics or chemistry, symbols for degrees, minutes and seconds in geographical tables, for male and female in biology or for logical operators in Russell's or Polish logic. Arabic numerals are a system of technical abbreviations which have become generally known. Telephone directories would hardly seem simpler without them.

A special kind of abbreviation is seen in the use of foreign quotations. Their use is not, as seems to be nowadays supposed, primarily phatic, a nod between gentlemen recognizing an old school tie, even though conventions relating to readers are kept in mind, since one may quote French untranslated but not Russian, and Greek is now less available than Latin. The advantage of writing *De gustibus non est disputandum* (or perhaps just its opening words) or *À chacun son goût* rather than 'Everyone to his taste' is that the support of antiquity or of a community acknowledged to be supremely civilized draws in a great many associations and modifications. It must be conceded that among the variants cited in this case the English version draws on the support and implications of popular wisdom, but an English equivalent is not always to hand. Latin is often succinct – to translate *Ex pede Herculem* as 'From his foot (you may know) Hercules, i.e. from a part you may judge the quality of the whole' brings a stylistic if not a semantic change. More serious is the loss of contextual association. *Delenda est Carthago* is not translated by the English words 'Carthage must be destroyed' for readers who do not know Carthage or Cato. In literary criticism, a writer mentioning the *utile* and the *dulce* does more than refer to usefulness and pleasure; he implies the whole Horatian refinement of classical literary theory.

The foreign quotation is a dying art because, no longer able to assume understanding, authors no longer bother to acquire the skill. It is not easy to recapture the outlook of an age in which Swift, seeing a lady accidentally brush a fiddle (a Cremona) from a table with her cloak (a mantle or Mantua) could aptly quote Vergil's line *Mantua, vae! miserae nimium vicina Cremonae* (Mantua, alas!, how much too near the unfortunate Cremona). By the time all the implications are elucidated for a modern reader, the flash of wit has become attenuated into the duller glow of an editorial exegesis. The educational austerity of a technological age has demanded that writers sacrifice the compression obtained by these economical references to established canons of taste and wisdom, though, strangely, at the same time, poets seem to have acquired an extended mandate to be allusive. T. S. Eliot expects you to know or get to know your Dante, and when Ezra Pound adds a prerequisite grounding in Chinese, nobody dares to protest.

Even within English, writers have an increasingly hard time of it. Knowledge of the Bible is no longer universal and after a fashionably allusive title a writer is safest if he does not depart from the better-known lines of Shakespeare in his allusions. There is the example of James Joyce, but Joyce, like the poets, has a special privilege and special guidebooks for the literary tourist willing to have a go at *Finnegans Wake* on five allusions a day. The Australian writer Joseph Furphy, a bullock driver with a Bible and Shakespeare in his swag, and no way of knowing that these advantages and the leisure to make use of them are not universal among the educated, has paid the penalty of over-estimating his audience. His too subtly interconnected moral satire *Such is Life* is usually read and enjoyed as an incoherent though realistic panorama of bush life.

A modern writer's best hope is that even if an allusion is missed the borrowed expression will at least pass as a neat one of his own. Professor I. A. Gordon begins the preface to his *The Movement of English Prose* with the sentence 'This study, first planned as an opus, has by degrees dwindled into a book', a witty allusion to Millamant's realistic view of marriage (to dwindle into a wife) in Congreve's *The Way of the World*, but even without thinking of Congreve, a reader may catch the neat contrast between the splendour of an ideal and the quieter security of the real.

Within the language of journalism, the need for brevity is most urgent in headlines. Many words otherwise rare or archaic have their special daily life as a result. Actresses *wed*, politicians *woo* voters, experts *probe* while more active citizens make *bids*. Colour is added by *Reds* and resulting *scares*. Events *loom*. The need for economy is reinforced by another function of headlines; they are not only messages but also headings or labels. Verbs are frequently nominalized, their subjects deleted. What in deep grammar might be analysed as (1) Someone tries to get X (2) X = 'Someone investigates Y' (3) Y = 'Communists frighten someone' is compressed into four monosyllables: Red Scare Probe Bid.

It is time to recall yet again the conversation of Mr Appleby and Mr Plumtree in the club-house. When Mr Plumtree said 'No, Roger's the hurdler. John runs', we can be sure that the name *Roger* had stress and moving tone but probably the name *John* did not. This is because Roger had not been mentioned before and John had. Situation, especially the linguistic context, affects language in another way then, not only by promoting brevity, but also by providing some elements of a discussion that are given and some that are new. Very often the subject of a sentence is the given element, announcing a topic rather than offering new information, and the predicate makes a comment, providing new information about the chosen subject. Accordingly a neutral or usual clause intonation is one with a moving tone on the predicate, as in a 'normal' pronunciation of 'John runs'. But this intonation is not universal as 'Roger's the hurdler' (in its context) reminds us; if it is the subject that provides the new element and the predicate recapitulates known information, the subject has a moving (falling) tone and the predicate either a rising inflection or no moving tone. There are some anomalous cases, notably in set expressions like 'The kettle's boiling' or 'The tap's running' or perhaps 'The dogs are barking', where subject and predicate seem to merge into a single unanalysed piece of information with moving (falling) tone on the subject.

Intonation is not the only device for distinguishing given and new. Perhaps inversion steers an emphatic word into final position with moving tone: 'That I don't know' (with added emphasis on the displaced *that* as well), or a passive emphasizes a retained agent: 'We were held up by a puncture', or a formula such as 'It is Roger who is the hurdler' emphasizes a subject. Poetic inversions sometimes control emphasis in this way: 'Us he devours' may be a poetic licence to vary not 'He devours us' but 'It is us that he devours' or, with more equal emphasis, 'As for us, he devours us'. But context may accurately dictate a shifted intonation so that words (say 'Age cannot wither her') normal in word order may be distinctive in intonation. Johnson seldom shifted intonation in this way in his writing, so that his conversation, though sometimes given a little extra balance by Boswell, is very different in flavour from his writing. This is spoken Johnson: 'You *may* abuse a tragedy, though you cannot write one. You may scold a carpenter who has made you a bad table, though you cannot make a table. It is not your trade to make tables.'

In another important way situation, this time the total situation, speaker, hearer, circumstances, linguistic context and cultural assumptions, may be of relevance to the understanding of language, and may modify the literal meaning of words to a point where they carry an opposite meaning from the literal one. We then talk of 'irony', and a speaker's intention is likely to cause most puzzlement and is most likely to be misunderstood when it is ironical. In simple cases, say the greeting 'Lovely weather!' on a nasty day, obvious discrepancy between the literal meaning of words and their situation reveals ironical intent clearly enough, but irony is usually subtler than this, relying on less obvious discrepancies between speech and the speaker's background, immediate situation or general situation, even perhaps the whole human situation as in Swift's *A Modest Proposal*.

Irony is not a property of language alone in isolation. It may even exist without language. During the great plague of London, cats were thought to be carriers of the disease and were killed, allowing rats to multiply. Reporting this, Defoe adds a note of irony to *The Journal of the Plague Year*, but this is not part of the language of that work. We may note that the fact, if true, was not ironical at the time; it is only to us, believing that rats carried plague, that irony is apparent. Irony depends on an audience and specifically on a double audience, one audience more informed than the other. A joke or mood of bitterness is shared with an enlightened audience at the expense of, or at least excluding, another more naïve audience actual or potential. Because the clues in a situation are not always easily understood or are unknown to some hearers, irony is selective of an elite audience.

It is not necessarily unkind. It is sometimes (though its use in this way has many dangers and may lead to a most objectionable archness) found in children's books. A forgiveable smile passes between the author and the adult who reads *Babar and Father Christmas* to a child when King Babar sets off without his wife to find Father Christmas: 'Celeste would have liked to go too, but Babar told her that it would be better if she stayed and ruled the country in his absence, and that mysterious people often did not like to be approached by several people at once.' To the child, two reasons are twice as convincing as one, but to adults the plural of *reason* is, in appropriate circumstances, *excuse*. Such complexities of communication are consistent with extreme simplicity in the linguistic form, so that the dullness for the teacher of 'graded readers' can be avoided, as it is in Else Minarik's *Little Bear* series: ' "Me tired?" said Grandfather Bear. "I am never tired!" He got up and did a little jig. "Never tired!" he said, and sat down.'

A play affords special opportunities for irony. The audience sees and hears all, but characters within the play need not all be present all the time, and may be supposed to lack some of the information available to the audience. They, like the child hearing the Babar story, represent the innocent audience of what is then said; the theatre audience, like the adult, is the wiser audience that sees more layers of meaning. Nowhere are the potentialities of this situation of a variously informed audience better brought out than in the famous 'screen scene' in Sheridan's *The School for Scandal*, where intruders successively hidden behind screens in Joseph's room have varying understanding of the situation while the theatre audience knows all. Everything that is said has complex layers of meaning appropriate to the various audiences on and off the stage. Sheridan richly exploits a power available to all dramatists, providing a memorable example of what is accordingly called 'dramatic irony'.

In a play, or in a novel, an author can give his audience the clues that make irony apparent. It is less easy in other works to make irony explicit, and since irony depends on at least a semblance of disguise, it is best not made explicit. Coleridge praised Defoe for not advertising an ironic intention by means of exclamation marks. Only the simpler forms of irony are advertised as such. Oliver St John Gogarty wrote a patriotic poem to celebrate the Boer War, but initial letters of the lines formed an acrostic sentence, 'The whores will be busy'. This must be regarded as unsubtle irony, though such tricks are amusing enough (and very dangerous, since the irony is provable) if played against more tyrannical regimes. Many students find that irony is too well disguised, however, in Swift's *A Modest Proposal* and would welcome less subtle clues than an occasional word from the vocabulary of animal husbandry to be sure that Swift did not seriously intend his proposal that the twin problems of too little food and too many people in Ireland could be solved by eating babies. I think they would like something like Artemus Ward's cautiously appended note 'N.B. This is wrote sarcasticul'.

Swift ran a risk because the most obvious clue to his ironical intention is the absurdity of his proposal. But students with little knowledge of history may not know whether such a proposal was absurd in Swift's day. Why do we not interpret Bernard Mandeville's *Fable of the Bees* with its thesis that private vices are 'Publick Benefits' as a similarly ironical exercise? Because his intentions were publicized in annotations to the poem which forms its nucleus? Or have we ruled intentions out of court? And why should Mandeville's annotations be less ironical than

Swift's elaborate arguments? If absurdity is always to indicate irony, how are we to interpret a notice on a door in our own age which reserves the doorway for non-whites only? The very force of Swift's satire comes from the number of less extreme analogues to his proposal which were generally accepted by his readers.

Anyone seriously in doubt about Swift's intentions may be referred to a stylistic analysis of *A Modest Proposal* by Edward P. J. Corbett, reprinted in *Contemporary Essays on Style*, edited by Glen A. Love and Michael Payne, where he will find statistical demonstration that the style in this work is not Swift's normal one but that he speaks through an assumed voice or 'persona', and will find that ironical intention is recognized less from the nature of the whole proposal than from the expression of its details, and that besides the well-known application of agricultural terms, there is a use of the language of scientific economists bordering on parody. The fact remains, of course, that an ironical intention is not always evident to all readers, as anyone who has ever been silly enough to write an ironical letter to a newspaper will well know. Defoe, whose *The Shortest Way with the Dissenters* offended those it was meant to help, will serve to prove that irony is always a risk.

A related risk is run today by an American school of 'deadpan' writers who betray no sense of shock as they record the shocking details of our own times, usually in a paratactic syntax which declines to present or arrange the raw details of the narrative. I was shocked at an early short story, 'Savannah River Payday', by Erskine Caldwell, describing two men carrying a dead 'nigger' on the running board of a car, finding gold in his teeth and extracting it with a monkey wrench and stopping for a game of pool on the way. The point was the completely callous and inhuman way of talking about the corpse; my shock came from a realization that a reader quickly becomes inured to the style and merely accepts the valuation of the insensitive men. Only thus, presumably, can crime thrillers be read; one is not invited to think of the corpse as a person once alive nor of the murderer as someone who will soon be dead. It is the reverse of Victorian sentimentality, where feeling was at least totally adequate to the situation. There our fear is that feeling may cease to be genuine; in the modern tough writing our fear is that an ironical intention may be so far forgotten that feeling is not aroused at all. From stories to newspapers, from newspapers to life is an easy enough transition to make possible the acceptance of barbarities which the writer presumably intended to prevent. Nobody can read any more Plato's remark about the unexamined life.

On the other side it must be conceded that barbarities are now widely publicized, are part of our twentieth-century experience and have to be understood. Kurt Vonnegut Jr in *Mother Night* recalls wartime Germany:

> He once saved his own life in the Second World War by playing so dead that a German soldier pulled out three of his teeth without suspecting that Mengel was not a corpse.
> The soldier wanted Mengel's three gold inlays.
> He got them.

Here are the 'deadpan' tricks, repetition, the laconic 'He got them', the simple unembroidered sentences. The facts. Perhaps such writing is necessary to begin to understand, but will greater understanding bring a clearer declaration of irony and a more explicit awareness of permanent humane values to represent the fuller understanding of a more enlightened audience? Science fiction, which at least should bring a more synoptic view, has so far seldom escaped from the 'deadpan' laconic or 'tough' school of writing.

Understatement can be an immense weapon. It is this possibility that gives an attractive plausibility to Sir Joshua Reynolds's belief that Lear's 'And my poor fool is hanged' is to be taken literally, as though the clown was all he could cope with when his dead daughter lay in his arms. But *Lear* is not all understatement. It is unrelieved understatement, particularly of emotional response, that leads to the styles strangely lacking in irony that are produced by an age which values irony. There is no reminder of other values, nothing to measure the terse style against, no 'double audience'. We are immersed in the unexamined life.

One source of the style is a failure of nerve, a retreat from the omniscience of the Victorian narrator. The preposterousness of the claim was amusingly brought to attention before Victoria's reign ended in Frank R. Stockton's little story 'The Lady or the Tiger?', in which a princess knows that in an arena her lover must open a door to release a tiger or a rival lady whom he must marry; she knows which door he should open and finds a way of telling him. Does she tell him the truth? Stockton confesses that his knowledge of feminine psychology does not equip him to decide, and the outcome of the story has never been told.

But again before the end of Victoria's reign another attack on a Victorian tradition, the lachrymose tradition this time, came in the preface to the third edition of Arthur Morrison's *A Child of the Jago*. Morrison declined to make 'public parade of his sympathy' for the people he described, merely to let readers 'keep their own sympathy for themselves and win comfort from the belief that they are eased of their just responsibility by vicarious snivelling'. None would now disagree with this, but Morrison reminds his readers of their 'just responsibility' by a continued irony, already very evident in the second chapter, and by a use of a standard literary style to provide a matrix for such ironical variations as 'Now he was of an age when most boys were thieving for themselves, and he owed money like a man' or 'the top-floor back, wherein he dwelt with his son Bob, Bob's wife and two sisters, and five children: an apartment in no way so clean as the united efforts of ten people might be expected to have made it'. It was not yet evident that the literary dialect used to translate the *Communist Manifesto* was an upper-class style.

What I have called 'deadpan irony' has permanent if limited usefulness. It is a necessary part of wartime slang. If a soldier calls a murderous battle 'a bit of a dust-up', it is because there is no danger among soldiers that the irony in the understatement will be misunderstood. Warfare and other harsh experiences need and produce popular laconic styles. Such styles are a feature of hard frontier life and appear in America and Australia as they appeared and became great literature in the early European frontier region, Iceland. Understatement is frequent in Anglo-

Saxon poetry, too, again a reflection of the 'heroic' way of life, perhaps.

These and other forms of irony are congenial to twentieth-century readers. John Fowles giving the Victorian hero of *The French Lieutenant's Woman* a modern consciousness in a past age gives him especially the gift (if it is a gift) of irony. It is a defence perhaps, our cultivation of irony, one we cannot imagine being without. We forestall attack by attacking ourselves as we go. Not for us pure solemnity separated from lighter moments of humour, a dichotomy we associate with the Victorians. Our serious moments admit wry fun as our humour is often very serious. We are rather surprised when Dryden, anticipating a Victorian view though following a classical one, blamed himself for an 'unnatural mingle' of the serious and comic in *The Spanish Friar*, 'for mirth and gravity destroy each other, and are no more to be allowed for decent than a gay widow laughing in a mourning habit'. Mercutio calling himself a 'grave man' would not have agreed, and today we would think a gay widow laughing in a mourning habit a very promising beginning for a story.

Some ironies become stereotyped, so that 'You're a fine one' is hardly ambiguous even out of context. Yet even these stereotypes have a residual ambiguity which can be activated. Readers of *Catch-22* may remember how General Dreedle's remark 'That's a really fine thing when a man of God begins hanging around a place like this with a bunch of dirty drunks and gamblers' was twice, on consecutive pages, misunderstood, in opposite ways, by the hapless Colonel Cathcart.

Irony may become multiplied as we waver between opposite interpretations of a statement, seeing deeper and deeper layers of meaning. What is the meaning in Shelley's *Ozymandias* of the famous 'Look on my works, ye mighty, and despair'? The inscription is the sole relic of the 'works' so that irony must be assumed. But is this enough? After all, we *do* know of Ozymandias and his works, though they are not extant: is this also the message? Must we first see an obvious irony and then by a second irony see that the inscription is, in a way, still valid? Perhaps, however, it is the inscriber of the message, the writer, who tells Ozymandias and his kind to despair? The uncertainties in the meaning support each other to provide a rich iridescent meaning not easily described exhaustively.

Irony in literature is of many kinds. Sometimes the naïve party is the speaker himself; Huckleberry Finn is a rather humourless fellow but Mark Twain allows him to tell a supremely amusing story. Not that we need an author in the background to share the joke, since few who enjoy Daisy Ashford's *The Young Visiters* suppose that the value of a book is delimited by its author's intention. Sometimes in life or literature irony which at first escapes both speaker and hearer emerges when it is realized that a topic of conversation thought too obvious to be announced was differently conceived by the participants. Examples are usually too long to quote, but readers will find one in the forty-fourth chapter of George Meredith's *The Egoist* in which Mr Dale and Dr Middleton are differently informed about an approaching marriage.

It will be seen that irony in my view is quite distinct from sarcasm. Sarcasm or abuse is a kind of negative-phatic use of language marked by an attitude to the hearer. It sets out to wound. Irony, too, will often wound, but this is not essential. Double meanings can be used to disguise adverse criticism under the form of praise and so wound more subtly and ignominiously, but with the same device of a double meaning a civilized writer may mock himself instead of or along with his reader. Irony might even be used to praise, and praise, like blame, may be enhanced by a witty deviousness. Beerbohm's concession of all the faults of Zuleika Dobson is praise under the disguise of adverse criticism and since there is a literal and a subtler interpretation the technique is akin to irony. Similarly, if more simply, Tony Weller in *Master Humphrey's Clock* describes a naughty boy who lives in his street, and his grandson knows well that this criminal catalogue expresses lively affection for the sinner, his grandson.

Before leaving the relations of language and situation, we must note that a part of the speech situation is language itself, and language may be used to discuss this part of the situation. That is, language may be used to discuss language itself. 'I don't like the way you said that' or 'Speak up; I can't hear you' draw attention to speech itself, and so indirectly might a remark such as 'Are you Australian?' Besides the audible or visible speech or writing of a particular act of communication, moreover, the situation includes a knowledge of a linguistic code shared by speaker and hearer, and language may be used to refer to this code, or, in technical terms, have a special 'metalinguistic' function. Organized into a technical subject of study such observations become the subject linguistics, but the metalinguistic function is an occasional function of ordinary language too. It is usually marked in written language by the presence of quotation marks or italics, but it is not easily indicated in spoken language. Meaning indicates metalinguistic reference in the spoken sentences 'How do you spell *diphthong*?' or 'How do you pronounce *p-h-t-h-i-s-i-s*?' but not in ' "This" is a four-lettered word'.

In the special written style of crossword-puzzle clues there may be a deliberate confusion of metalinguistic and normal reference as quotation marks or italics are withheld in strange collocations of words. 'Vehicle reverses before the Spanish' will immediately suggest to devotees the word *navel*, since a vehicle may be a van and *van* reversed is *nav-* and *the* in Spanish may be *el*. Shakespeare's often quoted 'But me no buts' should perhaps be discussed as a metalinguistic use of the word *but* rather than the use of a conjunction as verb and noun, though the reference is to a specific speech act as well as to the general code of English.

A metalinguistic reference in language need not be pure but can combine with an ordinary referential use. A special case of this is Pope's 'The reader's threatened (not in vain) with sleep', referring at once to a rhyming word and its meaning. More generally it is what happens when a pun is made. Besides the contextual meaning of a word, we are made aware of the word itself, and through the form of a word, of other possible and, if the pun is a good one, appropriate meanings. If we analyse our understanding of a reference in *Piers Plowman* to religious men who work for 'love of the cross', we find that we first interpret the word *cross* literally in context in its religious sense, then notice that the particular word *cross* is used, recall that it has another meaning as the name of a coin with a cross on the back of it and so more generally 'money', and that this second meaning is wryly appropriate in context and indeed obliterates the more obvious meaning in this case, though the obvious meaning is still important as a reminder of the true obligation of the clergy. Needless to say the pun, to be effective, must work more rapidly than this slow-motion analysis suggests.

In a subtle way there is a metalinguistic element in the concept of style itself, since particular words and their overtones are important rather than the reference of the words. Stylistics, to put it another way, moves on to a study of language in which words have complex reference, back to themselves as well as outward to situations. Metalinguistic uses of language are seldom translatable, unless the words used are international words with similar associations in another language, because to translate is by definition to change the vehicle of expression, and this vehicle of expression is itself the reference of a metalinguistic use of language. The style of an utterance may therefore be that part of it which is untranslatable. To render *Traduttore traditore* as 'Translators are betrayers' is to lose the point of the Italian statement, that there is very little difference between a translator and a betrayer, since in Italian this is underlined by the fortuitous similarity of the words. Henry James's title *The Portrait of a Lady* uses the words *portrait* and *lady* in a normal way but also hints at a commonly used title for a picture in an art gallery. The French translation *Portrait d'une femme* preserves the hint of an art gallery but does not exactly translate the implications of *lady*. It has kept the metalinguistic point, the use of a formula, by sacrificing exact reference.

In this and the two preceding chapters, I have gathered together the implications of various modern approaches to stylistics, mainly British ones, rather than accurately reporting any one of them. To do this I have adapted the grammatical concept of 'rank' to a study of situation, suggesting a model for the variation of language in its situation based on setting up three ranks, first varieties relating to time and place, secondly subvarieties relating to technicality, formality and the use of speech and writing, and a final analysis of the specific functions, declarative, interrogative, imperative, negative, performative, phatic, economical, emphatic, ironical, laconic or metalinguistic, which are described in this chapter. We must now note that occasionally there is a shift in function from one rank to another. A regional dialect may be used to assert solidarity with a person addressed, and so have phatic function; the language of an earlier time might be adopted in religious language and so mark a technicality with a ceremonial or highly formal dimension. Schoolboys make devastating use of polite language to exercise their genius for impudence while, more subtly, Lytton Strachey's *Eminent Victorians* makes use of impeccably respectful rhythms to develop the irony adumbrated in his title. We make our metalinguistic grids as tidy as we can, but they must not distract us from the salient truth in stylistic study, that language is infinitely rich and variable.

8. The Use of Stylistics

'By itself language is like water, tasteless and cold', wrote Walter Hilton, and a linguist is no less a scientist if he pauses to view the implications of his subject and his own social role. To fail in this is to justify the implications in the title of an inaugural address given by S. T. Alisjahbana in the University of Malaya in 1965: 'The Failure of Modern Linguistics in the Face of Linguistic Problems of the Twentieth Century'. Professor Alisjahbana thought especially of the problems of an emergent nation, the standardization of language, the formation of a written and literary language, the relations between linguistics and education, all problems more assiduously studied in the eighteenth century when they were urgent problems in Europe than by modern linguists. Linguistics in our time has been an exciting study in its theoretical advances; we have yet to work out fully the practical applications of its new insights.

Language is not a game but an adaptable means towards ends. Its rules may be changed and extended. Once in the accessible history of human language a revolutionary change added a whole new dimension to language with the invention of writing, but even in the most advanced communities writing is not yet fully the property of all users of language. Writing brings together people who would otherwise have no contact, making a reality of large cohesive political units and giving them a historical dimension longer and more exact than an oral tradition can maintain. It aids the process, already natural to language where there is contact among its speakers, of standardization, especially after the introduction of printing with its economic demand for large numbers of identical copies. Standardization promotes useful distinctions by retaining what is useful in contributing dialects and eliminating arbitrary distinctions, which impede communication both by revealing less than a speaker intends, since some of his forms are strange to the hearer, and more than he intends because he reveals a regional and social background which is usually irrelevant and often a basis of prejudice. Writing brings language nearer to an ideal condition where differences are internalized and all the potential range of the language is available to all of its speakers. Through writing, language approaches the condition of an ideally developed and ideally economical idiolect.

This thought brings into prominence a concept implied in the study of stylistics with its emphasis on the rich potentialities of language. This is the concept of 'development of idiolect', of central concern in educational theory. The concept resembles the ranges of variation we have already set up for language in that there is an infinite gradation from a smattering to an ideal mastery, divisible into categories, including children's language apart from the technicalities of children's activities, and in that at least some of the grades may be chosen – in a stylistic use of baby-talk for example. It even reintroduces in a new way a concept of class variation, since it is evident that power over the linguistic forms that bind society together is social power. A language with a written dimension is arguably richer than a necessarily more confined unwritten one, but it is less universally mastered by its users. Some lose an older oral culture without gaining a written one, and so have an assured place in society at the bottom. As a result, within certain geographical areas, especially within cities, though one might suspect that such a form of English was also transported from English cities to a new life in Australia, a restricted form of language is general enough to be virtually a dialect, and its laconic inarticulateness is even nostalgically looked back to by those who escape from it, as in the cult of the bush that grew up when Australians began to be more literate.

The development of the idiolect remains, however, rather a measure of the availability of the whole language to a speaker than a dimension of the whole language. To be illiterate in a literate community is not equivalent to illiteracy in an illiterate community. The culture of communities without writing is almost entirely lost to us, and though those most active in speaking up for people who are deprived of part of the available range of variety in English rightly stress that their restricted codes have a value and cohesion of their own and cannot be helpfully disturbed without tact, the choice today is finally between literacy and impoverishment. Unless a child develops with rich experience of the several varieties of adult language, he will remain permanently restricted in his linguistic experience and therefore in his participation in the wider community and its sources of power. In that case the extended range of variety in a modern civilized language will not appear to him as opportunity but as part of the impersonal complication of an age that has swallowed the village in the suburb, a nightmare department store where floorwalkers pounce snapping 'Don't split the infinitives' and the management lurks unseen.

As educationists become aware of the importance of language in relations between teachers and pupils and in the motivation and mastery of learning, they see at the same time that a return to thorough methods of teaching reading and writing is not enough. Writing is only one dimension of language and those who most lack it usually have further difficulty with the persuasive, phatic and polite dimensions of educated language. An important task in educational research is therefore a sociological study of all the forms of language used by educated people and the educationally deprived. Fruitful cooperation between linguists and educationists seems likely in this now developing study.

The teacher of English must train his students to be correct since accurate communication depends on agreed standards taught to writers and readers. The grammarian's preoccupation with the limiting rules of language has therefore commended him to the teacher. When English was learned indirectly and unselfconsciously through translation from Latin, and style was acquired by writing Latin proses in which clarity and economy were necessary virtues, the necessity of mastering a foreign tongue put an even greater premium on conformity. But some teachers have set up a rival aim in courses of 'creative writing', where the inhibiting preoccupation with correctness, which at its worst became a collection of rules of usage without theory or method, was supplanted by an ideal of self-expression. The stylistician may bring some comfort to this school, since his preoccupation is with the richness of language rather than a single ideal of correctness.

But though the use of language for conveying information and the expressive or phatic uses of language can be distinguished, they are not necessarily opposed. All writing must be aware of readers and must therefore be disciplined. Easy writing for the reader is difficult writing for the writer. It has the added art of concealing art. All writing organizes experience; we may dwell on the socially important need for organizing social experience, but the writer mastering the means of organizing social experience also organizes his own experience. In this sense the most disciplined writing is the most creative because what the writer creates is himself. Soviet psychologists, especially L. S. Vygotsky and A. R. Luria, have been especially illuminating in discussing this dual private and social function of language.

The stylistician has to point out that mastery of English includes mastery of the formal, technical and informative styles as well as the conversational and the confessional. In Brecht's words, the ideal is 'to write for the people in the language of kings', using all the resources built up in styles once confined to the upper classes and developed through centuries of civilization. Some will call this *élitist* – an argument I pass on to small boys looking for a brand-new reason for not having a bath. As an undeservedly forgotten writer George Willis put it in *The Philosophy of Speech* in 1919, 'An educated person . . . is simply one who understands his own language', and full understanding may include understanding older forms of the language used by Shakespeare or Chaucer and the Latin and French languages which have contributed the skeleton of what is distinctive in the learned and formal varieties of English. If this sounds like asking for baths with running water, it must be pointed out that where a non-bather offends a few non-smokers near him, a person deprived of his linguistic rights is at odds with all society.

Not all the details of the civilized varieties of English arise naturally from everyday speech, and so some concern with 'correctness', some theory of linguistic pathology, seems inevitable in English teaching, even for native speakers. The teacher is wise to emphasize the constructive rather than the destructive side of this need. Rules are most suspect when they set up a universal rule of usage and complain that is is 'frequently broken'. 'Hardly any speaker now uses the correct form "It is I".' Such statements, intended as cosmic complaints, may equally well be interpreted as opposing rules of usage. Statements with a statistical flavour are more persuasive, especially if research backs the generalizations. 'The expression "I've got a book" for "I have a book" is seldom used in formal writing' is not merely destructive. Best of all is the instruction designed to eliminate weaknesses by revealing the resources of language. The old device of teaching 'Latin roots' to children with no Latin had the merit of being constructive. It promoted an interest in words (rather than set phrases) and in the interconnections among scientific words, while unobtrusively helping with spelling. It ought to be revived and extended as a teaching method.

Weaknesses in writing are often easier to diagnose than to cure. A student who adds *definitely* to any statement he wishes to emphasize can be told to read more, to extend his vocabulary, to become sensitive to the rhythms which control emphasis in sentences; but no simple panacea is available. A student writes in a discussion of Jane Austen's *Sense and Sensibility*:

> Marianne's strength of emotion is further shown by her non-attempt to eat anything at breakfast, a point which Mrs Jennings fails to note due to Elinors (sic) steadying hand being able to get Mrs Jennings to devote her attention to Elinor during it.

The writer is a product of an educational system in which a strong antagonism to the classics coincided with an extreme antagonism to any formal teaching of grammar, so that the student was virtually insulated against the tradition of written English and invented a written language of his own based not on sentences but clauses. Most students in the same educational tradition produced much the same style. It shows skill and intelligence but lone-handed these students in a distant land did not happen on an instrument as delicate or adaptable as the style produced by generations of England's best writers.

The chief weakness is in connectives. Apart from *which*, an element in the colourless complex connective *a point which*, only prepositions and participles are used, so that a clotted collection of frozen nominal groups takes the place of finite verbs. The use of simple conjunctions (*because* rather than *due to . . . -ing*, 'when she does not attempt' rather than 'by her non-attempt') is a first step to lucidity. There are further awkwardnesses in pronoun reference and the precariously metaphorical 'steadying hand'. The sentence needs recasting. Since Marianne's emotion is already (as we see from the word *further*) the topic of discourse, it need not be mentioned again. The main new statement seems to be that Marianne does not eat breakfast and so we may begin (keeping the student's present tense) 'Marianne eats nothing at breakfast . . .' We now find that it is not easy to 'correct' a sentence like this, because we must make it more precise, and we have insufficient guidance. 'A point which' requires a conjunction to replace it, either *but* or *though* according to what was meant. Perhaps '. . . but Mrs Jennings does not notice because Elinor diverts her attention' omits nothing of value in the rest of the student's sentence. What seemed complicated was really a simple statement, capable, if necessary, of further modification.

In this discussion we have introduced a new dimension, 'good–bad', into the discussion of style. We are beginning to evaluate styles. This can never be scientific apart from the simplest rules of correctness, those which show whether an utterance conforms to a linguistic code or not, because values cannot be derived from facts without a jump at some point from statements of the form 'X is true' to a statement of the form 'I like X', where verification is of a different and non-scientific kind. With this proviso, we may legitimately argue 'I like old houses', 'This house is old', 'Therefore I like this house'. We may replace 'I like old houses' with 'Old houses are good' if we wish. Or we may reserve *good* for 'most people like' or 'I think most people like' or even 'most people ought to like', if we give a definition of *ought* (which will probably involve another statement of the type 'I like X' somewhere).

We evaluate styles according to criteria which give us a general basis for particular statements. In the judgement of a house in the preceding paragraph the criterion is age. A critic of writing may similarly equate good style with long-established styles, making age his criterion. If he has no other criterion, he will find the best English in the laws of Ine and the worst in the book in which he publishes his researches. Another critic may take complexity as his criterion. An argument 'Complex styles are good', 'This style is complex', 'Therefore this style is good' is quite valid and the conclusion true if the other two propositions are accepted as true.

Evaluation presupposes description. A style is described, a criterion of excellence announced, the presence of that criterion found in the style and the evaluation made. Needless to say, not all who use the word *good* in discussions of style are so explicit, but, now that we can no longer say *De gustibus* . . ., literary argument about values can be clarified only when the criteria underlying judgement are revealed. In 'correcting' the passage about *Sense and Sensibility*, my criteria, apart from requiring an apostrophe in *Elinor's* in accordance with the given code of written English, were, I suppose, clarity, economy, precision, persuasiveness (or interest) and the provision of a loose enough basic construction to allow qualifications and modifications if necessary, and I suppose all these criteria would enter into any judgement of informative prose. But there could be argument about this set of criteria and about how they are recognized, or linked with description, before assessment of individual passages begins. Is it, for example, a general truth that a relatively high proportion of finite verbs makes for interest?

To analyse fully my assumptions in judging one sentence, to separate factual from evaluative steps in my thought, and to prove the one and justify the other would require more time and hard thinking than a busy essay-marker is able to bring to his task. In practice examiners of English expression do not attempt to work exclusively by formulas and rules. Examiners are themselves evaluated by controlling examiners and their assessments subject to statistical controls. Perhaps, since so much depends on the evaluation of writing in public examinations, an attempt to write a grammar of evaluative judgements about language would nevertheless have considerable theoretical and possible practical interest.

It would need to be complex. A single sentence cannot finally be judged in isolation. It is part of a paragraph and the paragraph is part of an essay. In good writing there are echoes and reverberations back and forth. It is true that well-established techniques of 'practical criticism' appear to assume that writing can be evaluated by close attention to excerpts (*Ex pede Herculem*) and it is also true that very experienced examiners can usually check the assessment of a whole script pretty accurately by reading a sentence or two, but the methods of evaluating by excerpt are based on assumptions which our ideal grammar of evaluative judgements would need to assess carefully.

If we seek general truths, we are likely to make rules of style, and these may be more inhibiting to writers than rules of usage. Very often we find that the most successful writers break rules at the right time. We might agree on a simple stylistic rule that writers for children should use simple words, and yet admire Beatrix Potter's memorable use of the word *soporific* in *Peter Rabbit*. We understand Dryden's master rule 'Better to break a rule than lose a beauty'.

Rules of style are out of fashion but evaluation remains a prime objective of literary stylistics. We avoid making general rules because we allow that writers may have very various purposes and we are now prepared to assess the style of a particular work in relation to the purpose of that work. We may work with a knowledge of linguistics as precise as the mathematical basis of engineering or accountancy, but stylistic evaluation resembles the engineer's or businessman's less exact art of 'decision making'. I understand from writers on management theory that decision making in management is not mathematical or scientific in its definitions but assumes that one course of action is better than another and recognizes that this is an ethical decision. But it is not exclusively a matter of ethics or there would be no science of decision making. A rational theory is based on a distinction of means and ends; a decision is rational if it selects a means that leads to a given end. So it is with evaluative literary stylistics. It includes an aesthetic or non-scientific element, assuming one style better than another, but is rational in that it discusses whether a chosen style achieves or supports a given end, the purpose of the literary work. One writer, Bertrand Russell, uses clear connectives to marshall the details of an argument; another, George Meredith, omits connectives to make the reader work and make his own judgements about characters, so that he gains a stronger feeling of knowing them than he would have gained from a more explicitly connected description by the writer. (This detail of Meredith's method was observed by Vernon Lee.)

Any style might be justified if a purpose is found for it. A schoolboy begins an essay in a ghastly officialese, but it emerges that he is writing an autobiography of a railway-station poster, wittily exaggerating railway-notice style in line with his title, the set topic 'Nobody Understands Me'. The substandard 'I seen the little light' is a wonderfully effective last sentence in Katherine Mansfield's story 'The Doll's House'. We do not condemn Anthony Powell when his sentences are long or Hemingway when his are short, though we may be variously attracted by the purposes of these authors which control the length of their sentences.

We learn to take into account the controlling purposes of an age or country when assessing literary works, an exercise in sympathy which is among the chief values of literature. This is not to dispute Vernon Lee's contention that what literature organizes is the experience of readers; we find if we can appreciate past literature at all that some basic experiences are universal but that they take different forms and enter into different patterns at different times. Literary ideals change; today we think originality a virtue and to write *cliché* in the margin of an essay is to mark a fault, even if to the young writer the condemned turn of phrase has a freshness it lacks for the elderly examiner, but originality was not always so prized. Medieval authors usually claimed to follow a book even when we suspect that their work is original. The eighteenth century prized old figures with new twists, an outlook partially revived by the allusions of some modern poetry, though these usually have an ironical intention which, outside the special style of mock epic, would have been inappropriate in the eighteenth century. Each individual talent enters the tradition at a particular point in its growth, to discover and be judged by the next historically valid purpose.

Literary criticism is more than the study of style, and much of it extends beyond our present topic. The literary writer makes patterns with language but he also fabricates situations and makes patterns of them. The 'happy ending' or the tragic climax do not ultimately seek justification in truth to life; they complete a pattern in events. We wonder why Dickens clung so tenaciously to a belief that a man might die, as Krook did, from spontaneous combustion. He appealed to medicine but a better appeal is to critical theory. The event fitted his pattern of corruption perfectly.

The literary 'situation' is not stable but composed of disparate elements or factions producing movement and development ('plot'). The fortunes of the differently motivated elements rise and fall relative to each other, so that the movement of a story traces a pattern. E. M. Forster, in *Aspects of the Novel*, has noted a simple and regular 'hour-glass' shape in the plot of *Thais* by Anatole France, in which an ascetic, Paphnuce, attempts to save the courtesan Thais. He succeeds and she enters a convent but he, having met her, is damned. The characters converge and cross over. This is, as Forster emphasizes, a particularly patterned book, but a similar X-shaped development may be found in other stories. Forster finds it in Henry James's *The Ambassadors*. It is a very basic pattern in dramatic conflict; in comedy our sympathies follow the upstroke, or fortunes of the successful party; in tragedy, the downstroke. Sometimes a double X, a disturbance of a natural order followed by its reinstatement, is the pattern; *Hrafnkels Saga* is an unusually symmetrical example. Literary patterns of plot, like grammatical patterns, control emphasis and deploy a reader's attention. Ultimately their message is ethical; in a paradigmatic instance an action is seen to have an apparently inevitable outcome.

The writer, controlling events and judging the morality of his characters, not unnaturally sometimes feels he is in a position usually occupied by God. This is explicit in John Fowles's *The French Lieutenant's Woman*, where there is also an abnegation of the Divine function, as Fowles provides alternative endings and suggests that his characters had a choice and he does not know which choice they would make. In Chaucer's *Troilus and Criseyde* the characters are less free, and so was Chaucer. He was in the position of Boethius' God, uncertain whether it was possible to be both omniscient and omnipotent. He was omniscient because Boccaccio's story was his model and the outcome was before him. But he seemed unwilling to accept the judgement which the events he narrated put on Criseyde. He seemed to wish he could justify her. There arises a tension between the author's values and those of his story. Even writers without a 'book' before them feel this kind of tension and perhaps its presence is one of the marks of serious literature. Not promotion of a single preconceived value but a dramatic conflict of values marks such works. It is moral in purpose but an evaluation of morals rather than a tract.

If this takes us some way from stylistics, it shows us why literary critics do not always separate stylistic study from a wider theory of literature. The fabrication of situations and the resulting moral evaluation are the writer's purpose and this purpose cannot be entirely separated from style which is its means and its finer texture. The linguistic and literary patterns fuse as colour and composition in a painting fuse. An outline may be isolated in a black and white print or in a translation but the integrity of a work is not judged from a translation or a monochrome print.

Literature is not the only application of stylistics. The style of a legal document or a scientific paper, a publicity leaflet or the instructions for operating a washing machine, can be described and evaluated. In these cases as in literature (though perhaps more obviously) description must precede evaluation. In each case, as in literature (though again more obviously), evaluation will be based on some criteria which are not directly stylistic but relate to the purpose of the document.

There is need, then, for a general stylistics to inform stylistic judgements in all these and in other applications. It will not be an immediately practical subject, just as mathematics does not in itself tell us whether a bridge will stand or fall, but it will guide the several practical applications. Clearly this general study must be a department of linguistics.

The linguist may leave to the philosopher of language the ultimate definition of style, but he will assume that something he can call style exists. This can be disputed, and has been disputed recently by Bennison Gray in his book *Style: The Problem and its Solution* (The Hague, 1969). Gray suggests that a linguistic element 'style' has proved as difficult to locate as the physicist's 'ether', and he proposes a similar solution to the problem – to abandon the concept altogether. If style is conceived as an element 'in' a text, a last residue when phonology, grammar and lexicon have been abstracted, we must agree with Gray that such an absolute stylistic element is not to be found. But Gray is perhaps like a too eager physicist who wants to discard the concept of motion. An absolute standard for the measurement of motion is not available but relative motion is still a useful concept. So absolute 'style' in an isolated text may not be found by analysis, but texts differ in relation to each other and in relation to what they might have been, and this is what we mean by style and this is why most writers have assumed that style has to do with choice. We may compare texts, observing choices made, and on the basis of such comparisons and our knowledge of the language go on to compare actual with possible texts or compare a text with what it might have been, inferring a choice.

Choices are not entirely free and the stylistician can be reasonably scientific as he observes the conditions that determine a speaker's or writer's choices and erects a theory of situational variation. Here sociological linguistics is especially helpful, and a theory of varieties is already a skeleton theory of style. But as situation determines style sufficiently rigorously to allow us to talk of a science of stylistics, as it does perhaps in a report of a game of chess, a knitting pattern, an accountant's balance sheet and, to a lesser extent, a legal document or a scientific paper, the resulting style seems to be too uninteresting to merit the attention of anyone but a scientific linguist or the practitioners of the styles described. Our practical interest in style grows as the style is less easily explained, already in legal documents which might show skill in drafting or scientific papers which can certainly be well or badly presented, and increasingly in school exercises which are assessed for style as well as content, and supremely in literature. So important is the literary application of stylistics that many would reserve the name for this study and confine it further to those choices which appear to be made freely. For these writers, stylistics, like philosophy, could never be a science and, like philosophy, would celebrate its explanatory successes by abandoning the territory it has won to more exact sciences.

For the linguist, stylistics will include the conquered territory, the exactly describable styles of chess or accountancy, as well as the more challenging styles of literature. The linguist will try to discover hidden patterns in apparently free choices, building, like other scientists, a scheme of order where the layman sees only chance. He will devise means of describing the subtleties of tone, stress and rhythm in speech, construct ways of revealing ambiguities in syntax and show hidden patterns of association in vocabulary.

For this last task especially statistics will help him. I think that I use *someone* and *somebody* interchangeably, but will the statistician agree with me? If he can show me subtle correlations between these words and their contexts, he reveals to me laws I did not know about, just as phoneticians once convinced me after much effort that when speaking unselfconsciously I am very likely to call a cardboard box a 'carbboarb box'. Statistics offers a possibility of adding to the situational determination of the forms of language another kind of determination, that of the linguistic context considered purely as a form. Though not

explanatory in the way that the situation is, since they do not
explain the choice of one rather than another total style, statistical
methods may explain details of a style in relation to the inner
coherence of a whole text. This may be very important in literature, where texts are usually treated as whole texts independent of
the circumstances of their production.

Statistics entered the study of literary style as simple counting.
In the nineteenth century, studies of mean word length and
sentence length attempted to construct objective methods of
identifying works of disputed authorship, and statistical 'profiles'
have remained an important technique in attempts to identify
individual styles. An interesting practical application of such
counts, based on a skilled linguistic analysis of the relevant texts,
is seen in Professor Jan Svartvik's evidence at the reopened
'Evans case', where statistics were used to distinguish genuine
statements by Evans from statements constructed by the police.
Statistical methods have not, however, always been so successful
in identifying authors where the stylistic variation in texts is less
marked and the possible authors are more numerous.

In England, Vernon Lee was a pioneer in the statistical examination of literary texts. She linked statistics with grammar, making counts of the use of parts of speech, and went on to analyse
the effect on the reader resulting from different grammatical
choices in connectives, voice, tense or pronouns. Her writings
are still of considerable interest, though for her methods rather
than her judgements. G. U. Yule and a number of American
stylisticians have written statistical accounts of style in English,
but the most notable development of statistical stylistics has been
outside the English tradition, in the study of Slavonic literature.

The statistical approach to style makes demands on the critic
which are seldom met. Ideally the critic using these methods
should have the sensitivity to literature that any critic must have,
combined with a thorough knowledge of linguistics and an equally
sound knowledge of mathematics. In a single exercise he might
need to begin with the reliable impression of literary quality that
tells a critic what to look for, along with the literary man's
awareness of the ways in which a whole work relates to its details,

then go on to decide whether a transformational or another linguistic model best suits his descriptive purposes and carry out a grammatical description which is as complete and sensitive as modern methods allow in order to identify the elements to be counted, and then he must decide on sampling techniques and perhaps decide whether a Poisson or a negative binomial model or the use of Bayes's theorem best suits his statistical purpose. In practice a scholar is unlikely to advance more than one section of his study, though he needs to understand the other two. This means that his studies will not always advance literary criticism, though even when they do not, they may give a verifiable statement of what was formerly an impression only. Any critic can see that Gibbon's style is different from Hemingway's; the statistician can show that the differences are objective and measurable and can show exactly where they lie and how great they are.

The statistician cannot escape another kind of difficulty when he engages in literary criticism. His statistical discussion (and indeed his linguistic discussion) must be technical, and since this contrasts with the literary text which is also strongly in the reader's mind, its technical language will be unusually obtrusive, especially as his chosen audience is one unusually sensitive to style. An important and useful recent essay contains this sequence of quotation and comment:

> In mist or cloud, on mast or shroud,
> It perched for vespers nine.
> Whiles all the night, through fog-smoke white,
> Glimmered the white moon-shine.

If we expanded vertical statistics to further components of the language of the poetic text, we could find out, for instance, that in Coleridge's poem there is not only a parallelism in the distribution of stresses and long vowels (which is natural in an English text), but also one in stresses and positional lengths, that is, from accumulations of consonants, etc. (which is not usual in other English poems).

The usefulness of the study is apparent even in this brief excerpt chosen for another purpose, but the stylistic transition will seem to literary men who are not attuned to scientific writing harsh, and even, in texts where mathematical terms and formulae appear more densely, ludicrous. This is not the fault of the writer (though the work quoted is a translation and not the best model of scientific prose), but it illustrates a difficulty in introducing literary specialists to this kind of scientifically presented criticism – even though it is only a magnification of the stylistic contrast implied by any analytical discussion of literature.

It is not necessary that all students of style master all the techniques that are available for its study, but it is necessary that all are respectfully able to learn from everything that is going on. The grammarian has provided new insights by refining our concept of the linguistic elements to be measured. The transformational grammarian aids the statistician by providing a tidy model to relate a manageable number of basic syntactic patterns to a large number of derived patterns, and both aid the literary man in bringing exact methods to a study which has often lacked exactness. The grammarian not only describes more exactly what is evident in any case but reveals ambiguities not immediately obvious or allows them to be clearly stated to those who have not noticed them. At the same time he indicates the whole range of choice available at a particular point in a text. We all know that passive constructions are alternative to active ones; we sometimes forget that 'Caesar conquered Gaul' varies not only with 'Gaul was conquered by Caesar' but also with 'Caesar's conquest of Gaul' and 'The conquest of Gaul by Caesar' as well as 'The conquest of Gaul' and 'Caesar's conquest'. There are differences, of course, in emphasis and specification of tense and agency, but such differences are the subject matter of stylistics and give the subject its importance. It is a study of nuances. Even smaller nuances are accommodated in modern grammars, which can analyse such apparently completely synonymous sequences as 'Mr Appleby picked his glass up' and 'Mr Appleby picked up his glass'.

If one value of stylistic study is to be raised above others, it is its value in revealing the rich complexity of language. It reminds us that in linguistic behaviour so many choices intrude between a stimulus and its response that though a scientific stylistician will explain as many choices as he can in terms of situation and context, he feels himself in no danger of being left without a residue of the unpredictable large enough to justify a concept of 'free choice' or 'creativity' in language. There are demagogues who would trim the richness of language in the interests of ease of understanding, but democrats will prefer to admire the ingenuity of social man in devising an instrument of the subtlety, adaptability and inexhaustible wealth that modern linguistic study reveals. When we understand the full richness of language, we recognize that not everyone masters it equally well, and this implies a humane duty to enrich the language of others when we can. It is not a particularly unselfish duty since the power of our own language grows as it is more exactly understood. A study of style leads us to a faith in education, if this can promote a mastery of the linguistic tools of learning and go on to release the adventurous uses of language which distinguish men from the cleverest machines and even from those laboratory rats whose responses have too much dominated educational thought in our time.

A Note on Further Reading

Available books and articles relating to stylistics are so numerous that anyone wanting more than a very select guide should go straight to a complete bibliography of the subject, perhaps Richard W. Bailey and D. M. Burton, *English Stylistics: A Bibliography* (M.I.T. Press, 1968) or Richard W. Bailey and L. Doležel, *An Annotated Bibliography of Statistical Stylistics* (University of Michigan Press, 1968).

Too early to profit from transformational approaches to grammar, the collection *Style in Language* edited by Thomas Sebeok (M.I.T. Press, and London, Wiley, 1960) is already somewhat dated and some of the papers remind us uncomfortably of the difference between a stylistician and a stylist, but it is a well-indexed and comprehensive work which remains valuable as a source of detailed information and an indication of the scope of stylistics. More recent collections are Glen A. Love and Michael Payne (editors), *Contemporary Essays on Style* (Scott Foresman & Co, 1969) and Roger Fowler (ed.), *Essays on Style and Language* (Routledge, 1966).

For the study of style apart from its special application to literature, David Crystal and Derek Davy, *Investigating English Style* (Longman, 1969), is especially recommended for its emphasis on methods of studying style and its detailed analysis of a number of non-literary texts. Another volume in the same series (English Language Series), G. N. Leech, *A Linguistic Guide to English Poetry* (Longman, 1969), has the complementary virtue of applying modern stylistic study to a literary genre.This book has a very good bibliography. For prose there is David Lodge, *Language of Fiction: Essays in Criticism and Verbal Analysis of the English Novel* (Routledge, 1966).

R. Quirk, *The Use of English* (Longman, revised edition 1968), is full of observations of interest for stylistic study and is a very readable book. N. E. Enkvist, J. Spencer and M. Gregory, *Linguistics and Style* (O.U.P., 1965), offers two essays on the relationship of linguistic and literary studies, and interesting practical demonstrations of the use of linguistic approaches to literary problems will be found in some of the papers in A. McIntosh and M. A. K. Halliday, *Patterns of Language* (Longman, 1966). Stephen Ullmann, *Language and Style* (Blackwell, 1964) takes the reader beyond English literature into continental approaches to stylistic problems. Dialect is studied in G. L. Brook, *English Dialects* (Deutsch, 1963), which includes a chapter on dialect and literature.

The writings of those who approach style from the literary side should not be neglected by linguists. Perhaps most congenial to linguists is the theoretical approach of R. Wellek and A. Warren, *The Theory of Literature* (Cape, 1949), but much can still be learned from older literary discussions, notably Walter Raleigh, *Style* (Arnold, 1897), John Middleton Murry, *The Problem of Style* (O.U.P., 1922) and Vernon Lee (pseudonym of Violet Paget), *The Handling of Words* (John Lane, 1923). More recently Graham Hough has written an interesting short book, *Style and Stylistics* (Routledge, 1969), written from the point of view of a literary critic willing to find what linguistics can contribute to his subject.

Difficult to classify as linguists or literary critics (an enviable achievement!) are Ian Gordon, *The Movement of English Prose* (Longman, 1966), and Winifred Nowottny, *The Language Poets Use* (Athlone Press, 1962). I cannot agree with those who find Mrs Nowottny's book 'easy to read' but agree with all who mention her book that it is important.

For language in education, Denis Lawton, *Social Class, Language and Education* (Routledge, 1968), is a convenient introduction from the educational side, and M. A. K. Halliday, A. McIntosh and P. D. Strevens, *Linguistic Sciences and Language Teaching* (Longman, 1964) from the linguistic side.

Among more specialized linguistic studies relevant to style, mention may be made of Lubomir Doležel and Richard W. Bailey (editors), *Statistics and Style* (New York, Elsevier, 1968), for mathematical approaches to stylistics, and for an advanced study of the sound of language, David Crystal, *Prosodic Systems and Intonation in English* (C.U.P., 1969).

Acknowledgements

Grateful thanks are due to the following publishers for permission to reproduce extracts in this book: For 2 lines from 'For the Time Being' by W. H. Auden (p. 29) to Faber & Faber Ltd and Random House Inc.; for 2 lines from 'Autumn Song' from *Collected Shorter Poems 1930–1944* (p. 120) and 7 lines from 'The Wanderer' from *Collected Shorter Poems 1927–1957* (p. 129) by W. H. Auden to Faber & Faber Ltd; for 6 lines from 'Naming of Parts' from *A Map of Verona* by Henry Reed (p. 46) to Jonathan Cape Ltd; for 4 lines from 'Bagpipe Music' from *Eighty-five Poems* by Louis MacNeice (p. 62) to Faber & Faber Ltd and Oxford University Press, New York; for 3 lines from the 'Anxious Pooh Song' from *Winnie the Pooh* by A. A. Milne (p. 70) to Eyre Methuen Ltd; for 2 lines from *Poems* by A. D. Hope (p. 73) to Hamish Hamilton Ltd; for one line from *On the Frontier* by W. H. Auden and Christopher Isherwood (p. 80) to Faber & Faber Ltd and Curtis Brown Ltd (U.S. rights); for 4 lines from 'Any Complaints' from *Out Loud* by Adrian Mitchell (p. 81) to Cape Golliard Press; for 2 lines from 'Strange Meeting' from *The Collected Poems of Wilfred Owen* edited by C. Day Lewis (p. 83) to Chatto & Windus Ltd; for 13 lines from 'A Refusal to Mourn the Death, by Fire, of a Child in London' from *The Poems of Dylan Thomas* (p. 99) to J. M. Dent & Sons Ltd and New Directions Publishing Corporation, New York.

Person Index

Subject Index